LUCIA'S PROGRESS

With Lucia's fiftieth birthday looming, she takes stock of her life's achievements — and finds them lacking. Determined to take up a new pursuit, she dismisses flying across the Atlantic, writing a genius novel, or swimming the Channel. Then, not only does her eye alight on the obituary of a spinster who made a fortune on the Stock Exchange, but the notion of standing for the Town Council occurs to her . . . As Lucia gambles with shares and dives into the world of electioneering, her rival Miss Mapp — now Mrs Mapp-Flint, having finally ensnared her Major — remains dedicated to thwarting her ambitions . . .

Books by E. F. Benson
Published by Ulverscroft:

QUEEN LUCIA
MISS MAPP
LUCIA IN LONDON
MAPP AND LUCIA
TROUBLE FOR LUCIA

SPECIAL MESSAGE TO READERS

THE ULVERSCROFT FOUNDATION

: 264873)

funds for
eye diseases.
led by
re:-

orfields Eye

Unit at Great
Children
iseases and
hthalmology,

rch Group,

he Western

t the Royal
ogists

Foundation
legacy.
ved. If you
dation or
contact:

THE ULVERSCROFT FOUNDATION
The Green, Bradgate Road, Anstey
Leicester LE7 7FU, England
Tel: (0116) 236 4325

website: www.foundation.ulverscroft.com

E. F. BENSON

◆

LUCIA'S PROGRESS

Complete and Unabridged

ULVERSCROFT
Leicester

First published in Great Britain in 1935

This Large Print Edition
published 2017

The moral right of the author has been asserted

*A catalogue record for this book is available
from the British Library.*

ISBN 978–1–4448–3332–4

Published by
F. A. Thorpe (Publishing)
Anstey, Leicestershire

Set by Words & Graphics Ltd.
Anstey, Leicestershire
Printed and bound in Great Britain by
T. J. International Ltd., Padstow, Cornwall

This book is printed on acid-free paper

Cordially dedicated to the
Marquess of Carisbrooke

1

Mrs. Emmeline Lucas was walking briskly and elegantly up and down the cinder path which traversed her kitchen garden and was so conveniently dry underfoot even after heavy rain. This house of hers, called 'Grebe,' stood some quarter of a mile outside the ancient and enlightened town of Tilling, on its hill away to the west; in front there stretched out the green pasture-land of the marsh, flat and featureless, as far as the line of sand-dunes along the shore. She had spent a busy morning divided about equally between practising a rather easy sonata by Mozart and reading a rather difficult play by Aristophanes. There was the Greek on one page and an excellent English translation on the page opposite, and the play was so amusing that to-day she had rather neglected the Greek and pursued the English. At this moment she was taking the air to refresh her after her musical and intellectual labours, and felt quite ready to welcome the sound of that tuneful set of little bells in the hall which would summon her to lunch.

The January morning was very mild and

her keen bird-like eye noted that several imprudent and precocious polyanthuses (she spoke and even thought of them as 'polyanthi') were already in flower, and that an even more imprudent tortoiseshell butterfly had been tempted from its hybernating quarters and was flitting about these early blossoms. Presently another joined it, and they actually seemed to be engaged in a decrepit dalliance quite unsuitable to their faded and antique appearance. The tortoiseshells appeared to be much pleased with each other, and Lucia was vaguely reminded of two friends of hers, both of mature years, who had lately married and with whom she was to play Bridge this afternoon.

She inhaled the soft air in long breaths holding it in for five seconds according to the Yoga prescription and then expelling it all in one vigorous puff. Then she indulged in a few of those physical exercises, jerks and skippings and flexings which she found so conducive to health, pleased to think that a woman of her age could prance with such supple vigour. Another birthday would knock at her door next month, and if her birth certificate was correct (and there was no reason for doubting it) the conclusion was forced upon her that if for every year she had already lived, she lived another, she would then be a centenarian. For a brief moment the thought of the shortness of life and the all-devouring grave laid a chill on her spirit, as if a cold draught had blown round the corner of her house, but before she had time to shiver, her habitual intrepidity warmed her up again, and she resolved to make the most of the years that remained, although there might not be even fifty more in store for her. Certainly she would not indulge in senile dalliance, like those aged butterflies, for nothing made a woman so old as pretending to be young, and there would surely be worthier outlets for her energy than wantonness. Never yet had she been lacking in activity or initiative or even attack when necessary, as those ill-advised persons knew who from time to time had attempted to thwart her career, and these priceless gifts were still quite unimpaired.

It was a little over a year since the most remarkable adventure of her life so far had befallen her, when the great flood burst the river bank just across the road, and she and poor panic-stricken Elizabeth Mapp had been carried out to sea on the kitchen table. They had been picked up by a trawler in the Channel and had spent three weird but very interesting months with a fleet of cod-fishers on the Gallagher Bank. Lucia's undefeated vitality had pulled them through, but since then she had never tasted cod. On returning home at grey daybreak on an April morning they had found that a handsome cenotaph had been erected to their memories in the churchyard, for Tilling had naturally concluded that they must be dead. But Tilling was wrong, and the cenotaph was immediately removed.

But since then, Lucia sometimes felt, she had not developed her undoubted horse-power to its full capacity. She had played innumerable duets on the piano with Georgie Pillson: she had constituted herself instructress in physical culture to the ladies of Tilling, until the number of her pupils gradually dwindled away and she was left to skip and flex alone: she had sketched miles of marsh and been perfectly willing to hold classes in Contract Bridge: she had visited the wards in the local hospital twice a week, till the matron complained to Dr. Dobbie that the patients were unusually restless for the remainder of the day when Mrs. Lucas had been with them, and the doctor tactfully told her that her vitality was too bracing for them (which was probably the case). She had sung in the church choir; she had read for an hour every Thursday afternoon to the inmates of the workhouse till she had observed for herself that, long before the hour was over, her entire audience was wrapt in profound slumber; she had perused the masterpieces of Aristophanes, Virgil and Horace with the help of a crib; she had given a lecture on the 'Tendencies of Modern Fiction,' at the Literary Institute, and had suggested another on the 'Age of Pericles,' not yet delivered, as, most unaccountably, a suitable date could not be arranged; but looking back on these multifarious activities, she found that they had only passed the time for her without really extending her. To be sure there was the constant excitement of social life in Tilling, where crises, plots and counterplots were endemic rather than epidemic, and kept everybody feverish and with a high psychical temperature, but when all was said and done (and there was always a great deal to do, and a great deal more to say) she felt this morning, with a gnawing sense of self-reproach, that if she had written down all the achievements which, since her return from the Gallagher Bank, were truly worthy of mention, the chronicle would be sadly brief.

'I fear,' thought Lucia to herself, 'that the Recording Angel will have next to nothing in his book about me this year. I've been vegetating. *Molto cattiva!* I've been content (yet not quite content: I will say that for myself) to be occupied with a hundred trifles. I've been frittering my energies away over them, drugging myself with the fallacy that they were important. But surely a woman in the prime of life like me could have done all I have done as mere relaxations in her career. I must do something more monumental (*monumentum œre perennius*, isn't it?) in this coming year. I know I have the capacity for high ambition. What I don't know is what to be ambitious about. Ah, there's lunch at last.'

Lucia could always augur from the mode in which Grosvenor, her parlourmaid, played her prelude to food on those tuneful chimes, in what sort of a temper she was. There were six bells hung close together on a burnished copper frame, and they rang the first six notes of an ascending major scale. Grosvenor improvised on these with a small drumstick, and if she was finding life a harmonious business she often treated Lucia to charming dainty little tunes, quite a pleasure to listen to, though sometimes rather long. Now and then there was an almost lyrical outburst of melody, which caused Lucia a momentary qualm of anxiety, lest Grosvenor should have fallen in love, and would leave. But if she felt morose or cynical, she expressed her humour with realistic fidelity. To-day she struck two adjoining bells very hard, and then ran the drumstick up and down the peal, producing a most jangled effect, which meant that she was jangled too. 'I wonder what's the matter: indigestion perhaps,' thought Lucia, and she hurried indoors, for a jangled Grosvenor hated to be kept waiting.

'Mr. Georgie hasn't rung up?' she asked, as she seated herself.

'No, ma'am,' said Grosvenor.

'Nor Foljambe?'

'No, ma'am.'

'Is there no tomato sauce with the macaroni?'

'No, ma'am.'

Lucia knew better than to ask if she ached anywhere, for Grosvenor would simply have said 'No, ma'am' again, and, leaving her to stew in her own snappishness, she turned her mind to Georgie. For over a fortnight now he had not been to see her, and enquiries had only elicited the stark information that he was keeping the house, not being very well, but that there was nothing to bother about. With Georgie such a retirement might arise from several causes none of which need arouse anxiety. Some little contretemps, thought Lucia: perhaps there was dental trouble, and change must be made in the furnishings of his mouth. Or he might have a touch of

7

lumbago, and did not want to be seen hobbling and bent, instead of presenting his usual spry and brisk appearance. It was merely tactless when he assumed these invisibilities to ask the precise cause: he came out of them again with his hair more auburn than ever, or wreathed in smiles which showed his excellent teeth, and so one could guess.

But a fortnight was an unprecedentedly long seclusion, and Lucia determined to have a word with Foljambe when she came home in the evening. Foljambe was Georgie's peerless parlourmaid and also the wife of Lucia's chauffeur. She gave Cadman his early breakfast in the morning, and then went up to Georgie's house, Mallards Cottage, where she ministered all day to her master, returning home to her husband after she had served Georgie with his dinner. Like famous actresses who have married, she retained her maiden name, instead of becoming Mrs. Cadman (which she undoubtedly was in the sight of God) since her life's work was Foljambizing to Georgie . . . Then Grosvenor brought in the tomato sauce of which there was quantities, after Lucia had almost finished her macaroni, and by way of expressing penitence for her mistake, became more communicative, though hardly less morose.

'Foljambe won't say anything about Mr.

Georgie, ma'am,' she observed, 'except that he hasn't been outside his front door for over a fortnight nor seen anybody. Dr. Dobbie has been in several times. You don't think it's something mental, ma'am, do you?'

'Certainly not,' said Lucia. 'Why should I think anything of the kind?'

'Well, my uncle was like that,' said Grosvenor. 'He shut himself up for about the same time as Mr. Georgie, and then they took him away to the County Asylum, where he's thought himself to be the Prince of Wales ever since.'

Though Lucia poured scorn on this sinister theory, it made her more desirous of knowing what actually was the matter with Georgie. The news that the doctor had been to see him disposed of the theory that a new chestnut-coloured toupee was wanted, for a doctor would not have been needed for that, while if he had been paying a round of visits to the dentist, Foljambe would not have said that he had not been outside his own front door, and an attack of lumbago would surely have yielded to treatment before now. So, after telephoning to Georgie suggesting, as she had often done before, that she should look in during the afternoon, and receiving uncompromising discouragement, she thought she would walk into Tilling after lunch and find what other people made of this long retirement. It was Saturday and there would certainly be a good many friends popping in and out of the shops.

Lucia looked at her engagement book, and scribbled 'Mozart, Aristophanes,' as post-dated engagements for the morning of to-day. She was due to play Bridge at Mallards, next door to Mallards Cottage, this afternoon at half-past three with Major and Mrs. Mapp-Flint: tea would follow and then more Bridge. For the last year Contract had waged a deadly war with Auction, but the latter, like the Tishbites in King David's campaigns, had been exterminated, since Contract gave so much more scope for violent differences of opinion about honour-tricks and declarations and doublings and strong twos and takings-out, which all added spleen and savagery to the game. There were disciples of many schools of thought: one played Culbertson, another one club, another two clubs, and Diva Plaistow had a new system called 'Leeway,' which she could not satisfactorily explain to anybody, because she had not any clearness about it herself. So, before a couple of tables were started, there was always a gabble, as of priests of various denominations reciting the articles of their faith. Mrs. Mapp-Flint was 'strong two,' but her husband was 'one club.' Consequently when they cut together their opponents had to remember that when he declared one club, it meant that he had strong outside suits, but possibly no club at all, but that when his wife declared two clubs it meant that she certainly had good clubs and heaps of other honour-tricks as well. Lucia herself relied largely on psychic bids: in other words when she announced a high contract in any suit, her partner had to guess whether she held, say, a positive tiara of diamonds, or whether she was being psychic. If he guessed wrong, frightful disaster might result, and Elizabeth Mapp-Flint had once been justifiably sarcastic on the conclusion of one of these major debacles. 'I see, dear,' she said, 'when you declare four diamonds, it means you haven't got any, and want to be taken out. So sorry: I shall know better another time.'

Lucia, as she walked up to Tilling, ran over in her head the various creeds of the rest of the players she was likely to meet. The Padre and his wife Evie Bartlett were sure to be there: he was even more psychic than herself, and almost invariably declared his weakest suit first, just to show he had not got any. Evie, his wife, was obliging enough to play any system desired by her partner, but she generally forgot what it was. Then Algernon and Susan Wyse would certainly be there: they need not be reckoned with, as they only declared what they thought they could get and meant what they said. The eighth would probably be Diva with her 'Leeway,' of which, since she invariably held such bad cards, there was always a great deal to make up.

Lucia passed these systems in review, and then directed her stream of consciousness to her hostess, who, as Elizabeth Mapp, had been her timorous partner in the great adventure on the kitchen table a year ago. She, at any rate, had not vegetated since their return, for she had married Major Benjamin Flint, and since he had only an Army Pension, and she was a woman of substance in every sense of the word, and owner of Mallards, it was only proper that she should hyphenate her surname with his. The more satirical spirits of Tilling thought she would have preferred to retain her maiden name like Foljambe and famous actresses. At the marriage service she had certainly omitted the word 'obey' when she defined what sort of wife she would make him. But the preliminary exhortation had been read in full, though the Padre had very tactfully suggested to the bride that the portion of it which related to children need not be recited: Elizabeth desired to have it all.

Immediately after the marriage the 'young couple' had left Tilling, for Elizabeth had accepted the offer of a very good let for Mallards for the summer and autumn months, and they had taken a primitive and remote bungalow close to the golf links two miles away, where they could play golf and taste romance in solitude. Mr. and Mrs. Wyse had been there to lunch occasionally and though Mr. Wyse (such a gentleman) always said it had been a most enjoyable day, Susan was rather more communicative and let out that the food was muck and that no alcoholic beverage had appeared at table. On wet days the Major had occasionally come into Tilling by bus, on some such hollow pretext of having his hair cut, or posting a letter, and spent most of the afternoon at the Club where there was a remarkably good brand of port. Then Elizabeth's tenants had been so delighted with Mallards that they had extended their lease till the end of November, after which the Mapp-Flints, gorged with the gold of their rent-roll, had gone to the Riviera for the month of December, and had undoubtedly been seen by Mr. Wyse's sister, the Contessa Fariglione, at the Casino at Monte Carlo. Thus their recent return to Tilling was a very exciting event, for nothing was really known as to which of them had

13

established supremacy. Teetotalism at the bungalow seemed 'one up' to Elizabeth, for Benjy, as all Tilling knew, had a strong weakness in the opposite direction: on the other hand Mrs. Wyse had hinted that the bride exhibited an almost degrading affection for him. Then which of them was the leading spirit in those visits to the Casino? Or were they both gamblers at heart? Altogether it was a most intriguing situation: the ladies of Tilling were particularly interested in the more intimate and domestic side of it, and expressed themselves with great delicacy.

Lucia came up the steep rise into the High Street and soon found some nice food for constructive observation. There was Foljambe just going into the chemist's, and Lucia, remembering that she really wanted a toothbrush, followed her in, to hear what she ordered, for that might throw some light on the nature of Georgie's mysterious indisposition. But a packet of lint was vague as a clue, though it disposed of Grosvenor's dark suggestion that his illness was mental: lint surely never cured lunacy. A little further on there was quaint Irene Coles in trousers and a scarlet pullover, with her easel set up on the pavement, so that foot passengers had to step on to the roadway, making a highly impressionistic sketch of the street. Irene had an almost embarrassing *schwärm* for Lucia, and she flung her arms round her and upset her easel; but she had no news of Georgie, and her conjecture that Foljambe had murdered him and was burying him below the brick-pillar in his back garden had nothing to support it.

'But it might be so, beloved,' she said. 'Such things do happen, and why not in Tilling? Think of Crippen and Belle Elmore. Let's suppose Foljambe gets through with the burial today and replaces the pillar, then she'll go up there to-morrow morning just as usual and tell the police that Georgie has disappeared. Really I don't see what else it can be.'

Diva Plaistow scudded across the street to them. She always spoke in the style of a telegram, and walked so fast that she might be mistaken for a telegram herself. 'All too mysterious,' she said, taking for granted what they were talking about. 'Not seen since yesterday fortnight. Certainly something infectious. Going to the Mapp-Flints, Lucia? Meet again then,' and she whizzed away.

These monstrous suggestions did not arouse the least anxiety in Lucia, but they vastly inflamed her curiosity. If Georgie's ailment had been serious, she knew he would have told so old a friend as herself: it must

15

simply be that he did not want to be seen. But it was time to go to the Bridge party, and she retraced her steps a few yards (though with no definite scheme in her mind) and turned up from the High Street towards the church: this route, only a few yards longer, would lead her past Mallards Cottage, where Georgie lived. It was dusk now, and just as she came opposite that gabled abode, a light sprang up in his sitting-room which looked on to the street. There was no resisting so potent a temptation, and crossing the narrow cobbled way she peered stealthily in. Foljambe was drawing the curtains of the other window, and there was Georgie sitting by the fire, fully dressed, with his head turned a little away, doing his *petit-point*. At that very moment he shifted in his chair, and Lucia saw to her indescribable amazement that he had a short grey beard: in fact it might be called white. Just one glimpse she had, and then she must swiftly crouch down, as Foljambe crossed the room and rattled the curtains across the window into which she was looking. Completely puzzled but thrilled to the marrow, Lucia slid quietly away. Was he then in retirement only in order to grow a beard, feigning illness until it had attained comely if not venerable proportions? Common sense revolted at the notion, but common sense could not suggest any other theory.

Lucia rang the bell at Mallards, and was admitted into its familiar white-panelled hall which wanted painting so badly. On her first visit to Tilling, which led to her permanent residence here, she had taken this house for several months from Elizabeth Mapp and had adored it. Grebe, her own house, was very agreeable, but it had none of the dignity and charm of Mallards with its high-walled garden, its little square parlours, and, above all, with its entrancing garden-room, built a few yards away from the house itself, and commanding from its bow-window that unique view of the street leading down to the High Street, and, in the other direction, past Mallards Cottage to the church. The owner of Mallards ought not to let it for month after month and pig it in a bungalow for the sake of the rent. Mallards ought to be the centre of nodal life in Tilling. Really Elizabeth was not worthy of it: year after year she let it for the sake of the rent it brought her, and even when she was there she entertained very meagrely. Lucia felt very strongly that she was not the right person to live there, and she was equally strongly convinced as to who the right person was.

With a sigh she followed Withers out into the garden and up the eight steps into the garden-room. She had not seen the young couple since the long retirement of their honeymoon to the bungalow and to the garishness of Monte Carlo, and now even that mysterious phenomenon of Georgie with a grey, nearly white, beard faded out before the intense human interest of observing how they had adjusted themselves to matrimony . . . '*Chérie!*' cried Mrs. Elizabeth. 'Too lovely to see you again! My Benjy-boy and I only got back two days ago, and since then it's been 'upstairs and downstairs and in my lady's chamber,' all day, in order to get things shipshape and comfy and *comme il faut* again. But now we're settled in, *n'est ce pas?*'

Lucia could not quite make up her mind whether these pretty Gallicisms were the automatic result of Elizabeth's having spent a month in France, or whether they were ironically allusive to her own habit of using easy Italian phrases in her talk. But she scarcely gave a thought to that, for the psychological balance between the two was so much more absorbing. Certainly Elizabeth and her Benjy-boy seemed an enamoured couple. He called her Liz and Girlie and perched himself on the arm of her chair as they waited for the rest of the gamblers to gather, and she patted his hand and pulled his cuff straight. Had she surrendered to him,

Lucia wondered, had matrimony wrought a miraculous change in this domineering woman? The change in the room itself seemed to support the astounding proposition. It was far the biggest and best room in Mallards, and in the days of Elizabeth's virginity it had dripped with feminine knick-knacks, vases and china figures, and Tilling crockery pigs, screens set at angles, muslin blinds and riband-tied curtains behind which she sat in hiding to observe the life of the place. Here had been her writing-table close to the hot water pipes and here her cosy corner by the fire with her work-basket. But now instead of her water-colours on the walls were heads of deer and antelopes, the spoil of Benjy's sporting expeditions in India, and a trophy consisting of spears and arrows and rhinoceros-hide whips and an apron made of shells, and on the floor were his moth-eaten tiger-skins. A stern business table stood in the window, a leather chair like a hipbath in her cosy corner, a gun stand with golf clubs against the wall, and the room reeked of masculinity and stale cigar smoke. In fact, all it had in common with its old aspect was the big false bookcase in the wall which masked the cupboard, in which once, for fear of lack of food during a coal strike, the prudent Elizabeth had stored immense quantities of corned beef and other nutritious provisions. All this change looked like surrender: Girlie Mapp had given up her best room to Benjy-boy Flint. Their little pats and tweaks at each other might have been put on merely as Company-manners suitable to a newly-married couple, but the room itself furnished more substantial evidence.

The party speedily assembled: the Wyses' huge Rolls-Royce from their house fifty yards away hooted at the front door and Susan staggered in under the weight of her great sable coat, and the odour of preservatives from moth gradually overscored that of cigars. Algernon followed and made a bow and a polite speech to everybody. The Padre and Mrs. Bartlett arrived next: he had been to Ireland for his holiday, and had acquired a touch of brogue which he grafted on to his Highland accent, and the effect was interesting, as if men of two nationalities were talking together of whom the Irishman only got in a word or two edgeways. Diva Plaistow completed the assembly and tripped heavily over the head of a one-eyed tiger. The other eye flew out at the shock of the impact and she put it, with apologies, on the chimney-piece.

The disposition of the players was easily settled, for there were three married couples to be separated, and Diva and Lucia made the fourth at each of the tables. Concentration settled down on the room like the grip of some intense frost, broken, at the end of each hand, as if by a sudden thaw, by torrential postmortems. At Lucia's table, she and Elizabeth were partners against Mr. Wyse and the Padre. 'Begorra,' said he, 'the bhoys play the lassies. Eh, mon, there's a sair muckle job for the puir wee laddies agin the guid wives o' Tilling, begob.'

Though Elizabeth seemed to have surrendered to her Benjy-boy, it was clear that she had no thoughts of doing so to the other wee laddies, who, though vulnerable after the first hand were again and again prevented from winning the rubber by preposterously expensive bids on Elizabeth's part.

'Yes, dear Lucia,' she said, 'three hundred down I'm afraid, but then it's worth six hundred to prevent the adversary from going out. Let me see, *qui donne?*'

'Key what?' asked the Padre.

'Who gives: I should say, who deals?'

'You do, dear Elizabeth,' said Lucia, 'but I don't know if it's worth quite so many three hundreds. What do you think?'

Lucia picked up a hand gleaming with high honours, but psychic silences were often as valuable as psychic declarations. The laddies,

21

flushed with untold hundreds above would be sure to declare something in order to net so prodigious a rubber, and she made no bid. Far more psychic to lure them on by modest overbidding and then crush them under a staggering double. But the timorous laddies held their tongues, the hands were thrown in and though Lucia tried to mingle hers with the rest of the pack, Elizabeth relentlessly picked it out and conducted a savage post-mortem as if on the corpse of a regicide.

The rubber had to be left for the present, for it was long after tea-time. At tea a most intriguing incident took place, for it had been Major Benjy's invariable custom at these gatherings to have a whisky and soda or two instead of the milder refreshment. But to-day, to the desperate interest of those who, like Lucia, were intent on observing the mutual adjustments of matrimony, a particularly large cup was provided for him which, when everybody else was served, was filled to the brim by Elizabeth and passed to him. Diva noticed that, too, and paused in her steady consumption of nougat chocolates.

'And so *triste* about poor Mr. Georgie,' said Elizabeth. 'I asked him to come in this afternoon, and he telephoned that he was too unwell: hadn't been out of his *maison* for more than a fortnight. What's the matter with him? You'll know, Lucia.'

Lucia and everybody else wondered which of them would have been left out if Georgie had come, or whether Elizabeth had asked him at all. Probably she had not.

'But indeed I don't know,' she said. 'Nobody knows. It's all very puzzling.'

'And haven't even you seen him? Fancy!' said Elizabeth. 'He must be terribly ill.'

Lucia did not say that actually she had seen him, nor did she mention his beard. She intended to find out what that meant before she disclosed it.

'Oh, I don't think that,' she said. 'But men like to be left quite alone when they're not the thing.'

Elizabeth kissed her finger-tips across the table to her husband. Really rather sickening.

'That's not the way of my little Benjy-boy,' she said. 'Why, he had a touch of chill out at Monte, and *pas un moment* did I get to myself till he was better. Wasn't it so, mischief?'

Major Benjy wiped his great walrus-moustache which had been dipped in that cauldron of tea.

'Girlie is a wizard in the sick-room,' he said. 'Bucks a man up more than fifty tonics. Ring Georgie up, Liz: say you'll pop in after dinner and sit with him.'

Lucia waited for the upshot of this offer with some anxiety. Georgie would certainly be curious to see Elizabeth after her marriage and it would be too shattering if he accepted this proposal after having refused her own company. Luckily nothing so lamentable happened. Elizabeth returned from the telephone in a very short space of time, a little flushed, and, for the moment, forgetting to talk French.

'Not up to seeing people,' she said, 'so Foljambe told me. A rude woman I've always thought: I wonder Mr. Georgie can put up with her. Diva, dear, more chocolates? I'm sure there are plenty more in the cupboard. More tea, anybody? Benjy, dear, another cup? Shall we get back to our rubbers then? All so exciting!'

The wee laddies presently began to get as incautious as the guid wives. It was maddening to be a game up and sixty, and not to be allowed to secure one of the fattest scores above ever known in Sussex. Already it reached nearly to the top of the scoring-sheet, but now owing to penalties from their own over-bidding, a second sky-scraper was mounting rapidly beside the first. Then the guid wives got a game, and the deadly process began again.

'Très amusant!' exclaimed Elizabeth, sorting her hand with a fixed smile, because it was so amusing, and a trembling hand because it was so agonizing. 'Now let me see; *que faire?*'

'Hold your hand a wee bitty higher, Mistress Mapp-Flint,' said the Padre, 'or sure I can't help getting a keek o't.'

'*Monsieur*, the more you keeked the less you'd like it,' said Elizabeth, scanning a hand of appalling rubbish. Quite legitimate to say that.

At this precise moment when Elizabeth was wondering whether it might not pay to be psychic for once, Major Benjy at the other table laid down his hand as dummy, and cast just one glance, quick as a lizard at the knotted face of his wife. 'Excuse me,' he said and quietly stole from the room. Elizabeth, so thought Diva, had not noticed his exit, but she certainly noticed his return, though she had got frightfully entangled in her hand, for Lucia had been psychic, too, and God knew what would happen . . .

'Not kept you waiting, I hope,' said Benjy stealing back. 'Just a telephone message. Ha, we seem to be getting on, partner. Well, I must say, beautifully played.'

Diva thought these congratulations had a faint odour about them as if he had been telephoning to a merchant who dealt in spirituous liquors . . .

It was not till half-past seven that the great tussle came to an end, resulting in a complete wash-out, and the whole party, marvelling at the lateness of the hour left in a great hurry so as not to keep dinner (or a tray) waiting. Mr. Wyse vainly begged Lucia and Diva to be taken home in the Royce: it was such a dark night, he observed, but saw that there was a full moon, and it would be so wet underfoot, but he became aware that the pavements were bone-dry. So after a phrase or two in French from Elizabeth, in Italian from Lucia, in Scotch and Irish from the Padre, so that the threshold of Mallards resembled the Tower of Babel, Diva and Lucia went briskly down towards the High Street, both eager for a communing about the balance of the matrimonial equation.

'What a change, Diva!' began Lucia. 'It's quite charming to see what matrimony has done for Elizabeth. Miraculous, isn't it? At present there does not seem to be a trace left of her old cantankerousness. She seems positively to dote on him. Those little tweaks and dabs, and above all her giving up the garden-room to him: that shows there must be something real and heartfelt, don't you think? Fond eyes following him — '

'Not so sure about the fond eyes,' said Diva. 'Pretty sharp they looked when he came back from telephoning. Another kind of cup of tea was what he was after. That I'll swear to. Reeked!'

'No!' said Lucia. 'You don't say so!'

'Yes, I do. Teetotal lunches at the bungalow indeed! Rubbish. Whisky bottles, I bet, buried all over the garden.'

'Dear Diva, that's pure imagination,' said Lucia very nobly. 'If you say such things you'll get to believe them.'

'Ho! I believe them already,' said Diva. 'There'll be developments yet.'

'I hope they'll be happy ones, anyhow,' said Lucia. 'Of course, as the Padre would say, Major Benjy was apt to lift the elbow occasionally, but I shall continue to believe that's all done with. Such an enormous cup of tea: I never saw such a cup, and I think it's a perfect marriage. Perfect! I wonder — '

Diva chipped in.

'I know what you mean. They sleep in that big room overlooking the street. Withers told my cook. Dressing-room for Major Benjy next door; that slip of a room. I've seen him shaving at the window myself.'

Lucia walked quickly on after Diva turned into her house in the High Street. Diva was a little coarse sometimes, but in fairness Lucia had to allow that when she said 'I wonder,' Diva had interpreted what she wondered with absolute accuracy. If she was right about the precise process of Major Benjy's telephoning, it would look as if matrimony had not wrought so complete a change in him as in his bride, but perhaps Diva's sense of smell had been deranged by her enormous consumption of chocolates.

Then like a faint unpleasant odour the thought of her approaching fiftieth birthday came back to her. Only this morning she had resolved to make a worthy use of the few years that lay in front of her and of the energy that boiled inside her, and to couple the two together and achieve something substantial. Yet, even while that resolve was glowing within her, she had frittered four hours away over tea and Bridge, with vast expenditure of nervous force and psychic divination, and there was nothing to shew for it except weariness of the brain, a few dubious conclusions as to the effect of matrimony on the middle-aged and a distaste for small cards . . . Relaxation, thought Lucia in this sharp attack of moralizing, should be in itself productive. Playing duets with Georgie was productive because their fingers in spite of occasional errors, evoked the divine harmonies of Mozartino and Beethoven: when she made sketches of the twilight marsh her eye drank in the loveliness of Nature, but these hours of Bridge, however strenuous, had not really enriched or refreshed her, and it was no use pretending that they had.

'I must put up in large capital letters over my bed 'I am fifty',' she thought as she let herself into her house, 'and that will remind me every morning and evening that I've done nothing yet which will be remembered after I am gone. I've been busy (I will say that for myself) but beyond giving others a few hours of enchantment at the piano, and helping them to keep supple, I've done nothing for the world or indeed for Tilling. I must take myself in hand.'

        ★   ★   ★

The evening post had come in but there was nothing for her except a packet covered with seals which she knew must be her pass-book returned from the bank. She did not trouble to open it, and after a tray (for she had made a substantial tea) she picked up the evening paper, to see if she could find any hints about a career for a woman of fifty. Women seemed to be much to the fore: there was one flying backwards and forwards across the Atlantic, but Lucia felt it was a little late for her to take up flying: probably it required an immense amount of practice before you could, with any degree of confidence, start for New York alone, two or three thousand feet up in the air.

Then eight others were making a tour of pavilions and assembly rooms in towns on the South Coast, and entrancing everybody by their graceful exhibitions (in tights, or were their legs bare?) of physical drill; but on thinking it over, Lucia could not imagine herself heading a team of Tilling ladies, Diva and Elizabeth and Susan Wyse, with any reasonable hope of entrancing anybody. The pages of reviews of books seemed to deal entirely with novels by women, all of which were works of high genius. Lucia had long felt that she could write a marvellous novel, but perhaps there were enough geniuses already. Then there was a woman who, though it was winter, was in training to swim the Channel, but Lucia hated sea-bathing and could not swim. Certainly women were making a stir in the world, but none of their achievements seemed suited to the ambitions of a middle-aged widow.

Lucia turned the page. Dame Catherine Winterglass was dead at the age of fifty-five, and there was a long obituary notice of this remarkable spinster. For many years she had been governess to the children of a solicitor who lived at Balham, but at the age of forty-five she had been dismissed to make way for somebody younger. She had a capital of £500, and had embarked on operations on the Stock Exchange, making a vast fortune. At the time of her death she had a house in Grosvenor Square where she entertained Royalty, an estate at Mocomb Regis in Norfolk for partridge shooting, a deer forest in Scotland, and a sumptuous yacht for cruising in the Mediterranean; and from London, Norfolk, Ross-shire and the Riviera she was always in touch with the centres of finance. An admirable woman, too: hospitals, girl-guides, dogs' homes, indigent parsons, preventions of cruelty and propagations of the Gospel were the recipients of her noble bounty. No deserving case (and many undeserving) ever appealed to her in vain and her benefactions were innumerable. Right up to the end of her life, in spite of her colossal expenditure, it was believed that she grew richer and richer.

Lucia forgot all about nocturnal arrangements at Mallards, and read this account through again. What an extraordinary power money had! It enabled you not only to have everything you could possibly want yourself, but to do so much good, to relieve suffering, to make the world (as the Padre had said last Sunday) 'a better place.' Hitherto she had taken very little interest in money, being quite content every six months or so to invest a few hundred pounds from her constantly accruing balance in some gilt-edged security, the dividends from which added some negligible sum to her already ample income. But here was this woman who, starting with a total capital of a paltry five hundred pounds, had for years lived in Sybaritic luxury and done no end of good as well. 'To be sure,' thought Lucia, 'she had the start of me by five years, for she was only forty-five when she began, but still . . . '

Grosvenor entered.

'Foljambe's back from Mr. Georgie's ma'am,' she said. 'You told me you wanted to see her.'

'It doesn't matter,' said Lucia, deep in meditation about Dame Catherine. 'To-morrow will do.'

She let the paper drop, and fixed her gimlet eyes on the bust of Beethoven, for this conduced to concentration. She did not covet yachts and deer forests, but there were many things she would like to do for Tilling: a new organ was wanted at the church, a new operating theatre was wanted at the hospital and she herself wanted Mallards. She intended to pass the rest of her days here, and it would be wonderful to be a great benefactress to the town, a notable figure, a civic power and not only the Queen (she had no doubt about that) of its small social life. These benefactions and the ambitions for herself, which she had been unable to visualize before, outlined themselves with distinctness and seemed wreathed together: the one twined round the other. Then the parable of the talents occurred to her. She had been like the unprofitable servant who, distrusting his financial ability, had wrapped it up in a napkin, for really to invest money in Government Stock was comparable with that, such meagre interest did it produce.

She picked up her paper again and turned to the page of financial news, and strenuously applied her vigorous mind to an article on the trend of markets by the City Editor. Those tedious gilt-edged stocks had fallen a little (as he had foreseen) but there was great activity in Industrials and in gold shares. Then there was a list of the shares which the City Editor had recommended to his readers a month ago. All of them (at least all that he quoted) had experienced a handsome rise: one had doubled in price. Lucia ripped open the sealed envelope containing her pass-book and observed with a pang of retrospective remorse that it revealed that she had the almost indecent balance of twelve hundred pounds.

If only, a month ago, she had invested a thousand of it in that share recommended by this clever City Editor each pound would have made another pound!

But it was no use repining, and she turned to see what the wizard recommended now. Goldfields of West Africa were very promising, notably Siriami, and the price was eight to nine shillings. She did not quite know what that meant: probably there were two grades of shares, the best costing nine shillings, and a slightly inferior kind costing eight. Supposing she bought five hundred shares of Siriami and they behaved as those others had done, she would in a month's time have doubled the sum she had invested.

'I'm beginning to see my way,' she thought, and the way was so absorbing that she had not heard the telephone bell ring, and now Grosvenor came in to say that Georgie wanted to speak to her. Lucia wondered whether Foljambe had seen her peeping in at his window this afternoon and had reported this intrusion, and was prepared, if this was the case and Georgie resented it, not exactly to lie about it, but to fail to understand what he was talking about until he got tired of explaining. She adopted that intimate dialect of baby-language with a peppering of Italian words in which they often spoke together.

'Is zat 'oo, Georgino mio?' she asked.

'Yes,' said Georgie in plain English.

'Lubly to hear your voice again. *Come sta?* Better I hope.'

'Yes, going on all right, but very slow. All too tarsome. And I'm getting dreadfully depressed seeing nobody and hearing nothing.'

Lucia dropped dialect.

'But, my dear, why didn't you let me come and see you before? You've always refused.'

'I know.'

There was a long pause. Lucia with her psychic faculties alert after so much Bridge felt sure he had something more to say, and like a wise woman she refrained from pressing him. Clearly he had rung her up to tell her something, but found it difficult to bring himself to the point.

At last it came.

'Will you come in to-morrow then?'

'Of course I will. Delighted. What time?'

'Any time is the same to me,' said Georgie gloomily. 'I sit in this beastly little room all day.'

'About twelve then, after church?' she asked.

'Do. And I must warn you that I'm very much changed.'

('That's the beard,' thought Lucia.) She

made her voice register deep concern.

'My dear, what do you mean?' she asked with a clever tremolo.

'Nothing to be anxious about at all, though it's frightful. I won't tell you because it's so hard to explain it all. Any news?'

That sounded better: in spite of this frightful change Georgie had his human interests alive.

'Lots: quantities. For instance, Elizabeth says *n'est ce pas* and *chérie*, because she's been to France.'

'No!' said Georgie with a livelier inflexion. 'We'll have a good talk: lots must have happened. But remember there's a shocking change.'

'It won't shock *me*,' said Lucia. 'Twelve then, to-morrow. Good night, Georgino.'

'*Buona notte*,' said he.

2

Major Benjy was in church with his wife next morning: this was weighty evidence as regards her influence over him, for never yet had he been known to spend a fine Sunday morning except on the golf links. He sat with her among the auxiliary choir sharing her hymn-book and making an underground sort of noise during the hymns. The Padre preached a long sermon in Scotch about early Christianity in Ireland which was somehow confusing to the geographical sense. After service Lucia walked away a little ahead of the Mapp-Flints, so that they certainly saw her ring the bell at Mallards Cottage and be admitted, and Elizabeth did not fail to remember that Georgie had said only yesterday afternoon that he was not up to seeing anybody. Lucia smiled and waved her hand as she went in to make sure Elizabeth saw, and Elizabeth gave a singularly mirthless smile in answer. As it was Sunday, she tried to feel pleased that he must be better this morning, but with only partial success. However, she would sit in the window of the garden-room and see how long Lucia stayed.

Georgie was not yet down and Lucia had a few minutes alone in his sitting-room among the tokens of his handiwork. There were dozens of his water-colour sketches on the walls, the sofa was covered with a charming piece of *gros-point* from his nimble needle, and his new piece in *petit point*, not yet finished, lay on one of the numerous little tables. One window looked on to the street, the other on to a tiny square of flower garden with a patch of crazy pavement surrounding a brick pillar on the top of which stood a replica of the Neapolitan Narcissus. Georgie had once told Lucia that he had just that figure when he was a boy, and with her usual tact she had assured him he had it still. There were large soft cushions in all the chairs, there was a copy of *Vogue*, a work-basket containing wools, a feather brush for dusting, a screen to shut off all draughts from the door, and a glass case containing his bibelots, including a rather naughty enamelled snuff-box: two young people — Then she heard his slippered tread on the stairs and in he came.

He had on his new blue suit: round his neck was a pink silk scarf with an amethyst pin to keep it in place, and above the scarf his face, a shade plumper than Narcissus's, thatched by his luxuriant auburn hair and decorated with an auburn moustache turned up at the ends, was now framed in a short grey, almost white beard.

'My dear, it's too dreadful,' he said. 'I know I'm perfectly hidjus, but I shan't be able to shave for weeks to come, and I couldn't bear being alone any longer. I tried to shave yesterday. Agonies!'

Dialectic encouragement was clearly the first thing to administer.

'Georgino! 'Oo vewy naughty boy not to send for me before,' said Lucia. 'If I'd been growing a *barba* — my dear, not *at all* disfiguring: rather dignified — do you think I should have said I wouldn't see you? But tell me all about it. I know nothing.'

'Shingles on my face and neck,' said Georgie. 'Blisters. Bandages. Ointments. Aspirin. Don't tell anybody. So degrading!'

'*Povero!* But I'm sure you've borne it wonderfully. And you're over the attack?'

'So they say. But it will be weeks before I can shave, and I can't go about before I do that. Tell me the news. Elizabeth rang me up yesterday, and offered to come and sit with me after dinner.'

'I know. I was there playing Bridge and you, or Foljambe rather, said you weren't up to seeing people. But she saw me come in this morning.'

'No!' said Georgie. 'She'll hate that.'

Lucia sighed.

'An unhappy nature, I'm *afraid*,' she said. 'I waggled my hand and smiled at her as I stepped in, and she smiled back — how shall I say it? — as if she had been lunching on soused mackerel and pickles instead of going to church. And all those *n'est ce pas*-s as I told you yesterday.'

'But what about her and Benjy?' asked Georgie. 'Who wears the trousers?'

'Georgie: it's difficult to say: I felt a man's eye was needed. It looked to me as if they wore one trouser each. He's got the garden-room as his sitting-room: horns and savage aprons on the wall and bald tiger-skins on the floor. On the other hand he had tea instead of whisky and soda at tea-time in an enormous cup, and he was in church this morning. They dab at each other about equally.'

'How disgusting!' said Georgie. 'You don't know how you cheer me up.'

'So glad, Georgie. That's what I'm here for. And now I've got a plan. No, it isn't a plan, it's an order. I'm not going to leave you here alone. You're coming to stay with me at Grebe. You needn't see anybody but me and me only when you feel inclined. It's ridiculous your being cooped up here with no one to talk to. Have your lunch and tell

Foljambe to pack your bags and order your car.'

Georgie required very little persuasion. It was a daring proceeding to stay all alone with Lucia but that was not in its disfavour. He was the professional *jeune premier* in social circles at Tilling, smart and beautifully dressed and going to more tea-parties than anybody else, and it was not at all amiss that he should imperil his reputation and hers by these gay audacities. Very possibly Tilling would never know, as the plan was that he should be quite invisible till his clandestine beard was removed, but if Tilling did then or later find out, he had no objection. Besides, it would make an excellent opportunity for his cook to have her holiday, and she should go off to-morrow morning, leaving the house shut up. Foljambe would come up every other day or so to open windows and air it.

So Lucia paid no long visit, but soon left Georgie to make domestic arrangements. There was Elizabeth sitting at the window of the garden-room, and she threw it open with another soused mackerel smile as Lucia passed below.

'And how is our poor *malade*?' she asked. 'Better, I trust, since he is up to seeing friends again. I must pop in to see him after lunch.'

Lucia hesitated. If Elizabeth knew that he

41

was moving to Grebe this afternoon, she would think it very extraordinary that she was not allowed to see him, but the secret of the beard must be inviolate.

'He's not very well,' she said. 'I doubt if he would see anybody else to-day.'

'And what's the matter exactly, *chérie*?' asked Elizabeth, oozing with the tenderest curiosity. Major Benjy, Lucia saw, had crept up to the window too. Lucia could not of course tell her that it was shingles, for shingles and beard were wrapped up together in one confidence.

'A nervous upset,' she said firmly. 'Very much pulled down. But no cause for anxiety.'

Lucia went on her way, and Elizabeth closed the window.

'There's something mysterious going on, Benjy,' she said. 'Poor dear Lucia's face had that guileless look which always means she's playing hokey-pokey. We shall have to find out what really is the matter with Mr. Georgie. But let's get on with the crossword till luncheon: read out the next.'

By one of those strange coincidences, which admit of no explanation, Benjy read out:

'No. 3 down. A disease, often seen on the seashore.'

Georgie's move to Grebe was effected early

that afternoon without detection, for on Sunday, during the hour succeeding lunch, the streets of Tilling were like a city of the dead. With his head well muffled up, so that not a hair of his beard could be seen, he sat on the front seat to avoid draughts, and, since it was not worth while packing all his belongings for so short a transit, Foljambe sitting opposite him, was half buried under a loose moraine of coats, sticks, paint-boxes, music, umbrellas, dressing-gown, hot-water bottle and work-basket.

Hardly had they gone when Elizabeth, having solved the crossword except No. 3 down, which continued to baffle her, set about solving the mystery which, her trained sense assured her, existed, and she rang up Mallards Cottage with the intention of congratulating Georgie on being better, and of proposing to come in and read to him. Georgie's cook, who was going on holiday next day and had been bidden to give nothing away, answered the call. The personal pronouns in this conversation were rather mixed as in the correspondences between Queen Victoria and her Ministers of State.

'Could Mrs. Mapp-Flint speak to Mr. Pillson?'

'No, ma'am, she couldn't. Impossible just now.'

'Is Mrs. Mapp-Flint speaking to Foljambe?'

'No, ma'am, it's me. Foljambe is out.'

'Mrs. Mapp-Flint will call on Mr. Pillson about 4.30.'

'Very good, ma'am, but I'm afraid Mr. Pillson won't be able to see her.'

The royal use of the third person was not producing much effect, so Elizabeth changed her tactics, and became a commoner. She was usually an adept at worming news out of cooks and parlourmaids.

'Oh, I recognise your voice, cook,' she said effusively. 'Good afternoon. No anxiety, I hope, about dear Mr. Georgie?'

'No, ma'am, not that I'm aware of.'

'I suppose he's having a little nap after his lunch.'

'I couldn't say, ma'am.'

'Perhaps you'd be so very kind as just to peep, oh, so quietly, into his sitting-room and give him my message, if he's not asleep.'

'He's not in his sitting-room, ma'am.'

Elizabeth rang off. She was more convinced than ever that some mystery was afoot, and her curiosity passed from tender oozings to acute inflammation. Her visit at 4.30 brought her no nearer the solution, for Georgie's substantial cook blocked the doorway, and said he was at home to nobody. Benjy on his way back from golf met with no better luck, nor did Diva on her way to evening church. All these kind enquiries were telephoned to Georgie at Grebe: Tilling was evidently beginning to seethe, and it must continue to do so.

Lucia's household had been sworn to secrecy, and the two passed a very pleasant evening. They had a grand duet on the piano, and discussed the amazing romance of Dame Catherine Winterglass who had become enshrined in Lucia's mind as a shining example of a conscientious woman of middle-age determined to make the world a better place.

'Really, Georgie,' she said, 'I'm ashamed of having spent so many years getting gradually a little richer without being a proper steward of my money. Money is a power, and I have been letting it lie idle, instead of increasing it by leaps and bounds like that wonderful Dame Catherine. Think of the good she did!'

'You might decrease it by leaps and bounds if you mean to speculate,' observed Georgie. 'It's supposed to be the quickest short-cut to the workhouse, isn't it?'

'Speculation?' said Lucia. 'I abhor it. What I mean is studying the markets, working at finance as I work at Aristophanes, using one's brains, going carefully into all those prospectuses that are sent one. For instance, yesterday there was a strong recommendation in the evening paper to buy shares in a West African mine called Siriami, and this morning the City Editor of a Sunday paper gave the same advice. I collate those facts, Georgie. I reason that there are two very shrewd men recommending the same thing. Naturally I shall be very cautious at first, till I know the ropes, so to speak, and shall rely largely on my broker's advice. But I shall telegraph to him first thing to-morrow to buy me five hundred Siriami. Say they go up only a shilling — I've worked it all out — I shall be twenty-five pounds to the good.'

'My dear, how beautiful!' said Georgie. 'What will you do with it all?'

'Put it into something else, or put more into Siriami. Dame Catherine used to say that an intelligent and hard-working woman can make money every day of her life. She was often a bear. I must find out about being a bear.'

'I know what that means,' said Georgie. 'You sell shares you haven't got in order to buy them cheaper afterwards.'

Lucia looked startled.

'Are you sure about that? I must tell my broker to be certain that the man he buys my Siriami shares from has got them. I shall insist on that: no dealings with bears.'

Georgie regarded his needlework. It was a

French design for a chair back: a slim shepherdess in a green dress was standing among her sheep. The sheep were quite unmistakable but she insisted on looking like a stick of asparagus. He stroked the side of his beard which was unaffected by shingles.

'Tarsome of her,' he said. 'I must give her a hat or rip her clothes off and make her pink.'

'And if they went up two shillings I should make fifty pounds,' said Lucia absently.

'Oh, those shares: how marvellous!' said Georgie. 'But isn't there the risk of their going down instead?'

'My dear, the whole of life is a series of risks,' said Lucia sententiously.

'Yes, but why increase them? I like to be comfortable, but as long as I have all I want, I don't want anything more. Of course I hope you'll make tons of money, but I can't think what you'll do with it.'

'*Aspett'un po*', Georgino,' said she. 'Why it's half-past ten. The invalid must go to bed.'

'Half-past ten: is it really?' said Georgie. 'Why, I've been going to bed at nine, because I was so bored with myself.'

* * *

Next morning Tilling seethed furiously. Georgie's cook had left before the world was

47

astir, and Elizabeth, setting out with her basket about half-past ten to do her marketing in the High Street observed that the red blinds in his sitting-room were still down. That was very odd: Foljambe was usually there at eight, but evidently she had not come yet: possibly she was ill, too. That distressing (but interesting) doubt was soon set at rest, for there was Foljambe in the High Street looking very well. Something might be found out from her, and Elizabeth put on her most seductive smile.

'Good morning, Foljambe,' she said. 'And how is poor Mr. Georgie to-day?'

Foljambe's face grew stony, as if she had seen the Gorgon.

'Getting on nicely, ma'am,' she said.

'Oh, so glad! I was almost afraid you were ill, too, as his sitting-room blinds were down.'

'Indeed, ma'am,' said Foljambe, getting even more flintily petrified.

'And will you tell him I shall ring him up soon to see if he'd like me to look in?'

'Yes, ma'am,' said Foljambe.

Elizabeth watched her go along the street, and noticed she did not turn up in the direction of Mallards Cottage, but kept straight on. Very mysterious: where could she be going? Elizabeth thought of following her, but her attention was diverted by seeing Diva pop out of the hairdresser's establishment in that scarlet beret and frock which made her look so like a round pillar-box. She had taken the plunge at last after tortures of indecision, and had had her hair cropped quite close. The right and scathing thing to do, thought Elizabeth, was to seem not to notice any change in her appearance.

'Such a lovely morning, isn't it, dear Diva, for January,' she said. '*Si doux*. Any news?'

Diva felt there was enough news on her own head to satisfy anybody for one morning, and she wheeled so that Elizabeth should get a back view of it, where the change was most remarkable. 'I've heard none,' she said. 'Oh, there's Major Benjy. Going to catch the tram, I suppose.'

It was Elizabeth's turn to wheel. There had been a coolness this morning, for he had come down very late to breakfast, and had ordered fresh tea and bacon with a grumpy air. She would punish him by being unaware of him . . . Then that wouldn't do, because gossipy Diva would tell everybody they had had a quarrel, and back she wheeled again.

'Quick, Benjy-boy,' she called out to him, 'or you'll miss the tram. Play beautifully, darling. All those lovely mashies.'

Lucia's motor drew up close to them opposite the post office. She had a telegraph form in her hand, and dropped it as she got out. It bowed and fluttered in the breeze, and fell at Elizabeth's feet. Her glance at it, as she picked it up, revealing the cryptic sentence: 'Buy five hundred Siriami shares,' was involuntary or nearly so.

'Here you are, dear,' she said. 'En route to see poor Mr. Georgie?'

Lucia's eye fell on Diva's cropped head.

'Dear Diva, I like it immensely!' she said. 'Ten years younger.'

Elizabeth remained profoundly unconscious.

'Well, I must be trotting,' she said. 'Such a lot of commissions for my Benjy. So like a man, bless him, to go off and play golf, leaving wifie to do all his jobs. Such a scolding I shall get if I forget any.'

She plunged into the grocer's, and for the next half-hour, the ladies of Tilling, popping in and out of shops, kept meeting on doorsteps with small collision of their baskets, and hurried glances at their contents. Susan Wyse alone did not take part in this ladies' chain, but remained in the Royce, and butcher and baker and greengrocer and fishmonger had to come out and take her orders through the window. Elizabeth felt bitterly about this, for, in view of the traffic, which would otherwise have become congested, tradesmen ran out of their shops, leaving other customers to wait, so that Susan's Royce might not be delayed. Elizabeth had addressed a formal complaint about it to the Town Council, and that conscientious body sent a reliable time-keeper in plain clothes down to the High Street on three consecutive mornings, to ascertain how long, on the average, Mrs. Wyse's car stopped at each shop. As the period worked out at a trifle over twenty seconds they took the view that as the road was made for vehicular traffic, she was making a legitimate use of it. She could hardly be expected to send the Royce to the parking place by the Town Hall each time she stopped, for it would not nearly have got there by the time she was ready for it again. The rest of the ladies, not being so busy as Elizabeth, did not mind these delays, for Susan made such sumptuous orders that it gave you an appetite to hear them: she had been known, even when she and Algernon had been quite alone to command a hen-lobster, a pheasant, and a *pâté de foie gras* . . .

★   ★   ★

Elizabeth soon finished her shopping (Benjy-boy had only asked her to order him some shaving soap), and just as she reached her door, she was astonished to see Diva coming

51

rapidly towards her house from the direction of Mallards Cottage, thirty yards away, and making signs to her. After the severity with which she had ignored the Eton crop, it was clear that Diva must have something to say which overscored her natural resentment.

'The most extraordinary thing,' panted Diva as she got close, 'Mr. Georgie's blinds — '

'Oh, is his sitting-room blind still down?' asked Elizabeth. 'I saw that an hour ago, but forgot to tell you. Is that all, dear?'

'Nowhere near,' said Diva. '*All* his blinds are down. Perhaps you saw that too, but I don't believe you did.'

Elizabeth was far too violently interested to pretend she had, and the two hurried up the street and contemplated the front of Mallards Cottage. It was true. The blinds of his dining-room, of the small room by the door, of Georgie's bedroom, of the cook's bedroom, were all drawn.

'And there's no smoke coming out of the chimneys,' said Diva in an awed whisper. 'Can he be dead?'

'Do not rush to such dreadful conclusions,' said Elizabeth. 'Come back to Mallards and let's talk it over.'

But the more they talked, the less they could construct any theory to fit the facts.

Lucia had been very cheerful, Foljambe had said that Georgie was going on nicely, and even the two most ingenious women in Tilling could not reconcile this with the darkened and fireless house, unless he was suffering from some ailment which had to be nursed in a cold, dark room. Finally, when it was close on lunch time, and it was obvious that Elizabeth was not going to press Diva to stay, they made their thoughtful way to the front door, still completely baffled. Till now, so absorbed had they been in the mystery, Diva had quite forgotten Elizabeth's unconsciousness of her cropped head. Now it occurred to her again.

'I've had my hair cut short this morning,' she said. 'Didn't you notice it?'

'Yes, dear, to be quite frank, since we are such old friends, I did,' said Elizabeth. 'But I thought it far kinder to say nothing about it. Far!'

'Ho!' said Diva, turning as red as her beret, and she trundled down the hill.

Benjy came back very sleepy after his golf, and in a foul temper, for the Padre, who always played with him morning and afternoon on Monday, to recuperate after the stress of Sunday, had taken two half-crowns off him, and he was intending to punish him by not going to church next Sunday. In this morose mood he took only the faintest interest in what might or might not have happened to Georgie. Diva's theory seemed to have something to be said for it, though it was odd that if he was dead, there should not have been definite news by now. Presently Elizabeth gave him a little butterfly kiss on his forehead, to show she forgave him for his unpunctuality at breakfast, and left him in the garden-room to have a good snooze. Before his good snooze he had a good swig at a flask which he kept in a locked drawer of his business table.

* * *

Diva's theory was blown into smithereens next day, for Elizabeth from her bedroom window observed Foljambe letting herself into Mallards Cottage at eight o'clock, and a short stroll before breakfast shewed her that blinds were up and chimneys smoking, and the windows of Georgie's sitting-room opened for an airing. Though the mystery of yesterday had not been cleared up, normal routine had been resumed, and Georgie could not be dead.

* * *

After his sad lapse yesterday Benjy was punctual for breakfast this morning. Half-past eight was not his best time, for during his bachelor days he had been accustomed to get down about ten o'clock, to shout 'Quai-hai' to show he was ready for his food, and to masticate it morosely in solitude. Now all was changed: sometimes he got as far as 'Quai,' but Elizabeth stopped her ears and said 'There is a bell, darling,' in her most acid voice. And concerning half-past eight she was adamant: she had all her household duties to attend to, and then after she had minutely inspected the larder, she had her marketing to do. Unlike him she was quite at her best and brightest (which was saying a good deal) at this hour, and she hailed his punctual advent to-day with extreme cordiality to show him how pleased she was with him.

'Nice hot cup of tea for my Benjy,' she said, 'and dear me, what a disappointment — no, not disappointment: that wouldn't be kind — but what a surprise for poor Diva. Blinds up, chimneys smoking at Mr. Georgie's, and there was she yesterday suggesting he was dead. Such a pessimist! I shan't be able to resist teasing her about it.'

Benjy had entrenched himself behind the morning paper, propping it up against the teapot and the maiden-hair fern which stood in the centre of the table, and merely grunted. Elizabeth, feeling terribly girlish made a scratching noise against it, and then looked over the top.

'Peep-o!' she said brightly. 'Oh, what a sleepy face! Turn to the City news, love, and see if you can find something called Siriami.'

A pause.

'Yes: West African mine,' he said. 'Got any, Liz? Shares moved sharply up yesterday: gained three shillings. Oh, there's a note about them. Excellent report received from the mine.'

'Dear me! how lovely for the shareholders, I wish I was one,' said Elizabeth with singular bitterness as she multiplied Lucia's five hundred shares by three and divided them by twenty. 'And what about my War Loan?'

'Down half a point.'

'That's what comes of being patriotic,' said Elizabeth, and went to see her cook. She had meant to have a roast pheasant for dinner this evening, but in consequence of this drop in her capital, decided on a rabbit. It seemed most unfair that Lucia should have made all that money (fifteen hundred shillings minus commission) by just scribbling a telegram, and dropping it in the High Street. Memories of a golden evening at Monte Carlo came back to her, when she and Benjy returned to their *pension* after a daring hour in the Casino with five hundred francs between them and in such a state of reckless elation that he had an absinthe and she a vermouth before dinner. They had resolved never to tempt fortune again, but next afternoon, Elizabeth having decided to sit in the garden and be lazy while he went for a walk, they ran into each other at the Casino, and an even happier result followed and there was more absinthe and vermouth. With these opulent recollections in her mind she bethought herself, as she set off with her market-basket for her shopping, of some little savings she had earmarked for the expenses of a rainy day, illness or repair to the roof of Mallards. It was almost a pity to keep them lying idle, when it was so easy to add to them . . .

Diva trundled swiftly towards her with Paddy, her great bouncing Irish terrier, bursting with news, but Elizabeth got the first word.

'All your gloomy anticipations about Mr. Georgie quite gone phut, dear,' she said. 'Chimneys smoking, blinds up — '

'Oh, Lord, yes,' said Diva. 'I've been up to have a look already. You needn't have got so excited about it. And just fancy! Lucia bought some mining shares only yesterday, and she seems to have made hundreds and hundreds of pounds. She's telegraphing now to buy some more. What did she say the mine was? Syrian Army, I think.'

Elizabeth made a little cooing noise, expressive of compassionate amusement.

'I should think you probably mean Siriami, *n'est ce pas?*' she said. 'Siriami is a very famous gold mine somewhere in West Africa. *Mon vieux* was reading to me something about it in the paper this morning. But surely, dear, hundreds and hundreds of pounds is an exaggeration?'

'Well, quite a lot, for she told me so herself,' said Diva. 'I declare it made my mouth water. I've almost made up my mind to buy some myself with a little money I've got lying idle. Just a few.'

'I wouldn't if I were you, dear,' said Elizabeth earnestly. 'Gambling is such an insidious temptation. Benjy and I learned that at Monte Carlo.'

'Well, you made something, didn't you?' asked Diva.

'Yes, but I should always discourage anyone who might not be strong-minded enough to stop.'

'I'd back the strength of my mind against yours any day,' said Diva.

A personal and psychological discussion might have ensued, but Lucia at that moment came out of the post-office. She held in her hand a copy of the *Financial Post*.

'And have you bought some more Siriami?' asked Diva with a sort of vicarious greed.

Lucia's eyes wore a concentrated though far-away expression as if she was absorbed in some train of transcendent reasoning. She gave a little start as Diva spoke, and recalled herself to the High Street.

'Yes: I've bought another little parcel of shares,' she said. 'I heard from my broker this morning, and he agrees with me that they'll go higher. I find his judgment is usually pretty sound.'

'Diva's told me what a stroke of luck you've had,' said Elizabeth.

Lucia smiled complacently.

'No, dear Elizabeth, not luck,' she said. 'A little studying of the world-situation, a little inductive reasoning. The price of gold, you know: I should be much surprised if the price of gold didn't go higher yet. Of course I may be wrong.'

'I think you must be,' said Diva. 'There are always twenty shillings to the pound, aren't there?'

Lucia was not quite clear what was the answer to that. Her broker's letter, quite approving of a further purchase on the strength of the favourable news from the mine, had contained something about the price of gold, which evidently she had not grasped.

'Too intricate to explain, dear Diva,' she said indulgently. 'But I should be very sorry to advise you to follow my example. There is a risk. But I must be off and get back to Georgie.'

The moment she had spoken she saw her mistake. The only way of putting it right was to take the street that led up to Mallards Cottage and then get back to Grebe by a circuitous course, else surely Elizabeth would get on Georgie's track. Even as it was Elizabeth watched her till she had disappeared up the correct turning.

'So characteristic of the dear thing,' she said, 'making a lot of money in Siriami, and then advising you not to touch it! I shouldn't the least wonder if she wants to get all the shares herself and be created Dame Lucia Siriami. And then her airs, as if she was a great financier! Her views of the world-situation! Her broker who agrees with her about the rising price of gold! Why she hadn't the slightest idea what it meant, anyone could see that. Diva, *c'est trop*! I shall get on with my humble marketing instead of buying parcels of gold.'

But behind this irritation with Lucia,

Elizabeth was burning with the desire to yield to the insidious temptation of which she had warned Diva, and buy some Siriami shares herself. Diva might suspect her design if she went straight into the post-office, and so she crossed the street to the butcher's to get her rabbit. Out of the corner of her eye she saw Susan Wyse's car slowing up to stop at the same shop, and so she stood firm and square in the doorway, determined that that sycophantic vendor of flesh-food should not sneak out to take Susan's order before she was served herself, and that should take a long time. She would spin the rabbit out.

'Good morning, Mr. Worthington,' she said in her most chatty manner. 'I just looked in to see if you've got anything nice for me to give the Major for his dinner to-night. He'll be hungry after his golfing.'

'Some plump young pheasants, ma'am,' said Mr. Worthington. He was short, but by standing on tiptoe he could see that Susan's car had stopped opposite his shop, and that her large round face appeared at the window.

'Well, that does sound good,' said Elizabeth. 'But let me think. Didn't I give him a pheasant a couple of days ago?'

'Excuse me, ma'am, one moment,' said this harassed tradesman. 'There's Mrs. Wyse — '

Elizabeth spread herself a little in the

doorway with her basket to reinforce the barricade. Another car had drawn up on the opposite side of the street, and there was a nice congestion forming. Susan's chauffeur was hooting to bring Mr. Worthington out and the car behind him was hooting because it wanted to get by.

'You haven't got a wild duck, I suppose,' said Elizabeth, gloating on the situation. 'The Major likes a duck now and then.'

'No ma'am. Mallards, if you'll excuse me, is over.'

More hoots and then an official voice.

'Move on, please,' said the policeman on point duty to Susan's chauffeur. 'There's a block behind you and nothing in front.'

Elizabeth heard the purr of the Royce as it moved on, releasing the traffic behind. Half-turning she could see that it drew up twenty yards further on and the chauffeur came back and waited outside the doorway which she was blocking so efficiently.

'Not much choice then,' said Elizabeth. 'You'd better send me up a rabbit, Mr. Worthington. Just a sweet little bunny, a young one mind — '

'Brace of pheasants to Mrs. Wyse,' shouted the chauffeur through the window, despairing of getting in.

'Right-o,' called Mr. Worthington. 'One

rabbit then, ma'am; thank you.'

'Got such a thing as a woodcock?' called the chauffeur.

'Not fit to eat to-day,' shouted Mr. Worthington. 'Couple of snipe just come in.'

'I'll go and ask.'

'Oh, Mr. Worthington, why didn't you tell me you'd got a couple of snipe?' said Elizabeth. 'Just what the Major likes. Well, I suppose they're promised now. I'll take my bunny with me.'

All this was cheerful work: she had trampled on Susan's self-assumed right to hold up traffic till she lured butchers out into the street to attend to her, and with her bunny in her basket she crossed to the post-office again. There was a row of little boxes like mangers for those who wanted to write telegrams, and she took one of these, putting her basket on the floor behind her. As she composed this momentous telegram for the purchase of three hundred Siriami shares and the denuding of the rainy day fund, she heard a mixed indefinable hubbub at her back and looking round saw that Diva had come in with Paddy, and that Paddy had snatched bunny from the basket, and was playing with him very prettily. He tossed him in the air, and lay down with a paw on each side of him, growling in a menacing manner as he pretended to worry him. Diva who had gone to the counter opposite with a telegram in her hand was commanding Paddy to drop it, but Paddy leaped up, squeezed himself through the swing-door and mounted guard over his prey on the pavement. Elizabeth and Diva rushed out after him and by dint of screaming 'Trust, Paddy!' Diva induced her dog to drop bunny.

'So sorry, dear Elizabeth,' she said, smoothing the rumpled fur. 'Not damaged at all, I think.'

'If you imagine I'm going to eat a rabbit mangled by your disgusting dog — ' began Elizabeth.

'You shouldn't have left it lying on the floor,' retorted Diva. 'Public place. Not my fault.'

Mr. Worthington came nimbly across the street, unaware that he was entering a storm-centre.

'Mrs. Wyse doesn't need that couple of snipe, ma'am,' he said to Elizabeth. 'Shall I send them up to Mallards?'

'I'm surprised at your offering me Mrs. Wyse's leavings,' said Elizabeth. 'And charge the rabbit I bought just now to Mrs. Plaistow.'

'But I don't want a rabbit,' said Diva. 'As soon eat rats.'

'All I can say is that it's not mine,' said Elizabeth.

Diva thought of something rather neat.

'Oh, well, it'll do for the kitchen,' she said, putting it in her basket.

'Diva dear, don't let your servants eat it,' said Elizabeth. 'As likely as not it would give them hydrophobia.'

'Pooh!' said Diva. 'Bet another dog carried it when it was shot. Oh, I forgot my telegram.'

'I'll pick out a nice young plump one for you, ma'am, shall I?' said Mr. Worthington to Elizabeth.

'Yes, and mind you only charge one to me.'

The two ladies went back into the post-office with Paddy and the rabbit to finish the business which had been interrupted by that agitating scene on the pavement. Elizabeth's handwriting was still a little ragged with emotion when she handed her telegram in, and it was not (except the address which had been written before) very legible. In fact the young lady could not be certain about it.

'Buy 'thin bunkered Simiawi' is it?' she asked.

'No, three hundred Siriami,' said Elizabeth, and Diva heard. Simultaneously Diva's young lady asked: 'Is it Siriami?' and Elizabeth heard. So both knew.

They walked back together very amicably as far as Diva's house, quite resolved not to let a rabbit wreck or even threaten so long-standing a friendship. Indeed there was no cause for friction any more, for Diva had no objection to an occasional rabbit for the kitchen, and Elizabeth saw that her bunny was far the plumper of the two. As regards Siriami, Diva had a distinct handle against her friend, in case of future emergencies, for she knew that Elizabeth had solemnly warned her not to buy them and had done so herself: she knew, too, how many Elizabeth had bought, in case she swanked about her colossal holding, whereas nobody but the young lady to whom she handed her telegram, knew how many she had bought. So they both quite looked forward to meeting that afternoon for Bridge at Susan Wyse's.

Marketing had begun early this morning, and though highly sensational, had been brief. Consequently, when Elizabeth turned up the street towards Mallards, she met her Benjy just starting to catch the eleven o'clock tram for the golf links. He held a folded piece of paper in his hand, which, when he saw her, he thrust into his pocket.

'Well, boy o' mine, off to your game?' she asked. 'Look, such a plump little bunny for dinner. And news. Lucia has become a great financier. She bought Siriami yesterday and again to-day.'

Should she tell him she had bought Siriami too? On the whole, not. It was her own private rainy day fund she had raided, and if, by some inscrutable savagery of Providence, the venture did not prosper, it was better that he should not know. If, on the other hand, she made money, it was wise for a married woman to have a little unbeknownst store tucked away.

'Dear me, that's a bit of luck for her, Liz,' he said.

Elizabeth gave a gay little laugh.

'No, dear, you're quite wrong,' she said. 'It's inductive reasoning, it's study of the world-situation. How pleasant for her to have all the gifts. Bye-bye.'

She went into the garden-room, still feeling very sardonic about Lucia's gifts, and wondering in an undercurrent why Benjy had looked self-conscious. She could always tell when he was self-conscious, for instead of having a shifty eye, he had quite the opposite kind of eye; he looked at her, as he had done just now, with a sort of truculent innocence, as if challenging her to suspect anything. Then that piece of paper which he had thrust into his pocket, linked itself up. It was rather like a telegraph form, and instantly she wondered if he had been buying Siriami, too, out of his exiguous income. Very wrong of him, if he had, and most secretive of him not to have told her so. Sometimes she felt that he did not give her his full confidence, and that saddened her. Of course it was not actually proved yet that he had bought Siriami, but cudgel her brains as she might, she could think of nothing else that he could have been telegraphing about. Then she calculated afresh what she stood to win if Siriami went up another three shillings, and sitting down on the hot water pipes in the window which commanded so wide a prospect, she let her thoughts stray back to Georgie. Even as she looked out she saw Foljambe emerge from his door, and without a shadow of doubt she locked it after her.

The speed with which Elizabeth jumped up was in no way due to the heat of the pipes. A flood of conjectures simply swept her off them. Lucia had gone up to see Georgie less than half-an-hour ago, so had Foljambe locked her and Georgie up together? Or had Foljambe (in case Lucia had already left) locked Georgie up alone with his cook? She hurried out for the second time that morning to have a look at the front of the house. All blinds were down.

3

Confidence was restored between the young couple at Mallards next morning in a manner that the most ingenious could hardly have anticipated. Elizabeth heard Benjy go thumping downstairs a full five minutes before breakfast time, and peeping out from her bedroom door in high approval she called him a good laddie and told him to begin without her. Then suddenly she remembered something and made the utmost haste to follow. But she was afraid she would be too late.

Benjy went straight to the dining-room, and there on the table with the *Times* and *Daily Mirror*, were two copies of the *Financial Post*. He had ordered one himself for the sake of fuller information about Siriami, but what about the other? It seemed unlikely that the newsagent had sent up two copies when only one was ordered. Then hearing Elizabeth's foot on the stairs, he hastily sat down on one copy, which was all he was responsible for, and she entered.

'Ah, my *Financial Post*,' she said. 'I thought it would be amusing, dear, just to see what was happening to Lucia's gold mine. I take such an interest in it for her sake.'

She turned over the unfamiliar pages, and clapped her hands in sympathetic delight.

'Oh, Benjy-boy, isn't that nice for her?' she cried. 'Siriami has gone up another three shillings. Quite a fortune!'

Benjy was just as pleased as Elizabeth, though he marvelled at the joy that Lucia's enrichment had given her.

'No! That's tremendous,' he said. 'Very pleasant indeed.'

'Lovely!' exclaimed Elizabeth. 'The dear thing! And an article about West African mines. Most encouraging prospects, and something about the price of gold: the man expects to see it higher yet.'

Elizabeth grew absorbed over this, and let her poached egg get cold.

'I see what it means!' she said. 'The actual price of gold itself is going up, just as if it was coals or tobacco, so of course the gold they get out of the mine is worth more. Poor muddle-headed Diva, thinking that the number of shillings in a pound had something to do with it! And Diva will be pleased too. I know she bought some shares yesterday, after the rabbit, for she sent a telegram, and the clerk asked if a word was Siriami.'

'Did she indeed?' asked Benjy. 'How many?'

'I couldn't see. Ring the bell, dear, and don't shout *Quai-hai*. Withers has forgotten the pepper.'

Exultant Benjy forgot about his copy of the *Financial Post*, on which he was sitting, and disclosed it.

'What? Another *Financial Post?*' cried Elizabeth. 'Did you order one, too? Oh, Benjy, make a clean breast of it. Have you been buying Siriami as well as Lucia and Diva?'

'Well, Liz, I had a hundred pounds lying idle. And not such a bad way of using them after all. A hundred and fifty shares. Three times that in shillings. Pretty good.'

'Secretive one!' said Elizabeth. 'Naughty!'

Benjy had a brain-wave.

'And aren't you going to tell me how many you bought?' he asked.

Evidently it was no use denying the imputation. Elizabeth instinctively felt that he would not believe her, for her joy for Lucia's sake must already have betrayed her.

'Three hundred,' she said. 'Oh, what fun! And what are we to do next? They think gold will go higher. Benjy, I think I shall buy some more. What's the use of, say, a hundred pounds in War Loan earning three pound ten a year? I shouldn't miss three pound ten a year . . . But I must get to my jobs. Not sure that I won't treat you to a woodcock to-night, if Susan allows me to have one.'

In the growing excitement over Siriami, Elizabeth got quite indifferent as to whether the blinds were up or down in the windows of Georgie's house. During the next week the shares continued to rise, and morning after morning Benjy appeared with laudable punctuality at breakfast, hungry for the *Financial Post*. An unprecedented extravagance infected both him and Elizabeth: sometimes he took a motor out to the links, for what did a few shillings matter when Siriami was raining so many on him, and Elizabeth vied with Susan in luxurious viands for the table. Bridge at threepence a hundred, which had till lately aroused the wildest passions, failed to thrill, and next time the four gamblers, the Mapp-Flints and Diva and Lucia, met for a game, they all agreed to play double the ordinary stake, and even at that enhanced figure a recklessness in declaration, hitherto unknown, manifested itself. They lingered over tea discussing gold and the price of gold, the signification of which was now firmly grasped by everybody, and there were frightful searchings of heart on the part of the Mapp-Flints and Diva as to whether to sell out and realize their gains, or to invest more in hopes of a further rise. And never had Lucia shewn herself more nauseatingly Olympian. She referred to her 'few shares' when everybody knew she had bought five hundred to begin with and had made one if not two more purchases since, and she held forth as if she was a City Editor herself.

'I was telephoning to my broker this morning,' she began.

'What? A trunk call?' interrupted Diva. 'Half-a-crown, isn't it?'

'Very likely: and put my view of the situation about gold before him. He agreed with me that the price of gold was very high already, and that if, as I suggested, America might come off the gold standard — however, that is a very complicated problem; and I hope to hear from him to-morrow morning about it. Then we had a few words about English rails. Undeniably there have been much better traffic returns lately, and I am distinctly of the opinion that one might do worse — '

Diva was looking haggard. She ate hardly any chocolates, and had already confessed that she was sleeping very badly.

'Don't talk to me about English rails,' she said. 'The price of gold is worrying enough.'

Lucia spread her hands wide with a gesture of infinite capacity.

'You should enlarge your horizon, Diva,' she said. 'You should take a broad, calm view of world-conditions. Look at the markets, gold, industrials, rails as from a mountain height; get a panoramic view. My few shares in Siriami have certainly given me a marvellous profit, and I am beginning to ask myself whether there is not more chance of capital-appreciation, if you follow me, elsewhere. Silver, for instance, is rising — nothing to do with the number of pennies in a shilling — one has to consider that. I feel very responsible, for Georgie has bought a little parcel — we call it — of Siriami on my advice. If one follows silver, I don't think one could do better — and my broker agrees — than to buy a few Burma Corporation. I am thinking seriously of clearing out of Siriami, and investing there. Wonderfully interesting, is it not?'

'It's so interesting that it keeps me awake,' said Diva. 'From one o'clock to two this morning, I thought I would buy more, and from six to seven I thought I would sell. I don't know which to do.'

Elizabeth rose. Lucia's lecture was quite intolerable. Evidently she was constituting herself a central bureau for the dispensing of financial instruction. So characteristic of her: she must boss and direct everybody. There had been her musical parties at which all

Tilling was expected to sit in a dim light and listen to her and Georgie play endless sonatas. There had been her gymnastic class, now happily defunct, for the preservation of suppleness and slimness in middle-age, and when Contract Bridge came in she had offered to hold classes in that. True, she had been the first cause of the enrichment of them all by the purchase of Siriami, but no one could go on being grateful for ever, and Elizabeth's notable independence of character revolted against the monstrous airs she exhibited, and inwardly she determined that she would do exactly the opposite of anything Lucia recommended.

'Thank you, dear,' she said, 'for all you've told us. Most interesting and instructive. How wonderfully you've grasped it all! Now do you think we may go back to our Bridge before it gets too late to begin another rubber? And I declare I haven't asked about *notre pauvre ami*, Mr. Georgie. One hasn't seen him about yet, though Foljambe always tells me he's much better. And such odd things happen at his house. One day all his blinds will be down, as if the house was empty, and the next there'll be Foljambe coming at eight in the morning as usual.'

'No! What a strange thing!' said Lucia.

Diva managed to eat just one of those

nougat chocolates of which she generally emptied the dish. It was lamentable how little pleasure it gave her, and how little she was thrilled by the mystery of those drawn blinds.

'I noticed that too,' she said. 'But then I forgot all about it.'

'Not before you suggested he was dead, dear,' said Elizabeth. 'I only hope Foljambe looks after him properly.'

'I saw him this morning,' said Lucia. 'He has everything he wants.'

The Bridge was of a character that a week ago would have aroused the deepest emotions. Diva and Lucia played against the family and won three swift rubbers at these new dizzy points. There were neither vituperations between the vanquished nor crows of delight from the victors, and though at the end Diva's scoring, as usual, tallied with nobody's, she sacrificed a shilling without insisting that the others should add up again. There was no frenzy, there was no sarcasm even when Benjy doubled his adversaries out or when Elizabeth forgot he always played the club convention, and thought he had some. All was pale and passionless; the sense of the vast financial adventures going on made it almost a matter of indifference who won. Occasionally, at the end of a hand Lucia gave a short exposition of the psychic bid which had so flummoxed her

76

opponents, but nobody cared.

Diva spent the evening alone without appetite for her tray. She took Paddy out for his stroll observing without emotion that someone, no doubt in allusion to him, had altered the notice of 'No Parking' outside her house to 'No Barking.' It scarcely seemed worth while to erase that piece of wretched bad taste, and as for playing Patience to beguile the hour before bedtime, she could not bother to lay the cards out, but sat in front of her fire re-reading the City news in yesterday's and to-day's paper. She brooded over her note of purchase of Siriami shares: she made small addition sums in pencil on her blotting-paper: the greed of gold caused her to contemplate buying more: the instinct of prudence prompted her to write a telegram to her broker to sell out her entire holding. 'Which shall I do? Oh, which shall I do?' she muttered to herself. Ten struck and eleven: it was long after her usual bedtime on solitary evenings, and eventually she fell into a doze. From that she passed into deep sleep and woke with her fire out and her clock on the stroke of midnight, but with her mind made up. 'I shall sell two of my shares and keep the other three,' she said aloud.

For the first time for many nights she slept beautifully till she was called, and woke fresh and eager for the day. There on her dressing-table lay the three half-crowns which she had taken from Elizabeth the evening before. They had seemed then but joyless and negligible tokens; now they gleamed with their accustomed splendour. 'And to think that I won all that without really enjoying it,' thought Diva, as she performed a few of those salubrious flexes and jerks which Lucia had taught her. Just glancing at the *Financial Post* she saw that Siriami had gone up another sixpence, but she did not falter in her prudent determination to secure some part of her profits.

The same crisis which, for Diva, had sucked all the sweetness out of life but supplied Lucia with grist for the Imitation of Dame Catherine Winterglass. Georgie, with a white pointed beard (that clever Foljambe had trimmed it for him, as neatly as if she had been a barber all her life) came down to breakfast for the first time this morning, and pounced on the *Financial Post*.

'My dear, another sixpence up!' he exclaimed. 'What shall I do?'

Lucia already knew that: she had taken a swift glance at the paper before he came down, and had replaced it as if undisturbed. She shook a finger at him.

'Now, Georgie, what about my rule that we have no business talk at meals? How are you?

That's much more important.'

'Beautiful night,' said Georgie, 'except that I dreamt about a gold mine and the bottom fell out of it, and all the ore slid down to the centre of the earth.'

'That will never do, Georgie. You must not let money get on your mind. I'll attend to your interests when I get to work after breakfast. And are your face and neck better?'

'Terribly sore still. I don't know when I shall be able to shave.'

Lucia gave him a glance with head a little tilted, as if he was a landscape she proposed to paint. That neat beard gave character and distinction to his face. It hid his plump second chin and concealed the slightly receding shape of the first: another week's growth would give it a greater solidity. There was something Stuart-like, something van Dyckish about his face. To be sure the colour of his beard contrasted rather strangely with his auburn hair and moustache, in which not the faintest hint of grey was manifest, but that could be remedied. It was not time, however, to say anything about that yet.

'Don't think about it then,' she said. 'And now for to-day. I really think you ought to get some air. It's so mild and sunny. Wrap up well and come for a drive with me before lunch.'

'But they'll see me,' said Georgie.

'Not if you lean well back till we're out of the town. I shall walk up there when I've gone into my affairs and yours, for I'm sure to have a telegram to send, and the car shall take you and Foljambe straight up to your house. I shall join you, so that we shall appear to be starting from there. Now I must get to work. I see there's a letter from my broker.'

Lucia's voice had assumed that firm tone which Georgie knew well to betoken that she meant to have her way, and that all protest was merely a waste of nervous force. Off she went to the little room once known as the library, but now more properly to be called the Office. This was an inviolable sanctuary: Grosvenor had orders that she must never be disturbed there except under stress of some great emergency, such as a trunk-call from London. The table where Lucia used to sit with her Greek and Latin dictionaries and the plays of Aristophanes and the Odes of Horace with their English translations was now swept clean of its classical lore, and a ledger stood there, a bundle of prospectuses, some notes of purchase and a clip of communications from her broker. She opened the letter she had received this morning, and read it with great care. The rise in gold (and in consequence in gold mines) he thought had gone far enough and he repeated his suggestion that home-rails and silver merited attention. There lay the annual report of Burma Corporation, and a very confusing document she found it, for it dealt with rupees and annas instead of pounds and shillings, and she did not know the value of an anna or what relation it bore to a rupee: they might as well have been drachmas and obols. Then there was a statement about the earnings of the Great Western Railway (Lucia had no idea how many people went by train), and another about the Southern Railway shewing much improved traffics. Once more she referred to her broker's last two letters, and then, with the dash and decision of Dame Catherine, made up her mind. She would sell out her entire holding in Siriami, and Burma Corporation and Southern Rails Preferred should enact a judgment of Solomon on the proceeds and each take half. She felt that she was slighting that excellent line, the Great Western, but it must get on without her support. Then she wrote out the necessary telegram to her broker, and touched the bell on her table. Grosvenor, according to orders, only opened the door an inch or two, and Lucia sent for Georgie.

Like a client he pulled a high chair up to the table.

'Georgie, I've gone very carefully into the

monetary situation,' she said, 'and I am selling all my Siriami. As you and others in Tilling followed me in your little purchases, I feel it my duty to tell you all what I am doing.'

Georgie gave a sigh of relief, as when a very rapid movement in a piano duet came to an end.

'I shall sell, too, then,' he said. 'I'm very glad. I'm not up to the excitement after my shingles. It's been very pleasant because I've made fifty pounds, but I've had enough. Will you take a telegram for me when you go?'

Lucia closed her ledger, put a paper-weight on her prospectuses, and clipped Mammoncash's letter into its sheaf.

'I think — I say I think — that you're right, Georgie,' she said. 'The situation is becoming too difficult for me to advise about, and I am glad you have settled to clear out, so that I have no further responsibility. Now I shall walk up to Tilling — I find these great decisions very stimulating — and a quarter of an hour later, you will start in the car with Foljambe. I think — I say I think — that Mammoncash, my broker you know, telegraphic address, will approve my decision.'

As he had already strongly recommended this course, it was probable he would do so, and Lucia walked briskly up to the High Street. Then, seeing Benjy and Elizabeth hanging about outside the post-office, she assumed a slower gait and a rapt, financial face.

'*Bon jour, chérie,*' said Elizabeth, observing that she took two telegrams out of her bag. 'Those sweet Siriamis. Up another sixpence.'

Lucia seemed to recall her consciousness from an immense distance, and broke the transition in Italian.

'*Ah, si, si! Buono piccolo Siriami!* . . . So glad, dear Elizabeth and Major Benjy that my little pet has done well for you. But I've been puzzling over it this morning and I think the price of gold is high enough. That's my impression — '

Diva whizzed across the road from the greengrocer's. All her zest and brightness had come back to her.

'Such a relief to have made up my mind, Lucia,' she said. 'I've telegraphed to sell two-thirds of my Siriami shares, and I shall keep the rest.'

'Very likely you're right, dear,' said Lucia. 'Very likely I'm wrong, but I'm selling all my little portfolio of them.'

Diva's sunny face clouded over.

'Oh, but that's terribly upsetting,' she said. 'I wonder if I'm too greedy. Do tell me what you think.'

Lucia had now come completely out of her remote financial abstraction, and addressed the meeting.

'Far be it from me to advise anybody,' she said. 'The monetary situation is too complicated for me to take the responsibility. But my broker admits — I must say I was flattered — that there is a great deal to be said for my view, and since you all followed my lead in your little purchases of Siriami, I feel bound to tell you what I am doing to-day. Not one share of Siriami am I keeping, and I'm reinvesting the whole — I beg of you all *not* to consider this advice in any way — in Burma Corporation and Southern Railway Preferred, Prefs as we call them. I have given some study to the matter, and while I don't think anyone would go far wrong in buying them, I should be sorry if any of you followed me blindly, without going into the matter for yourselves — '

Elizabeth simply could not stand it a moment longer.

'Sweet of you to tell us, dear,' she said, 'but pray don't make yourself uneasy about any responsibility for us. My Benjy and I have been studying too, and we've made up our minds to buy some more Siriami. So set your mind at ease.'

Diva moaned.

'Oh, dear me! Must begin thinking about it all over again,' she said, as Lucia, at this interruption from the meeting, went into the post-office.

Elizabeth waited till the swing-door had shut.

'I'm more and more convinced,' she said, 'that the dear thing has no more idea what she's talking about than when she makes psychic bids. I shall do the opposite of whatever she recommends.'

'Most confusing,' moaned Diva again. 'I wish I hadn't begun to make money at all.'

Elizabeth followed Lucia into the post-office, and Benjy went to catch the tram, while Diva, with ploughed and furrowed face, walked up and down the pavement in an agony of indecision as to whether to follow Lucia's example and sell her three remaining shares or to back Elizabeth and repurchase her two.

'Whatever I do is sure to be wrong,' she thought to herself, and then her attention was switched off finance altogether. Along the High Street came Lucia's motor. Cadman turned to go up the street leading to the church and Mallards Cottage, but had to back again to let Susan's Royce come down. Foljambe was sitting by her husband on the box, and for an instant there appeared at the window of the car the face of a man curiously like Georgie. Yet it couldn't be he, for he had a neat white beard. Perhaps Lucia had a friend staying with her, but, if so, it was very odd that nobody had heard about him. 'Most extraordinary,' thought Diva. 'Who can it possibly be?'

She got no second glimpse for the head was withdrawn in a great hurry, and Lucia came out of the post-office as calm as if she had been buying a penny stamp instead of conducting these vast operations.

'So that's done!' she said lightly, 'and now I must go and see whether I can persuade Georgie to come out for a drive.'

'Your car has just gone by,' said Diva.

'*Tante grazie.* I must hurry.'

Lucia went up to Mallards Cottage, and found Georgie had gone into his house, for fear that Elizabeth might peer into the car if she saw it standing there.

'And I was a little imprudent,' he said, 'for I simply couldn't resist looking out as we turned up from the High Street to see what was going on, and there was Diva standing quite close. But I don't think she could have recognised me.'

In view of this contingency, however, the re-embarkation was delayed for a few minutes, and then conducted with great caution. This was lucky, for Diva had told Elizabeth of that puzzling apparition at the window of the car, and Elizabeth, after a brilliant and sarcastic suggestion that it was Mr. Montagu Norman who had come down to consult Lucia as to the right policy of the Bank of England in this world crisis, decided that the matter must be looked into at once. So the two ladies separated and Diva hurried up to the Church Square in case the car left Georgie's house by that route, while Elizabeth went up to Mallards, where, from the window of the garden-room she could command the other road of exit . . . So, before Georgie entered the car again, Foljambe reconnoitred this way and that, and came back with the alarming intelligence that Diva was lurking in Church Square, and that Elizabeth was in her usual lair behind the curtains. Cadman and Foljambe therefore stood as a screen on each side of Georgie's doorstep while he, bending double, stole into the car. They passed under the window of the garden-room, and Lucia, leaning far forward to conceal Georgie, kissed and waved her hand to the half-drawn curtains to show Elizabeth that she was perfectly aware who was in ambush behind them.

'That's thwarted them,' she said, as she put down the window when danger-points were passed. 'Poor Elizabeth couldn't have seen you, and Diva may hide in Church Square till Doomsday. Let's drive out past the golf links along the road by the sea and let the breeze blow away all these pettinesses.'

She sighed.

'Georgie, how glad I am that I've taken up finance seriously,' she said. 'It gives me real work to do at last. It's time I had some, for I'm fifty next week. Of course I shall give a birthday party, and I shall have a cake with fifty-one candles on it, so as to prepare me for my next birthday. After all, it isn't the years that give the measure of one's age, but energy and capacity for enterprise. Achievement. Adventure.'

'I'm sure you were as busy as any woman could be,' said Georgie.

'Possibly, but about paltry things, scoring off Elizabeth when she was pushing and that *genus omne*. I shall give all that up. I shall dissociate myself from all the petty gossip of the place. I shall — '

'Oh, look,' interrupted Georgie. 'There's Benjy playing golf with the Padre. There! He missed the ball completely, and he's stamping with rage.'

'No! So it is!' cried Lucia, wildly interested. 'Pull up a minute, Cadman. There now he's hit it again into a sandpit, and the Padre's arguing with him. I wonder what language he's talking.'

'That's the best of Tilling,' cried Georgie enthusiastically, throwing prudence to the sea-winds, and leaning out of the window.

'There's always something exciting going on. If it isn't one thing it's another, and very often both!'

Benjy dealt the sand-pit one or two frightful biffs and Lucia suddenly remembered that she had done with such paltry trifles.

'Drive on, Cadman,' she said. 'Georgie, I'm afraid Major Benjy's nature has not been broadened and enriched by marriage. Marriage, one hoped, might have brought that about, but I don't see the faintest sign of it. Indeed I can't make up my mind about their marriage at all. They dab and stroke each other, and they're Benjy-boy and Girlie, but is it more than lip-service and finger-tips? Some women, I know, have had their greatest triumphs when youth was long, long past: Diane de Poictiers was fifty, was she not, when she became the King's mistress, but she was an enchantress, and you could not reasonably call Elizabeth an enchantress. Of course you haven't seen them together yet, but you will at my birthday party.'

Georgie gingerly fingered the portion of beard on the ailing side of his face.

'Not much chance of it,' he said. 'I don't suppose I shall get rid of this by then. Too tarsome.'

Lucia looked at him again with a tilted head.

'Well, we shall see,' she said. 'My dear, the sun glinting on the sea! Is that what Homer — or was it Æschylus? — meant by the 'numberless laughter of ocean?' An immortal phrase.'

'I shouldn't wonder if it was,' said Georgie. 'But about Benjy and Elizabeth. I can't see how you could expect anybody to be broadened and enriched by marrying Elizabeth. Nor by marrying Benjy for that matter.'

'Perhaps I was too sanguine. I hope they won't come to grief over their speculations. They're ignorant of the elements of finance. I told them both this morning what I was going to do. So they went and did exactly the opposite.'

'It's marvellous the way you've picked it up,' said Georgie. 'I'm fifty pounds richer by following your advice — '

'No, Georgie, not advice. My lead, if you like.'

'Lead then. I'm not sure I shan't have another go.'

'I wouldn't,' said she. 'It began to get on your mind: you dreamed about gold mines. Don't get like Diva: she was wringing her hands on the pavement in agony as to what she should do.'

'But how can you help thinking about it?'

'I do think about it,' she said, 'but calmly,

as if finance was a science, which indeed it is. I study, I draw my conclusions, I act. By the way, do you happen to know how much a rupee is worth?'

'No idea,' said Georgie, 'but not very much, I believe. If you have a great many of them, they make a lakh. But I don't know how many it takes, nor what a lakh is when they've made it.'

* * *

No startling developments occurred during the next week. Siriami shares remained steady, but the continued strain so told on Diva that, having bought seven more because the Mapp-Flints were making further purchases she had a nervous crisis one morning when they went down sixpence, sold her entire holding (ten shares) and with the help of a few strychnine pills regained her impaired vitality. But she watched with the intensest interest the movements of the market, for once again, as so often before, a deadly duel was in progress between Elizabeth and Lucia, but now it was waged as on some vast battlefield consisting of railway lines running between the shafts of gold mines. Lucia, so to speak, on the footboard of an engine on the Southern railway shrieked by, drawing a freight of Burma Corporation, while Elizabeth put lumps of ore from Siriami on the metals to wreck her train. For Southern Railway Prefs began to move: one morning they were one point up, another morning they were three, and at Mallards the two chagrined operators snatched up their copies of the *Financial Post* and ate with a poor appetite. It was known all over Tilling that this fierce fight was in progress, and when, next Sunday morning, the sermon was preached by a missionary who had devoted himself to the enlightenment of the heathen both in Burma and West Africa, Lucia, sitting among the auxiliary choir on one side of the church and the Mapp-Flints on the other seemed indeed to be the incarnations of those dark countries. Mr. Wyse, attending closely to the sermon thought that was a most extraordinary coincidence: even missionary work in foreign lands seemed to be drawn into the vortex.

Next morning on the breakfast table at Mallards was Lucia's invitation to the Mapp-Flints to honour her with their presence at dinner on Friday next, the occasion of her Jubilee. Southern Prefs had gone up again and Siriami down, but, so Elizabeth surmised, 'all Tilling' would be there, and if she and Benjy refused, which seemed the proper way to record what they felt about it, all Tilling would certainly conclude that they had not been asked.

'It's her *ways* that I find it so hard to bear,' said Elizabeth, cracking the top of her boiled egg with such violence that the rather under-cooked contents streamed on to her plate. 'Her airs, her arrogance. Even if she says nothing about Siriami I shall know she's pitying us for not having followed her lead, and buying those wild-cat shares of hers. What has Bohemian Corporation, or whatever it is, been doing? I didn't look.'

'Up sixpence,' said Benjy, gloomily.

Elizabeth moistened her lips.

'I suspected as much, and you see I was right. But I suppose we had better go to her Jubilee, and perhaps we shall learn something of this mystery about Georgie. I'm sure she's keeping something dark: I feel it in my bones. Women of a certain age are like that. They know that they are getting on in years and have become entirely unattractive, and so they make mysteries in order to induce people to take an interest in them a little longer, poor things. There was that man with a beard whom Diva saw in her car; there's a mystery which has never been cleared up. Probably it was her gardener, who has a beard, dressed up, and she hoped we might think she had someone staying with her whom we were to know nothing about. Just a mystery.'

'Well, she made no mystery about selling Siriami and buying those blasted Prefs,' said Benjy.

'My fault then, I suppose,' said Elizabeth bitterly, applying the pepper pot to the pool of egg on her plate, and scooping it up with her spoon. 'I see: I ought to have followed Lucia's lead, and have invested my money as she recommended. And curtsied, and said 'Thank your gracious Majesty.' Quite.'

'I didn't say you ought to have done anything of the kind,' said Benjy.

Elizabeth had applied pepper with too lavish a hand, and had a frightful fit of sneezing before she could make the obvious rejoinder.

'No, but you implied it, Benjy, which, if anything, is worse,' she answered hoarsely.

'No I didn't. No question of 'ought' about it. But I wish to God I had done as she suggested. Southern Prefs have risen ten points since she told us.'

'We won't discuss it any further, please,' said Elizabeth.

★   ★   ★

Everyone accepted the invitation to the Jubilee, and now Lucia thought it time to put into action her scheme for getting Georgie to make his re-entry into the world of Tilling. He was quite himself again save for the pointed white beard which Foljambe had once more trimmed very skilfully, his cook was returning from her holiday next day, and he would be going back to shut himself up in his lonely little house until he could present his normal face to his friends. On that point he was immovable: nobody should see him with a little white beard, for it would be the end of his *jeune* premiership of Tilling: no *jeune premier* ever had a white beard, however little. And Dr. Dobbie had told him not to think of 'irritating the nerve-ends' with the razor until they were incapable of resentment. In another three weeks or so, Dr. Dobbie thought. This verdict depressed Georgie: there would be three weeks more of skulking out in his motor, heavily camouflaged, and of return to his dreary solitude in the evening. He wanted to hear the Padre mingle Irish with Scotch, he wanted to see Diva with her Eton crop, he wanted to study the effect of matrimony on Mapp and Flint, and what made him miss this daily bread the more was that Lucia was very sparing in supplying him with it, for she was rather strict in her inhuman resolve to have done with petty gossip. Taken unawares, she could still manifest keen interest in seeing Benjy hit a golf ball into a bunker, but she checked herself in an annoying manner and became lofty again. Probably her inhumanity would wear off, but it was tarsome that when he so particularly thirsted for local news, she should be so parsimonious with it.

However, they dined very comfortably that night, though she had many far-away glances, as if at distant blue hills, which indicated that she was thinking out some abstruse problem: Georgie supposed it was some terrific financial operation of which she would not speak at meals. Then she appeared to have solved it, for the blue-hill-look vanished, she riddled him with several gimlet-glances, and suddenly gabbled about the modern quality of the Idylls of Theocritus. 'Yet perhaps modern is the wrong word,' she said. 'Let us call it the timeless quality, Georgie, *senza tempo* in fact. It is characteristic, don't you think of all great artists: van Dyck has it pre-eminently. What timeless distinction his portraits have! His Lady Castlemaine, the Kéroualle, Nell Gwynn — '

'But surely van Dyck was dead before their time,' began Georgie. 'Charles I, you know, not Charles II.'

'That may be so, possibly you are right,' said Lucia with her habitual shamelessness. 'But my proposition holds. van Dyck is timeless, he shows the dignity, the distinction which can be realized in every age. But I always maintain — I wonder if you will agree with me — that his portraits of men are far, far finer than his women. More perception: I doubt if he ever understood women really. But his men! That coloured print I have of his Gelasius in the next room by the piano. Marvellous! Have you finished your coffee? Let us go.'

Lucia strolled into the drawing-room, glanced at a book on the table, and touched a few notes on the piano as if she had forgotten all about Gelasius.

'Shall we give ourselves a holiday to-night, Georgie, and not tackle that dwefful diffy Brahms?' she asked. 'I shall have to practise my part before I am fit to play it with you. Wonderful Brahms! As Pater says of something else, 'the soul with all its maladies' has entered into his music.'

She closed the piano, and casually pointed to a coloured print that hung on the wall above it beside a false Chippendale mirror.

'Ah, there's the Gelasius I spoke of,' she said. 'Rather a dark corner. I must find a worthier place for him.'

Georgie came across to look at it. Certainly it was a most distinguished face: high eye-browed with a luxuriant crop of auburn hair and a small pointed beard. A man in early middle life, perhaps forty at the most. Georgie could not remember having noticed it before, which indeed was not to be wondered at, since Lucia had bought it that very afternoon. She had seen the great resemblance to Georgie, and her whole magnificent scheme had flashed upon her.

'Dear me, what a striking face,' he said. 'Stupid of me never to have looked at it before.'

Lucia made no answer, and turning, he saw that she was eagerly glancing first at the picture and then at him, and then at the picture again. Then she sat down on the piano stool and clasped her hands.

'Absolutely too *straordinario*,' she said as if speaking to herself.

'What is?' asked Georgie.

'*Caro*, do not pretend to be so blind! Why it's the image of you. Take a good look at it, then move a step to the right and look at yourself in the glass.'

Georgie did as he was told, and a thrill of rapture tingled in him. For years he had known (and lamented) that his first chin receded and that a plump second chin was

98

advancing from below, but now his beard completely hid these blemishes.

'Well, I do see what you mean,' he said.

'Who could help it? Georgie, you *are* Gelasius, which I've always considered van Dyck's masterpiece. And it's your beard that has done it. Unified! Harmonised! And to think that you intend to shut yourself up for three weeks more and then cut it off! It's murder. Artistic murder!'

Georgie cast another look at Gelasius and then at himself. All these weeks he had taken only the briefest and most disgusted glances into his looking-glass because of the horror of his beard, and had been blind to what it had done for him. He felt a sudden stab of longing to be a permanent Gelasius, but there was one frightful snag in the way, irrespective of the terribly shy-making moment when he should reveal himself to Tilling so radically altered. The latter, with such added distinction to shew them, he thought he could tone himself up to meet. But —

'Well?' asked Lucia rather impatiently. She had her part ready.

'What's so frightfully tarsome is that my beard's so grey that you might call it white,' he said. 'There's really not a grey hair on my head or in my moustache, and the stupid thing has come out this colour. No colour at all, in fact. Do you think it's because I'm run down?'

Lucia pounced on this: it was a brilliant thought of Georgie's, and made her part easier.

'Of course that's why,' she said. 'As you get stronger, your beard will certainly get its colour back. Just a question of time. I think it's beginning already.'

'But what am I to do till then?' asked Georgie. 'Such an odd appearance.'

She laughed.

'Fancy asking a woman that!' she said. 'Dye it, Georgino. Temporarily of course, just anticipating Nature. There's that barber in Hastings you go to. Drive over there to-morrow.'

Actually, Georgie had got a big bottle upstairs of the precise shade, and had been touching up with it this morning. But Lucia's suggestion of Hastings was most satisfactory. It implied surely that she had no cognizance of these hidden practices.

'I shouldn't quite like to do that,' said he.

Lucia had by now developed her full horse-power in persuasiveness. She could quite understand (knowing Georgie) why he intended to shut himself up for another three weeks, sooner than shew himself to Tilling with auburn hair and a white beard (and indeed, though she personally had got used to it, he was a very odd object). Everyone would draw the inevitable conclusion that he dyed his hair, and though they knew it perfectly well already, the public demonstration of that fact would be intolerable to him, for the poor lamb evidently thought that this was a secret shared only by his bottle of hair-dye. Besides, she had now for over a fortnight concealed him like some Royalist giving a hiding place to King Charles, and while he had been there, she had not been able to ask a single one of her friends to the house, for fear they should catch a glimpse of him. Her kindliness revolted at the thought of his going back to his solitude, but she had had enough of his undiluted company. He had been a charming companion: she had even admitted to herself that it would be pleasant to have him always here, but not at the price of seeing nobody else . . . She opened the throttle.

'But how perfectly unreasonable,' she cried. 'Dyeing it is only a temporary measure till it resumes its colour. And the improvement! My dear, I never saw such an improvement. Diva's not in it! And how can you contemplate going back to solitary confinement, for indeed it's that, for weeks and weeks more, and then at the end to scrap it? The distinction, Georgie, the dignity, and, to be quite frank, the complete disappearance of your chin, which was the one weak feature in your face. And it's in your power to be a living van Dyck masterpiece, and you're hesitating whether you shall madly cast away, as the hymn says, that wonderful chance. Hastings to-morrow, directly after breakfast, I implore you. It will be dry by lunch-time, won't it? Why, a woman with the prospect of improving her appearance so colossally would be unable to sleep a wink to-night from sheer joy. Oh, *amico mio*,' she said, lapsing into the intimate dialect, 'Oo will vex *povera* Lucia vewy, vewy much if you shave off *vostra bella barba. Di grazia!* Georgie.'

'Me must fink,' said Georgie. He left his chair and gazed once more at Gelasius and then at himself, and wondered if he had the nerve to appear without warning in High Street even if his beard was auburn.

'I believe you're right,' he said at length. 'Fancy all this coming out of my shingles. But it's a tremendous step to take . . . Yes, I'll do it. And I shall be able to come to your birthday party after all.'

'It wouldn't be a birthday party without you,' said Lucia warmly.

Georgie's cook having returned, he went back to his own house after the operation next morning. He had taken a little hand-glass with him to Hastings, and all the way home he had constantly consulted it in order to get used to himself, for he felt as if a total stranger with a seventeenth century face was sharing the car with him, and his agitated consciousness suggested that anyone looking at him at all closely would conclude that this lately discovered van Dyck (like the Carlisle Holbein) was a very doubtful piece. It might be after van Dyck, but assuredly a very long way after. Foljambe opened the door of Mallards Cottage to him, and she considerably restored his shattered confidence. For the moment her jaw dropped, as if she had been knocked out, at the shock of this transformation, but then she recovered completely, and beamed up at him.

'Well, that is a pleasant change, sir,' she said, 'from your white beard, if you'll pardon me,' and Georgie hurried upstairs to get an ampler view of himself in the big mirror in his bedroom than the hand-glass afforded. He then telephoned to Lucia to say that the operation was safely over and she promised to come up directly after lunch and behold.

The nerve-strain had tired him and so did the constant excursions upstairs to get fresh impressions of himself. Modern costume was a handicap, but a very pretty little cape of his with fur round the neck had a Gelasian effect, and when Lucia arrived he came down in this. She was all applause: she walked slowly round him to get various points of view, ejaculating, 'My *dear*, what an improvement,' or 'My dear, *what* an improvement,' to which Georgie replied, 'Do you really like it?' until her iteration finally convinced him that she was sincere. He settled to rest for the remainder of the day after these fatigues, and to burst upon all Tilling at the marketing hour next morning.

'And what do you seriously think they'll all think?' he asked. 'I'm terribly nervous as you may imagine. It would be good of you if you'd pop in to-morrow morning, and walk down with me. I simply couldn't pass underneath the garden-room window, with Elizabeth looking out, alone.'

'Ten forty-five, Georgie,' she said. '*What* an improvement!'

★　★　★

The afternoon and evening dragged after she was gone. It was pleasant to see his bibelots again, but he missed Lucia's companionship. Intimate as they had been for many years, they had never before had each other's undivided company for so long. A book, and a little conversation with Foljambe made dinner tolerable, but after that she went home to her Cadman, and he was alone. He polished up the naughty snuffbox, he worked at his *petit-point* shepherdess. He had stripped her nakeder than Eve, and replaced her green robe with pink, and now instead of looking like a stick of asparagus she really might have been a young lady who, for reasons of her own, preferred to tend her sheep with nothing on; but he wanted to show her to somebody and he could hardly discuss her with his cook. Or a topic of interest occurred to him, but there was no one to share it with, and he played beautifully on his piano, but nobody congratulated him. It was dreary work to be alone, though no doubt he would get used to it again, and dreary to go up to bed with no chattering on the stairs. Often he used to linger with Lucia at her bedroom door, finishing their talk, and even go in with her by express invitation. To-night he climbed up stairs alone, and heard his cook snoring.

Lucia duly appeared next morning, and they set off under the guns of the garden-room window. Elizabeth was there as usual, and after fixing on them for a moment her opera glass which she used for important objects at a distance, she gave a squeal that caused Benjy to drop the *Financial Post* which recorded the ruinous fall of two shillings in Siriami.

'Mr. Georgie's got a beard,' she cried, and hurried to get her hat and basket and follow them down to the High Street. Diva, looking out of her window was the next to see him, and without the hint Elizabeth had had of observing his exit from his own house quite failed to recognise him at first. She had to go through an addition sum in circumstantial evidence before she arrived at his identity: he was with Lucia, he was of his own height and build, the rest of his face was the same and he had on the well-known little cape with the fur collar. Q.E.D. She whistled to Pat, she seized her basket, and taking a header into the street ran straight into Elizabeth who was sprinting down from Mallards.

'He's come out. Mr. Georgie. A beard,' she said.

Elizabeth was out of breath with her swift progress.

'Oh yes, dear,' she panted. 'Didn't you know? Fancy! Where have they gone?'

'Couldn't see. Soon find them. Come on.'

Elizabeth, chagrined at not being able to announce the news to Diva, instantly determined to take the opposite line, and not shew the slightest interest in this prodigious transformation.

'But why this excitement, dear?' she said. 'I

cannot think of anything that matters less. Why shouldn't Mr. Georgie have a beard? If you had one now — '

A Sinaitic trumpet-blast from Susan's Royce made them both leap on to the pavement, as if playing Tom Tiddler's ground.

'But don't you remember — ' began Diva almost before alighting — 'there we're safe — don't you remember the man with a white beard whom I saw in Lucia's car? Must be same man. You said it was Mr. Montagu Norman first and then Lucia's gardener disguised. The one we watched for, you at your window and me in Church Square.'

'Grammar, dear Diva. 'I' not 'me',' interrupted Elizabeth to gain time, while she plied her brain with crucial questions. For if Diva was right, and the man in Lucia's car had been Georgie (white beard), he must have been driving back to Mallards Cottage in Lucia's car from somewhere. Could he have been living at Grebe all the time while he pretended (or Lucia pretended for him) to have been at home too ill to see anybody? But if so, why, on some days, had his house appeared to be inhabited, and on some days completely deserted? Certainly Georgie (auburn beard) had come out of it this morning with Lucia. Had they been staying with each other alternately? Had they been living in sin? . . . Poor shallow Diva had not the slightest perception of these deep and probably grievous matters. Her feather-pated mind could get no further that the colour of beards. Before Diva could frame an adequate reply to this paltry grammatical point a positive eruption of thrills occurred. Lucia and Georgie came out of the post office, Paddy engaged in a dog fight, and the Padre and Evie Bartlett emerged from the side street opposite, and, as if shot from a catapult, projected themselves across the road just in front of Susan's motor.

'Oh, dear me, they'll be run over!' cried Diva. 'PADDY! And there are Mr. Georgie and Lucia. What a lot of things are happening this morning!'

'Diva, you're a little overwrought,' said Elizabeth with kindly serenity. 'What with white beards and brown beards and motor accidents ... Oh, *voilà*! There's Susan actually got out of her car, and she's almost running across the road to speak to Mr. Georgie, and quaint Irene in shorts. What a fuss! For goodness sake let's be dignified and go on with our shopping. The whole thing has been staged by Lucia, and I won't be a super.'

'But I must go and say I'm glad he's better,' said Diva.

'*Certainement*, dear, if you happen to think he's been ill. I believe it's all a hoax.'

But she spoke to the empty air for Diva had thumped Paddy in the ribs with her market-basket and was whizzing away to the group on the pavement where Georgie was receiving general congratulations on his recovery and his striking appearance. The verdict was most flattering, and long after his friends had gazed their fill he continued to walk up and down the High Street and pop into shops where he wanted nothing, in order that his epiphany which he had been so nervous about, and which he found purely enjoyable, might be manifest to all. For a long time Elizabeth, determined to take no part in a show which she was convinced was run by Lucia, succeeded in avoiding him, but at last he ran her to earth in the greengrocer's. She examined the quality of the spinach till her back ached, and then she had to turn round and face him.

'Lovely morning, isn't it, Mr. Georgie,' she said. 'So pleased to see you about again. Sixpennyworth of spinach, please, Mr. Twistevant. Looks so good!' and she hurried out of the shop, still unconscious of his beard.

'Tarsome woman,' thought Georgie. 'If there is a fly anywhere about she is sure to put it in somebody's ointment . . . ' But there had been so much ointment on the subject that he really didn't much mind about Elizabeth's fly.

4

Elizabeth Mapp-Flint had schemes for her husband and meant to realize them. As a bachelor, with an inclination to booze and a very limited income, inhabiting that small house next to Mallards, it was up to him, if he chose, to spend the still robust energies of his fifty-five years in playing golf all day and getting slightly squiffy in the evening. But his marriage had given him a new status: he was master, though certainly not mistress, of the best house in Tilling, he was, through her, a person of position, and it was only right that he should have a share in municipal government. The elections to the Town Council were coming on shortly, and she had made up her mind, and his for him, that he must stand. The fact that, if elected, he would make it his business to get something done about Susan Wyse's motor causing a congestion of traffic every morning in the High Street was not really a leading motive. Elizabeth craved for the local dignity which his election would give not only to him but her, and if poor Lucia (always pushing herself forward) happened to turn pea-green with envy, that would be her misfortune and not Elizabeth's fault. As yet the programme which he should present to the electors was only being thought out, but municipal economy (Major Mapp-Flint and Economy) with reduction of rates would be the ticket.

The night of Lucia's birthday party was succeeded by a day of pelting rain, and, no golf being possible, Elizabeth, having sent her cook (she had a mackintosh) to do the marketing for her, came out to the garden-room after breakfast for a chat. She always knocked at the door, opening it a chink and saying, 'May I come in, Benjy-boy?' in order to remind him of her nobility in giving it him. To-day a rather gruff voice answered her, for economy had certainly not been the ticket at Lucia's party, and there had been a frightful profusion of viands and wine: really a very vulgar display, and Benjy had eaten enormously and drunk far more wine than was positively necessary for the quenching of thirst. There had been a little argument as they drove home, for he had insisted that there were fifty-one candles round the cake and that it had been a remarkably jolly evening: she said that there were only fifty candles, and that it was a very mistaken sort of hospitality which gave guests so much more than they wanted to eat or should want to drink. His lack of appetite at breakfast might prove that he had had enough to eat the night before to last him some hours yet, but his extraordinary consumption of tea could not be explained on the same analogy. But Elizabeth thought she had made sufficient comment on that at breakfast (or tea as far as he was concerned) and when she came in this morning for a chat, she had no intention of rubbing it in. The accusation, however, that he had not been able to count correctly up to fifty or fifty-one, still rankled in his mind, for it certainly implied a faintly camouflaged connection with sherry, champagne, port and brandy.

'Such a pity, dear,' she said brightly, 'that it's so wet. A round of golf would have done you all the good in the world. Blown the cobwebs away.'

To Benjy's disgruntled humour, this seemed an allusion to the old subject, and he went straight to the point.

'There were fifty-one candles,' he said.

'*Cinquante*, Benjy,' she answered firmly. 'She is fifty. She said so. So there must have been fifty.'

'Fifty-one. Candles I mean. But what I've been thinking over is that you've been thinking, if you follow me, that I couldn't count. Very unjust. Perhaps you'll say I saw a hundred next. Seeing double, eh? And why should a round of golf do me all the good in the world to-day? Not more good than any other day, unless you want me to get pneumonia.'

Elizabeth sat down on the seat in the window as suddenly as if she had been violently hit behind the knees, and put her handkerchief up to her eyes to conceal the fact that there was not a vestige of a tear there. As he was facing towards the fire he did not perceive this manœuvre and thought she had only gone to the window to make her usual morning observations. He continued to brood over the *Financial Post*, which contained the news that Siriami had been weak and Southern Prefs remarkably strong. These items were about equally depressing.

Elizabeth was doubtful as to what to do next. In the course of their married life, there had been occasional squalls, and she had tried sarcasm and vituperation with but small success. Benjy-boy had answered her back or sulked, and she was left with a sense of imperfect mastery. This policy of being hurt was a new one, and since the first signal had not been noticed she hoisted a second one and sniffed.

'Got a bit of a cold?' he asked pacifically.

No answer, and he turned round.

'Why, what's wrong?' he said.

'And there's a *jolie chose* to ask,' said

113

Elizabeth with strangled shrillness. 'You tell me I want you to catch pneumonia, and then ask what's wrong. You wound me deeply.'

'Well, I got annoyed with your nagging at me that I couldn't count. You implied I was squiffy just because I had a jolly good dinner. And there were fifty-one candles.'

'It doesn't matter if there were fifty-one million,' cried Elizabeth. 'What matters is that you spoke to me very cruelly. I planned to make you so happy, Benjy, by giving up my best room to you and all sorts of things, and all the reward I get is to be told one day that I ought to have let Lucia lead me by the nose and almost the next that I hoped you would die of pneumonia.'

He came across to the window.

'Well, I didn't mean that,' he said. 'You're sarcastic, too, at times and say monstrously disagreeable things to me.'

'Oh, that's a wicked lie,' said Elizabeth violently. 'Never have I spoken disagreeably to you. *Jamais!* Firmly sometimes, but always for your good. *Toujours!* Never another thought in my head but your true happiness.'

Benjy was rather alarmed: hysterics seemed imminent.

'Yes, girlie, I know that,' he said soothingly. 'Nothing the matter? Nothing wrong?'

She opened her mouth once or twice like a

gasping fish, and recovered her self-control.

'Nothing, dear, that I can tell you yet,' she said. 'Don't ask me. But never say I want you to get pneumonia again. It hurt me cruelly. There! All over! Look, there's Mr. Georgie coming out in this pelting rain. Do you know, I like his beard, though I couldn't tell him so, except for that odd sort of sheen on it, like the colours on cold boiled beef. But I daresay that'll pass off. Oh, let's put up the window and ask him how many candles there were . . . Good morning, Mr. Georgie. What a lovely, no, disgusting morning, but what a lovely evening yesterday! Do you happen to know for certain how many candles there were on Lucia's beautiful cake?'

'Yes, fifty-one,' said Georgie, 'though she's only fifty. She put an extra one, so that she may get used to being fifty-one before she is.'

'What a pretty idea! So like her,' said Elizabeth, and shut the window again.

Benjy with great tact pretended not to have heard, for he had no wish to bring back those hysterical symptoms. A sensational surmise as to the cause of them had dimly occurred to him, but surely it was impossible. So tranquillity being restored, they sat together 'ever so cosily,' said Elizabeth, by the fire (which meant that she appropriated his hip-bath chair and got nearly all the heat) and began plotting out the campaign for the coming municipal elections.

'Better just get quietly to work, love,' said she, 'and not say much about it at first, for Lucia's sadly capable of standing, too, if she knows you are.'

'I'm afraid I told her last night,' said Benjy.

'Oh, what a blabbing boy! Well, it can't be helped now. Let's hope it'll put no jealous ambitions into her head. Now, *l'Économie* is the right slogan for you. Anything more reckless than the way the Corporation has been spending money I can't conceive. Just as if Tilling was Eldorado. Think of pulling down all those pretty little slums by the railway and building new houses! Fearfully expensive, and spoiling the town: taking all its quaintness away.'

'And then there's that new road they're making that skirts the town,' said Benjy, 'to relieve the congestion in the High Street.'

'Just so,' chimed in Elizabeth. 'They'd relieve it much more effectually if they didn't allow Susan to park her car, positively across the street, wherever she pleases, and as long as she pleases. It's throwing money about like that which sends up the rates by leaps and bounds; why, they're nearly double of what they were when I inherited Mallards from sweet Aunt Caroline. And nothing to shew for it except a road that nobody wants and some ugly new houses instead of those picturesque old cottages. They may be a little damp, perhaps, but, after all, there was a dreadful patch of damp in my bedroom last year, and I didn't ask the Town Council to rebuild Mallards at the public expense. And I'm told all those new houses have got a bathroom in which the tenants will probably keep poultry. Then, they say, there are the unemployed. Rubbish, Benjy! There's plenty of work for everybody, only those lazy fellows prefer the dole and idleness. We've got to pinch and squeeze so that the so-called poor may live in the lap of luxury. If I didn't get a good let for Mallards every year we shouldn't be able to live in it at all, and you may take that from me. Economy! That's the ticket! Talk to them like that and you'll head the poll.'

A brilliant notion struck Benjy as he listened to this impassioned speech. Though he liked the idea of holding public office and of the dignity it conferred, he knew that his golf would be much curtailed by his canvassing, and, if he was elected, by his duties. Moreover, he could not talk in that vivid and vitriolic manner . . .

He jumped up.

'Upon my word, Liz, I wish you'd stand instead of me,' he said. 'You've got the gift of the gab; you can put things clearly and forcibly, and you've got it all at your fingers' ends. Besides, you're the owner of Mallards, and these rates and taxes press harder on you than on me. What do you say to that?'

The idea had never occurred to her before: she wondered why. How she would enjoy paying calls on all the numerous householders who felt the burden of increasing rates, and securing their votes for her programme of economy! She saw herself triumphantly heading the poll. She saw herself sitting in the Council Room, the only woman present, with sheaves of statistics to confute this spendthrift policy. Eloquence, compliments, processions to church on certain official occasions, a status, a doctorial-looking gown, position, power. All these enticements beckoned her, and from on high, she seemed to look down on poor Lucia as if at the bottom of a disused well, fifty years old, playing duets with Georgie, and gabbling away about all the Aristophanes she read and the callisthenics she practised, and the principles of psychic bidding, and the advice she gave her broker, while Councillor Mapp-Flint was as busy with the interests of the Borough. A lesson for the self-styled Queen of Tilling.

'Really, dear,' she said, 'I hardly know what to say. Such a new idea to me, for all this was

118

the future I planned for you, and how I've lain awake at night thinking of it. I must adjust my mind to such a revolution of our plans. But there is something in what you suggest. That house to house canvassing: perhaps a woman is more suited to that than a man. A cup of tea, you know, with the mother and a peep at baby. It's true again that as owner of Mallards, I have a solider stake in property than you. Dear me, yes, I begin to see your point of view. Sound, as a man's always is. Then again what you call the gift of the gab — such a rude expression — perhaps forcible words do come more easily to me, and they'll be needful indeed when it comes to fighting the spendthrifts. But first you would have to promise to help me, for you know how I shall depend on you. I hope my health will stand the strain, and I'll gladly work myself to the bone in such a cause. Better to wear oneself out than rust in the scabbard.'

'You're cut out for the job,' said Benjy enthusiastically. 'As for wearing yourself out, hubby won't permit that!'

Once more Elizabeth recalled her bright visions of power and the reduction of rates. The prospect was irresistible.

'I give you your way as usual, Benjy-boy,' she said. 'How I spoil you! Such a bully!

119

What? *Dejeuner* already, Withers? Hasn't the morning flown?'

The morning had flown with equal speed for Lucia. She had gone to her office after breakfast, the passage to which had now been laid with india-rubber felting, so that no noise of footsteps outside could distract her when she was engaged in financial operations. This insured perfect tranquillity, unless it so happened that she was urgently wanted, in which case Grosvenor's tap on the door startled her very much since she had not heard her approach; this risk, however, was now minimised because she had a telephone extension to the office. Today there were entries to be made in the ledger, for she had sold her Southern Prefs at a scandalous profit, and there was a list of recommendations from that intelligent Mammoncash for the re-investment of the capital released.

She drew her chair up to the fire to study this. High-priced shares did not interest her much: you got so few for your money. 'The sort of thing I want,' she thought, 'is quantities of low-priced shares, like those angelic Siriamis, which nearly doubled their value in a few weeks,' but the list contained nothing to which Mammoncash thought this likely to happen. He even suggested that she might do worse than put half her capital into gilt-edged stock. He could not have made a duller suggestion: Dame Catherine Winterglass, Lucia felt sure, would not have touched Government Loans with the end of a barge-pole. Then there was 'London Transport 'C.'' Taking a long view, Mammoncash thought that in a year's time there should be a considerable capital appreciation . . .

Lucia found her power of concentration slipping from her, and her thoughts drifted away to her party last night. She had observed that Benjy had seldom any wine in his glass for more than a moment, and that Elizabeth's eye was on him. Though she had forsworn any interest in such petty concerns, food for serious thought had sprung out of this, for, getting expansive towards the end of dinner, he had told her that he was standing for the Town Council. He and Elizabeth both thought it was his duty. 'It'll mean a lot of work,' he said, 'but thank God, I'm not afraid of that, and something must be done to check this monstrous municipal extravagance. Less golf for me, Mrs. Lucas, but duty comes before pleasure. I shall hope to call on you before long and ask your support.'

Lucia had not taken much interest in this project at the time, but now ideas began to bubble in her brain. She need not consider the idea of his being elected — for who in his senses could conceivably vote for him? — and she found herself in violent opposition to the programme of economy which he had indicated. Exactly the contrary policy recommended itself: more work must somehow be found for the unemployed: the building of decent houses for the poor ought to be quickened up. There was urgent and serious work to be done, and, as she gazed meditatively at the fire, personal and ambitious day-dreams began to form themselves. Surely there was a worthy career here for an energetic and middle-aged widow. Then the telephone rang and she picked it off the table. Georgie.

'Such a filthy day: no chance of its clearing,' he said. 'Do come and lunch and we'll play duets.'

'Yes, Georgie, that will be lovely. What about my party last night?'

'Perfect. And weren't they all astonished when I told them about my shingles. Major Benjy was a bit squiffy. Doesn't get a chance at home.'

'I rather like to see people a little, just a little squiffy at my expense,' observed Lucia. 'It makes me feel I'm being a good hostess. Any news?'

'I passed there an hour ago,' said Georgie, 'and she suddenly threw the window up and asked me how many candles there were on your cake, and when I said there were fifty-one she banged it down again quite sharply.'

'No! I wonder why she wanted to know that and didn't like it when you told her,' said Lucia, intrigued beyond measure, and forgetting that such gossip could not be worth a moment's thought.

'Can't imagine. I've been puzzling over it,' said Georgie.

Lucia recollected her principles.

'Such a triviality in any case,' she said, 'whatever the explanation may be. I'll be with you at one-thirty. And I've got something very important to discuss with you. Something quite new: you can't guess.'

'My dear, how exciting! More money?'

'Probably less for all of us if it comes off,' said Lucia enigmatically. 'But I must get back to my affairs. I rather think, from my first glance at the report, that there ought to be capital appreciation in Transport 'C'.'

'Transport by sea?' asked Georgie.

'No, the other sort of sea. A. B. C.'

'Those tea-shops?' asked the intelligent Georgie.

'No, trams, buses, tubes.'

She rang off, but the moment afterwards so brilliant an idea struck her that she called him up again.

'Georgie: about the candles. I'm sure I've

got it. Elizabeth believed that there were fifty. That's a clue for you.'

She rang off again, and meditated furiously on the future.

Georgie ran to the door when Lucia arrived and opened it himself before Foljambe could get there.

' — and Benjy said there were fifty-one and she thought he wasn't in a state to count properly,' he said all in one breath. 'Come in, and tell me at once about the other important thing. Lunch is ready. Is it about Benjy?'

Georgie at once perceived that Lucia was charged with weighty matter. She was rather overwhelming in these humours: sometimes he wished he had a piece of green baize to throw over her as over a canary, when it will not stop singing. ('Foljambe, fetch Mrs. Lucas's baize,' he thought to himself.)

'Yes, indirectly about him, and directly about the elections to the Town Council. I think it's my duty to stand, Georgie, and when I see my duty clearly, I do it. Major Benjy is standing, you see; he told me so last night, and he's all out for the reduction of rates and taxes — '

'So am I,' said Georgie.

Lucia laid down her knife and fork, and let her pheasant get cold to Georgie's great annoyance.

'You won't be if you listen to me, my dear,' she said. 'Rates and taxes are high, it's true, but they ought to be ever so much higher for the sake of the unemployed. They must be given work, Georgie: I know myself how demoralizing it is not to have work to do. Before I embarked on my financial career, I was sinking into lethargy. It is the same with our poorer brethren. That new road, for instance. It employs a fair number of men, who would otherwise be idle and on the dole, but that's not nearly enough. Work helps everybody to maintain his — or her — self-respect: without work we should all go to the dogs. I should like to see that road doubled in width and — well in width, and however useless it might appear to be, the moral salvation of hundreds would have been secured by it. Again, those slums by the railway: it's true that new houses are being built to take the place of hovels which are a disgrace to any Christian town. But I demand a bigger programme. Those slums ought to be swept away, at once. All of them. The expense? Who cares? We fortunate ones will bear it between us. Here are we living in the lap of luxury, and just round the corner, so to speak, or, at any rate, at the bottom of the hill are those pig-sties, where human beings are compelled to live. No bathroom, I believe;

125

think of it, Georgie! I feel as if I ought to give free baths to anybody who cares to come and have one, only I suppose Grosvenor would instantly leave. The municipal building plans for the year ought to be far more comprehensive. That shall be my ticket: spend, spend, spend. I'm too selfish: I must work for others, and I shall send in my name as standing for the Town Council, and set about canvassing at once. How does one canvass?'

'You go from house to house asking for support I suppose,' said Georgie.

'And you'll help me, of course. I know I can rely on you.'

'But I don't want rates to be any higher,' said Georgie. 'Aren't you going to eat any pheasant?'

Lucia took up her knife and fork.

'But just think, Georgie. Here are you and I eating pheasant — *molto bene e bellissime* cooked — in your lovely little house, and then we shall play on your piano, and there are people in this dear little Tilling who never eat a pheasant or play on a piano from Christmas Day to New Year's Day, I mean the other way round. I hope to live here for the rest of my days, and I have a duty towards my neighbours.'

Lucia had a duty towards the pheasant,

too, and wolfed it down. Her voice had now assumed the resonant tang of compulsion, and Georgie, like the unfortunate victim of the Ancient Mariner 'could not choose but hear.'

'Georgie, you and I — particularly I — are getting on in years, and we shall not pass this way again. (Is it Kingsley, dear?) Anyhow we must help poor little lame dogs over stiles. Ickle you and me have been spoiled. We've always had all we wanted and we must do ickle more for others. I've got an insight into finance lately, and I can see what a power money is, what one can do with it unselfishly, like the wonderful Winterglass. I want to live, just for the few years that may still be left me, with a clear conscience, quietly and peacefully — '

'But with Benjy standing in the opposite interest, won't there be a bit of friction instead?' asked Georgie.

'Emphatically not, as far as I am concerned,' said Lucia, firmly. 'I shall be just as cordial to them as ever — I say 'them', because of course Elizabeth's at the bottom of his standing — and I give them the credit of their policy of economy being just as sincere as mine.'

'Quite,' said Georgie, 'for if taxes were much higher, and if they couldn't get a thumping good let for Mallards every year, I don't suppose they would be able to live there. Have to sell.'

An involuntary gleam lit up Lucia's bird-like eyes, just as if a thrush had seen a fat worm. She instantly switched it off.

'Naturally I should be very sorry for them,' she said, 'if they had to do that, but personal regrets can't affect my principles. And then, Georgie, more schemes seem to outline themselves. Don't be frightened: they will bring only me to the workhouse. But they want thinking out yet. I seem to see — well, never mind. Now let us have our music. Not a moment have I had for practice lately, so you mustn't scold me. Let us begin with deevy Beethoven's fifth symphony. Fate knocking at the door. That's how I feel, as if there was one clear call for me.'

The window of Georgie's sitting-room, which looked out on to the street, was close to the front door. Lucia, as usual, had bagged the treble part, for she said she could never manage that difficult bass, omitting to add that the treble was far the more amusing to play, and they were approaching the end of the first movement, when Georgie, turning a page, saw a woman's figure standing on the doorstep.

'It's Elizabeth,' he whispered to Lucia.

'Under an umbrella. And the bell's out of order.'

'*Uno, due.* So much the better, she'll go away,' said Lucia with a word to each beat.

She didn't. Georgie occasionally glancing up saw her still standing there and presently the first movement came to an end.

'I'll tell Foljambe I'm engaged,' said Georgie, stealing from his seat. 'What can she want? It's too late for lunch and too early for tea.'

It was too late for anything. The knocker sounded briskly, and before Georgie had time to give Foljambe this instruction, she opened the door, exactly at the moment that he opened his sitting-room door to tell her not to.

'Dear Mr. Georgie,' said Elizabeth. 'So ashamed, but I've been eavesdropping. How I enjoyed listening to that lovely music. Wouldn't have interrupted it for anything!'

Elizabeth adopted the motion she called 'scriggling.' Almost imperceptibly she squeezed and wriggled till she had got past Foljambe, and had a clear view into George's sitting-room.

'Why! There's dear Lucia,' she said. 'Such a lovely party last night, *chérie*: all Tilling talking about it. But I know I'm interrupting. Duet wasn't it? May I sit in a corner, mum as a mouse, while you go on? It would be such a treat. That lovely piece: I seem to know it so well. I should never forgive myself if I broke into it, besides losing such a pleasure. *Je vous prie!*'

It was of course quite clear to the performers that Elizabeth had come for some purpose beyond that of this treat, but she sank into a chair by the fire, and assumed the Tilling musical face (Lucia's patent) smiling wistfully, gazing at the ceiling, and supporting her chin on her hand, as was the correct attitude for slow movements.

So Georgie sat down again, and the slow movement went on its long deliberate way, and Elizabeth was surfeited with her treat pages before it was done. Again and again she hoped it was finished, but the same tune (rather like a hymn, she thought) was presented in yet another aspect, till she knew it inside out and upside down: it was like a stage army passing by, individually the same, but with different helmets, or kilts instead of trousers. At long last came several loud thumps, and Lucia sighed and Georgie sighed, and before she had time to sigh too, they were off again on the next instalment. This was much livelier and Elizabeth abandoned her wistfulness for a mien of sprightly pleasure, and, in turn, for a mien of scarcely concealed impatience. It seemed odd that two people should be so selfishly absorbed in that frightful noise as to think that she had come in to hear them practise. True, she had urged them to give her a treat, but who could have supposed that such a gargantuan feast was prepared for her? Bang! Bang! Bang! It was over and she got up.

'Lovely!' she said. 'Bach was always a favourite composer of mine. *Merci!* And such luck to have found you here, dear Lucia. What do you think I came to see Mr. Georgie about? Guess! I won't tease you. These coming elections to the Town Council. Benjy-boy and I both feel very strongly — I believe he mentioned it to you last night — that something must be done to check the monstrous extravagance that's going on. *Tout le monde* is crippled by it: we shall all be bankrupt if it continues. We feel it our duty to fight it.'

Georgie was stroking his beard: this had already become a habit with him in anxious moments. There must be a disclosure now, and Lucia must make it. It was no use being chivalrous and doing so himself: it was her business. So he occupied himself with putting on the rings he had taken off for fate knocking at the door and stroked his beard again.

'Yes, Major Benjy told me something of his plans last night,' said Lucia, 'and I take quite the opposite line. Those slums, for instance, ought to be swept away altogether, and new houses built *tutto presto*.'

'But such a vandalism, dear,' said Elizabeth. 'So picturesque and, I expect, so cosy. As to our plans, there's been a little change in them. Benjy urged me so strongly that I yielded, and I'm standing instead of him. So I'm getting to work *toute suite*, and I looked in to get promise of your support, *monsieur*, and then you and I must convert dear Lucia.'

The time had come.

'Dear Elizabeth,' said Lucia very decisively, 'you must give up all idea of that. I am standing for election myself on precisely the opposite policy. Cost what it may we must have no more slums and no more unemployment in our beloved Tilling. A Christian duty. Georgie agrees.'

'Well, in a sort of way — ' began Georgie.

'Georgie, *tuo buon' cuore* agrees,' said Lucia, fixing him with the compulsion of her gimlet eye. 'You're enthusiastic about it really.'

Elizabeth ignored Lucia, and turned to him.

'Monsieur Georgie, it will be the ruin of us all,' she said, 'the Town Council is behaving as I said *à mon mari* just now, as if Tilling was Eldorado and the Rand.'

'Georgie, you and I go to-morrow to see those cosy picturesque hovels of which dear Elizabeth spoke,' said Lucia, 'and you will feel more keenly than you do even now that they must be condemned. You won't be able to sleep a wink at night if you feel you're condoning their continuance. Whole families sleeping in one room. Filth, squalor, immorality, insanitation — '

In their growing enthusiasm both ladies dropped foreign tongues.

'Look in any time, Mr. Georgie,' interrupted Elizabeth, 'and let me show you the figures of how the authorities are spending your money and mine. And that new road which nobody wants has already cost — '

'The unemployment here, Georgie,' said Lucia, 'would make angels weep. Strong young men willing and eager to get work, and despairing of finding it, while you and dear Elizabeth and I are living in ease and luxury in our beautiful houses.'

Georgie was standing between these two impassioned ladies, with his head turning rapidly this way and that, as if he was watching lawn tennis. At the same time he felt as if he was the ball that was being slogged to and fro between these powerful players, and he was mentally bruised and battered by their alternate intensity. Luckily, this last violent drive of Lucia's diverted Elizabeth's attack to her.

'Dear Lucia,' she said. 'You, of course, as a comparatively new resident in Tilling can't know very much about municipal expenditure, but I should be only too glad to show you how rates and taxes have been mounting up in the last ten years, owing to the criminal extravagance of the authorities. It would indeed be a pleasure.'

'I'm delighted to hear they've been mounting,' said Lucia. 'I want them to soar. It's a matter of conscience to me that they should.'

'Naughty and reckless of you,' said Elizabeth, trembling a little. 'You've no idea how hardly it presses on some of us.'

'We must shoulder the burden,' said Lucia. 'We must make up our minds to economise.'

Elizabeth with that genial air which betokened undiluted acidity, turned to Georgie, and abandoned principles for personalities, which had become irresistible.

'Quite a coincidence, isn't it, Mr. Georgie,' she said, 'that the moment Lucia heard that my Benjy-boy was to stand for the Town Council, she determined to stand herself.'

Lucia emitted the silvery laugh which

betokened the most exasperating and child-like amusement.

'Dear Elizabeth!' she said. 'How can you be so silly?'

'Did you say 'silly,' dear?' asked Elizabeth, white to the lips.

Georgie intervened.

'O, dear me!' he said. 'Let's all have tea. So much more comfortable than talking about rates. I know there are muffins.'

They had both ceased to regard him now: instead of being driven from one to the other, he lay like a ball out of court, while the two advanced to the net with brandished rackets.

'Yes, dear, I said 'silly,' because you are silly,' said Lucia, as if she was patiently explaining something to a stupid child. 'You certainly implied that my object in standing was to oppose Major Benjy *qua* Major Benjy. What made me determined to stand myself, was that he advocated municipal economy. It horrified me. He woke up my conscience, and I am most grateful to him. Most. And I shall tell him so on the first opportunity. Let me add that I regard you both with the utmost cordiality and friendliness. Should you be elected, which I hope and trust you won't, I shall be the first to congratulate you.'

Elizabeth put a finger to her forehead.

'Too difficult for me, I'm afraid,' she said.

'Such niceties are quite beyond my simple comprehension . . . No tea for me, thanks, Mr. Georgie, even with muffins. I must be getting on with my canvassing. And thank you for your lovely music. So refreshing. Don't bother to see me out, but do look in some time and let me show you my tables of figures.'

She gave a hyena-smile to Lucia, and they saw her hurry past the window, having quite forgotten to put up her umbrella, as if she welcomed the cooling rain. Lucia instantly and without direct comment sat down at the piano again.

'Georgino, a little piece of celestial Mozartino, don't you think, before tea?' she said. 'That will put us in tune again after those discords. Poor woman!'

The campaign began in earnest next day, and at once speculative investments, Lucia's birthday party and George's beard were, as topics of interest, as dead as Queen Anne. The elections were coming on very soon, and intensive indeed were the activities of the two female candidates. Lucia hardly set foot in her office, letting Transport 'C' pursue its upward path unregarded, and Benjy, after brief, disgusted glances at the *Financial Post*, which gave sad news of Siriami, took over his wife's household duties and went shopping in the morning instead of her, with her market-basket on his arm. Both ladies made some small errors: Lucia, for instance, exercised all her powers of charm on Twistevant the greengrocer, and ordered unheard of quantities of forced mushrooms, only to find, when she introduced the subject of her crusade and spoke of those stinking (no less) pigsties where human beings were forced to dwell, that he was the owner of several of them and much resented her disparagement of his house property. 'They're very nice little houses indeed, ma'am,' he said, 'and I should be happy to live there myself. I will send the mushrooms round at once . . . ' Again, Elizabeth, seeing Susan's motor stopping the traffic (which usually made her see red), loaded her with compliments on her sable cloak (which had long been an object of derision to Tilling) and made an appointment to come and have a cosy talk at six that afternoon, carelessly oblivious of the fact that, a yard away, Georgie was looking into the barber's window. Hearing the appointment made, he very properly told Lucia, who therefore went to see Susan at exactly the hour named. The two candidates sat and talked to her, though not to each other, about everything else under the sun for an hour and a half, each of them being determined not to leave the other in possession of the field. At half-past seven Mr. Wyse joined them to remind Susan that she must go and dress, and the candidates left together without having said a single word about the election. As soon as they had got outside Elizabeth shot away up the hill, rocking like a ship over the uneven cobbles of the street. That seemed very like a 'cut,' and when Lucia next day, in order to ascertain that for certain, met the mistress of Mallards in the High Street and wished her good morning, Elizabeth might have been a deaf mute. They were both on their way to canvass Diva, and crossed the road neck to neck, but Lucia by a dexterous swerve established herself on Diva's doorstep and rang the bell. Diva was just going out with her market-basket, and opened the door herself.

'*Diva mia*,' said Lucia effusively, 'I just popped in to ask you to dine to-morrow: I'll send the car for you. And have you two minutes to spare now?'

'I'll look in presently, sweet Diva,' called Elizabeth shrilly over Lucia's shoulder. 'Just going to see the Padre.'

Lucia hurried in and shut the door.

'May I telephone to the Padre?' she asked. 'I want to get him, too, for to-morrow night. Thanks. I'll give you a penny in a moment.'

138

'Delighted to dine with you,' said Diva, 'but I warn you — '

'Tilling 23, please,' said Lucia. 'Yes, Diva?'

'I warn you I'm not going to vote for you. Can't afford to pay higher rates. Monstrous already.'

'Diva, if you only saw the state of those houses — Oh, is that the Padre? I hope you and Evie will dine with me to-morrow. Capital. I'll send the car for you. And may I pop in for a minute presently? . . . Oh, she's with you now, is she. Would you ring me up at Diva's then, the moment she goes?'

'It's a squeeze to make ends meet as it is,' said Diva. 'Very sorry for unemployed, and all that, but the new road is sheer extravagance. Money taken out of my pocket. I shall vote for Elizabeth. Tell you frankly.'

'But didn't you make a fortune over my tip about Siriamis?' asked Lucia.

'That would be over-stating it. It's no use your canvassing me. Talk about something else. Have you noticed any change, any real change, in Elizabeth lately?'

'I don't think so,' said Lucia thoughtfully. 'She was very much herself the last time I had any talk with her at Georgie's a few days ago. She seemed to take it as a personal insult that anyone but herself should stand for the Town Council, which is just what one would expect.

Perhaps a shade more acid than usual, but nothing to speak of.'

'Oh, I don't mean that,' said Diva. 'No change there: I told you about the rabbit, didn't I?'

'Yes, so characteristic,' said Lucia. 'One hoped, of course, that matrimony might improve her, mellow her, make a true woman of her, but eagerly as I've looked out for any signs of it, I can't say — '

Lucia broke off, for a prodigious idea as to what might be in Diva's mind had flashed upon her.

'Tell me what you mean,' she said, boring with her eye into the very centre of Diva's secret soul. 'Not — not *that*?'

Diva nodded her head eight times with increasing emphasis.

'Yes, that,' she said.

'But it can't be true!' cried Lucia. 'Quite impossible. Tell me precisely why you think so?'

'I don't see why it shouldn't be true,' said Diva, 'for I think she's not more than forty-three, though of course it's more likely that she's only trying to persuade herself of it. She was in here the other day. Twilight. She asked me what twilight sleep was. Then hurriedly changed the subject and talked about the price of soap. Went back to subject again. Said there were such pretty dolls in the toy shop. Had a mind to buy one. It's odd her talking like that. May be something in it. I shall keep an open mind about it.'

The two ladies had sat down on the window-seat, where the muslin curtains concealed them from without, but did not obstruct from them a very fair view of the High Street. Their thrilling conversation was now suddenly broken by the loud ringing, as of a dinner-bell, not far away to the right.

'That's not the muffin-man,' said Diva. 'Much too sonorous and the town-crier has influenza, so it's neither of them. I think there are two bells, aren't there? We shall soon see.'

The bells sounded louder and louder, evidently there were two of them, and a *cortège* (no less) came into view. Quaint Irene led it. She was dressed in her usual scarlet pullover and trousers, but on her head she wore a large tin helmet, like Britannia on a penny, and she rang her dinner-bell all the time, turning round and round as she walked. Behind her came four ragged girls eating buns and carrying a huge canvas banner painted with an impressionist portrait of Lucia, and a legend in gold letters 'Vote for Mrs. Lucas, the Friend of the Poor.' Behind them walked Lucy, Irene's six-foot maid, ringing a second dinner-bell and chanting in

141

a baritone voice, 'Bring out your dead.' She was followed by four ragged boys, also eating buns, who carried another banner painted with a hideous rendering of Elizabeth and a legend in black, 'Down with Mrs. Mapp-Flint, the Foe of the Poor.' The whole procession was evidently enjoying itself prodigiously.

'Dear me, it's too kind of Irene,' said Lucia in some agitation, 'but is it quite discreet? What will people think? I must ask her to stop it.'

She hurried out into the street. The revolving Irene saw her, and, halting her procession, ran to her.

'Darling, you've come in the nick of time,' she said. 'Isn't it noble? Worth hundreds of votes to you. We're going to march up and down through all the streets for an hour, and then burn the Mapp-Flint banner in front of Mallards. Three cheers for Mrs. Lucas, the Friend of the Poor!'

Three shrill cheers were given with splutterings of pieces of bun and frenzied ringing of dinner-bells before Lucia could get a word in. It would have been ungracious not to acknowledge this very gratifying enthusiasm, and she stood smiling and bowing on the pavement.

'Irene, dear, most cordial and sweet of you,' she began when the cheers were done, 'and what a charming picture of me, but — '

'And three groans for the Foe of the Poor,' shouted Irene.

Precisely at that tumultuous moment Major Benjy came down one side-street from Mallards on his marketing errands, and Elizabeth down the next on her way from her canvassing errand to the Padre. She heard the cheers, she heard the groans, she saw the banners and the monstrous cartoon of herself, and beckoned violently to her Benjy-boy, who broke into a trot.

'The enemy in force,' shrieked Irene. 'Run, children.'

The procession fled down the High Street with bells ringing and banners wobbling frightfully. Major Benjy restrained an almost overwhelming impulse to hurl his market-basket at Lucy, and he and Elizabeth started in pursuit. But there was a want of dignity about such a race and no hope whatever of catching the children. Already out of breath, they halted, the procession disappeared round the far end of the street, and the clamour of dinner-bells died away.

Shoppers and shop-keepers, post-office clerks, errand boys, cooks and housemaids and private citizens had all come running out into the street at the sound of the cheers and groans and dinner-bells, windows had been

143

thrown open, and heads leaned out of them, goggle-eyed and open-mouthed. Everyone cackled and chattered: it was like the second act of *The Meistersinger*. By degrees the excitement died down, and the pulse of ordinary life, momentarily suspended, began to beat again. Cooks went back to their kitchens, housemaids to their brooms, shop-keepers to their customers, and goggle-faces were withdrawn and windows closed. Major Benjy, unable to face shopping just now, went to play golf instead, and there were left standing on opposite pavements of the High Street the Friend of the Poor and the Foe of the Poor, both of whom could face anything, even each other.

Lucia did not know what in the world to do. She was innocent of all complicity in Irene's frightful demonstration in her favour, except that mere good manners had caused her weakly to smile and bow when she was cheered by four small girls, but nothing was more certain than that Elizabeth would believe that she had got up the whole thing. But, intrepid to the marrow of her bones, she walked across the street to where a similar intrepidity was standing. Elizabeth fixed her with a steely glance, and then looked carefully at a point some six inches above her head.

'I just popped across to assure you,' said

Lucia, 'that I knew nothing about what we have just seen until — well, until I saw it.'

Elizabeth cocked her head on one side, but remained looking at the fixed point.

'I think I understand,' she said, 'you didn't see that pretty show until you saw it. Quite! I take your word for it.'

'And I saw it first when it came into the High Street,' said Lucia. 'And I much regret it.'

'I don't regret it in the least,' said Elizabeth with shrill animation. 'People, whoever they are, who demean themselves either to plan or to execute such gross outrages only hurt themselves. I may be sorry for them, but otherwise they are nothing to me. I do not know of their existence. *Ils n'existent pas pour moi.*'

'Nor for me either,' said Lucia, following the general sentiment rather than the precise application, '*Sono niente.*'

Then both ladies turned their backs on each other, as by some perfectly executed movement in a ballet, and walked away in opposite directions. It was really the only thing to do.

Two days still remained before the poll, and these two remarkable candidates redoubled (if possible) their activities. Major Benjy got no golf at all, for he accompanied his wife everywhere, and Georgie formed a corresponding bodyguard for Lucia: in fact the feuds of

145

the Montagues and Capulets were but a faint historical foreshadowing of this municipal contest. The parties, even when they met on narrow pavements in mean streets, were totally blind to each other, and, pending the result, social life in Tilling was at a standstill. As dusk fell on the eve of the poll, Lucia and Georgie, footsore with so much tramping on uneven cobblestones, dragged themselves up the hill to Mallards Cottage for a final checking of their visits and a reviving cup of tea. They passed below the windows of the garden-room, obscured by the gathering darkness, and there, quite distinctly against the light within, were the silhouettes of the enemy, and Elizabeth was drinking out of a wineglass. The silhouette of Benjy with a half-bottle of champagne in his hand showed what the refreshment was.

'Poor Elizabeth, taken to drink,' said Lucia, in tones of the deepest pity. 'I always feared for Benjy's influence on her. Tired as I am, Georgie — and I can't remember ever being really tired before — have you ever known me tired?'

'Never!' said Georgie in a broken voice.

'Well, tired as I am, nothing would induce me to touch any sort of stimulant. Ah, how nice it will be to sit down.'

Foljambe had tea ready for them and Lucia

lay down full length on Georgie's sofa.

'Very strong, please, Georgie,' she said. 'Stir the teapot up well. No milk.'

The rasping beverage rapidly revived Lucia; she drank two cups, the first out of her saucer, then she took her feet off the sofa, and the familiar gabbling *timbre* came back to her voice.

'Completely restored, Georgie, and we've got to think what will happen next,' she said. 'Elizabeth and I can't go on being totally invisible to each other. And what more can I do? I definitely told her that I had nothing to do with dear, loyal Irene's exhibition, and she almost as definitely told me that she didn't believe me. About the election itself I feel very confident, but if I get in at the top of the poll, and she is quite at the bottom, which I think more than likely, she'll be worse than ever. The only thing that could placate her would be if she was elected and I wasn't. But there's not the slightest chance of that happening as far as I can see. I have a *flair*, as Elizabeth would say, about such things. All day I have felt a growing conviction that there is a very large body of public opinion behind me. I can feel the pulse of the place.'

Sheer weariness had made Georgie rather cross.

'I daresay Elizabeth feels precisely the

same,' he said, 'especially after her booze. As for future plans, for goodness sake let us wait till we see what the result is.'

Lucia finished her tea.

'How right you are, Georgino,' she said. 'Let us dismiss it all. What about *un po' di musica?*'

'Yes, do play me something,' said Georgie. 'But as to a duet, I can't. Impossible.'

'*Povero!*' said Lucia. 'Is 'oo *fatigato?* Then 'oo shall rest. I'll be going back home, for I want two hours in my office. I've done hardly anything all this week. *Buon riposo.*'

The result of the poll was declared two mornings later with due pomp and circumstance. The votes had been counted in the committee room of the King's Arms Hotel in the High Street, and thither at noon came the Mayor and Corporation in procession from the Town Hall clad in their civic robes and preceded by the mace-bearers. The announcement was to be made from the first floor balcony overlooking the High Street. Traffic was suspended for the ceremony and the roadway was solid with folk, for Tilling's interest in the election, usually of the tepidest, had been vastly stimulated by the mortal rivalry between the two lady candidates and by Irene's riotous proceedings. Lucia and Georgie had seats in Diva's drawing-room window, for that would be a conspicuous place from which to bow to the crowd: Elizabeth and Benjy were wedged against the wall below, and that seemed a good omen. The morning was glorious, and in the blaze of the winter sun the scarlet gowns of Councillors, and the great silver maces dazzled the eye as the procession went into the hotel.

'Really a very splendid piece of pageantry,' said Lucia, the palms of whose hands, despite her strong conviction of success, were slightly moist. 'Wonderful effect of colour, marvellous maces; what a pity, Georgie, you did not bring your paint-box. I have always said that there is no more honourable and dignified office in the kingdom than that of the Mayor of a borough. The word 'mayor,' I believe, is the same as Major — poor Major Benjy.'

'There's the list of the Mayors of Tilling from the fifteenth century onwards painted up in the Town Hall,' said Georgie.

'Really! A dynasty indeed!' said Lucia. Her fingers had begun to tremble as if she was doing rapid shakes and trills on the piano. 'Look, there's Irene on the pavement opposite, smoking a pipe. I find that a false note. I hope she won't make any fearful demonstration when the names are read out, but I see she has got her dinner-bell. Has a woman ever been Mayor of Tilling, Diva?'

'Never,' said Diva. 'Not likely either. Here they come.'

The mace-bearers emerged on to the balcony, and the mayor stepped out between them and advanced to the railing. In his hand he held a drawing-board with a paper pinned to it.

'That must be the list,' said Lucia in a cracked voice.

The town-crier (not Irene) rang his bell.

'Citizens of Tilling,' he proclaimed. 'Silence for the Right Worshipful the Mayor.'

The Mayor bowed. There were two vacancies to be filled, he said, on the Town Council, and there were seven candidates. He read the list with the number of votes each candidate had polled. The first two had polled nearly three hundred votes each. The next three, all close together, had polled between a hundred and fifty and two hundred votes.

'Number six,' said the Mayor, 'Mrs. Emmeline Lucas. Thirty-nine votes. Equal with her, Mrs. Elizabeth Mapp-Flint, also thirty-nine votes. God save the King.'

He bowed to the assembled crowd and, followed by the mace-bearers, disappeared within. Presently the procession emerged again, and returned to the Town Hall.

'A most interesting ceremony, Diva. Quite mediæval,' said Lucia. 'I am very glad to have seen it. We got a wonderful view of it.'

The crowd had broken up when she and Georgie came out into the street.

'That noble story of Disraeli's first speech in the House of Commons,' she began —

5

The cause that chiefly conduced to the reconciliation of these two ultimate candidates was not Christian Charity so much as the fact that their unhappy estrangement wrecked the social gaieties of Tilling, for Georgie and Lucia would not meet Mallards and Mallards would not meet Irene as long as it continued, and those pleasant tea-parties for eight with sessions of Bridge before and after, could not take place. Again, both the protagonists found it wearing to the optic nerve to do their morning's shopping with one eye scouting for the approach of the enemy, upon which both eyes were suddenly smitten with blindness. On the other hand the Padre's sermon the next Sunday morning, though composed with the best intentions, perhaps retarded a reconciliation, for he preached on the text, 'Behold, how good and joyful a thing it is, brethren, to dwell together in unity,' and his allusions to the sad dissensions which arose from the clash of ambitions, highly honourable in themselves, were unmistakable. Both protagonists considered his discourse to be in the worst possible taste, and Elizabeth entirely refused to recognise either him or Evie when next they met, which was another wedge driven into Tilling. But inconvenience, dropping like perpetual water on a stone, eventually wore down dignity, and when, some ten days after the election, the market-baskets of Lucia and Elizabeth came into violent collision at the door of the fishmonger's, Lucia was suddenly and miraculously healed of her intermittent blindness. 'So sorry, dear,' she said, 'quite my fault,' and Elizabeth, remembering with an effort that Lent was an appropriate season for self-humiliation, said it was quite hers. They chatted for several minutes, rather carefully, with eager little smiles, and Diva who had observed this interesting scene, raced up and down the street, to tell everybody that an armistice at least had been signed. So Bridge parties for eight were resumed with more than their usual frequency, to make up for lost time, and though Lucia had forsworn all such petty occupations, her ingenuity soon found a formula, which justified her in going to them much as usual.

'Yes, Georgie, I will come with pleasure this afternoon,' she said, 'for the most industrious must have their remissions. How wonderfully Horace puts it: '*Non semper arcum tendit Apollo.*' I would give anything to have known Horace. Terse and witty and

153

wise. Half-past three then. Now I must hurry home, for my broker will want to know what I think about a purchase of Imperial Tobacco.'

That, of course, was her way of putting it, but put it as you liked, the fact remained that she had been making pots of money. An Industrial boom was on, and by blindly following Mammoncash's advice, Lucia was doing exceedingly well. She was almost frightened at the speed with which she had been growing richer, but remembered the splendid career of great Dame Catherine Winterglass, whose picture, cut out of an illustrated magazine, now stood framed on the table in her office. Dame Catherine had made a fortune by her own skill in forecasting the trend of the markets; that was not due to luck but to ability, and to be afraid of her own ability was quite foreign to Lucia's nature.

The financial group at Mallards, Mapp & Flint, was not displaying the same acumen, and one day it suffered a frightful shock. There had been a pleasant Bridge-party at Diva's, and Elizabeth shewed how completely she had forgiven Lucia, by asking her counsel about Siriami. The price of the shares had been going down lately, like an aneroid before a typhoon, and, as it dwindled, Elizabeth had continued to buy. What did Lucia think of this policy of averaging?

Lucia supported her forehead on her hand in the attitude of Shakespeare and Dame Catherine.

'Dear me, it is so long since I dealt in Siriami,' she said. 'A West African gold mine, I seem to recollect? The price of gold made me buy, I am sure. I remember reasoning it out and concluding that gold would go up. There were favourable reports from the mine too. And why did I sell? How you all work my poor brain! Ah! Eureka! I thought I should have to tie up my capital for a long time: my broker agreed with me, though I should say most decidedly that it is a promising lock-up. Siriami is still in the early stage of development, you see, and no dividend can be expected for a couple of years — '

'Hey, what's that?' asked Benjy.

'More than two years, do you think?' asked Lucia. 'I am rusty about it. Anyone who holds on, no doubt, will reap a golden reward in time.'

'But I shan't get any dividends for two years?' asked Elizabeth in a hollow voice.

'Ah, pray don't trust my judgment,' said Lucia. 'All I can say for certain, is that I made some few pounds in the mine, and decided it was too long a lock-up of my little capital.'

Elizabeth felt slightly unwell. Benjy had acquired a whisky and soda and she took a sip of it without it even occurring to her that he had no business to have it.

'Well, we must be off,' she said, for though the reconciliation was so recent, she felt it might be endangered if she listened to any more of this swank. 'Thanks, dear, for your views. All that four shillings mine? Fancy!'

It was raining hard when they left Diva's house, and they walked up the narrow pavement to Mallards in single file, with a loud and dismal tattoo drumming on their umbrellas, and streams of water pouring from the ends of the ribs. Arrived there, Elizabeth led the way out to the garden-room and put her dripping umbrella in the fender. It had been wet all afternoon and before going to Diva's, Benjy had smoked two cigars there.

'Of course, this is your room, dear,' said Elizabeth, 'and if you prefer it to smell like a pothouse, it shall. But would you mind having the window open a chink for a moment, for unless you do, I shall be suffocated.'

She fanned herself with her handkerchief, and took two or three long breaths of the brisker air.

'Thank you. Refreshed,' she said. 'And now we must talk Siriami. I think Lucia might have told us about its not paying dividends before, but don't let us blame her much. It merely isn't the way of some people to

156

consider others — '

'She told you she was selling all the Siriami shares she held,' said Benjy.

'If you've finished championing her, Benjy, perhaps you'll allow me to go on. I've put two thousand pounds into that hole in the ground, for, as far as I can see, it's little more than that. And that means that for the next two years my income will be diminished by seventy pounds.'

'God bless me,' ejaculated Benjy. 'I had no idea you had invested so heavily in it.'

'I believe a woman, even though married, is allowed to do what she likes with her money,' said Elizabeth bitterly.

'I never said she wasn't. I only said that I didn't know it,' said Benjy.

'That was why I told you. And the long and short of it is that we had better let this house as soon as we can for as long as we can, because we can't afford to live here.'

'But supposing Mrs. Lucas is wrong about it? I've known her wrong before now — '

'So have I,' interrupted Elizabeth, 'usually, in fact: but we must be prepared for her being right for once. As it is, I've got to let Mallards for three or four months in the year in order to live in it at all. I shall go to Woolgar & Pipstow's to-morrow and put it in their hands, furnished (all our beautiful things!) for six months. Perhaps with option of a year.'

'And where shall we go?' asked Benjy.

Elizabeth rose.

'Wherever we can. One of those little houses, do you think, which Lucia wanted to pull down. And then, perhaps, as I told you, there'll be another little mouth to feed, dear.'

'I wish you would go to Dr. Dobbie and make sure,' he said.

'And what would Dr. Dobbie tell me? 'Have a good rest before dinner.' Just what I'm going to do.'

With the re-establishment of cordial relations between the two leading ladies of Tilling, the tide of news in the mornings flowed on an unimpeded course, instead of being held up in the eddies of people who would speak to each other, and being blocked by those who wouldn't, and though as yet there was nothing definite on the subject to which Elizabeth and Benjy had thus briefly alluded, there were hints, there were signs and indications that bore on it, of the very highest significance. The first remarkable occurrence was that Major Benjy instead of going to play golf next morning, according to his invariable custom, came shopping with Elizabeth, as he had done when she was busy canvassing and carried his wife's basket. There was a solicitous, a tender air about the way he gave her an arm as she mounted the two high steps into Twistevant's shop. Diva was the first to notice this strange phenomenon, and naturally she stood rooted to the spot in amazement, intent on further observation. When they came out there was not the shadow of doubt in her mind that Elizabeth had let out the old green skirt that everyone knew so well. It fell in much ampler folds than ever before, and Diva vividly recollected that strange talk about dolls and twilight sleep: how pregnant it seemed now, in every sense of the word! The two popped into another shop, and at the moment the Padre and Evie debouched into the High Street, a few yards away, and he went into the tobacconist's, leaving Evie outside. Diva uprooted herself with difficulty, hurried to her, and the two ladies had a few whispered remarks together. Then the Mapp-Flints came out again, and retraced their way, followed by four eager detective eyes.

'But no question whatever about the skirt,' whispered Evie, 'and she has taken Major Benjy's arm again. *So unusual.* What an event if it's really going to happen! Never such a thing before in our circle. She'll be quite a heroine. There's Mr. Georgie. What a pity we can't tell him about it. What beautiful clothes!'

Georgie had on his fur-trimmed cape and a

new bright blue beret which he wore a little sideways on his head. He was coming towards them with more than his usual briskness, and held his mouth slightly open as if to speak the moment he got near enough.

'Fiddlesticks, Evie,' said Diva. 'You don't expect that Mr. Georgie, at his age, thinks they're found under gooseberry bushes. Good morning, Mr. Georgie. Have you seen Elizabeth — '

'Skirt,' he interrupted. 'Yes, of course. Three inches I should think.'

Evie gave a little horrified squeal at this modern lack of reticence in talking to a gentleman who wasn't your husband, on matters of such extreme delicacy, and took refuge in the tobacconist's.

'And Major Benjy carrying her basket for her,' said Diva. 'So it must be true, unless she's deceiving him.'

'Look, they've turned down Malleson Street,' cried Georgie. 'That's where Dr. Dobbie lives.'

'So do Woolgar & Pipstow,' said Diva.

'But they wouldn't be thinking of letting Mallards as early as March,' objected Georgie.

'Well, it's not likely. Must be the doctor's. I'm beginning to believe it. At first when she talked to me about dolls and twilight sleep, I thought she was only trying to make herself interesting, instead of being so — '

'I never heard about dolls and twilight sleep,' said Georgie, with an ill-used air.

'Oh, here's Irene on her motor-bicycle, coming up from Malleson Street,' cried Diva. 'I wonder if she saw where they went. What a row she makes! And so rash. I thought she must have run into Susan's Royce, and what a mess there would have been.'

Irene, incessantly hooting, came thundering along the High Street, with foul fumes pouring from the open exhaust. She evidently intended to pull up and talk to them, but miscalculated her speed. To retard herself, she caught hold of Georgie's shoulder, and he tittuped along, acting as a brake, till she came to a standstill.

'My life-preserver!' cried Irene fervently, as she dismounted. 'Georgie, I adore your beard. Do you put it inside your bedclothes or outside? Let me come and see some night when you've gone to bed. Don't be alarmed, dear lamb, your sex protects you from any frowardness on my part. I was on my way to see Lucia. There's news. Give me a nice dry kiss and I'll tell you.'

'I couldn't think of it,' said Georgie. 'What would everybody say?'

'Dear old grandpa,' said Irene. 'They'd say you were a bold and brazen old man. That would be a horrid lie. You're a darling old lady, and I love you. What were we talking about?'

'You were talking great nonsense,' said Georgie, pulling his cape back over his shoulder.

'Yes, but do you know why? I had a lovely idea. I thought how enlightening it would be to live a day backwards. So when I got up this morning, I began backwards as if it was the end of the day instead of the beginning. I had two pipes and a whisky and soda. Then I had dinner backwards, beginning with toasted cheese, and I'm slightly tipsy. When I get home I shall have tea, and go out for a walk and then have lunch, and shortly before going to bed I shall have breakfast and then some salts. Do you see the plan? It gives you a new view of life altogether; you see it all from a completely different angle. Oh, I was going to tell you the news. I saw the Mapp-Flints going into the house agent's. She appeared not to see me. She hasn't seen me since dinner-bell day. I hope you understand about living backwards. Let's all do it: one and all.'

'My dear, it sounds too marvellous,' said Georgie, 'but I'm sure it would upset me and I should only see it from the angle of being sick . . . Diva, they were only going into Woolgar & Pipstow's.'

Diva had trundled up to them.

'Not the doctor's, then,' she said. 'I'm disappointed. It would have made it more conclusive.'

'Made what more conclusive?' asked Irene.

'Well, it's thought that Elizabeth's expecting — ' began Diva.

'You don't say so!' said Irene. 'Who's the co-respondent? Georgie, you're blushing below your beard. Roguey-poguey-Romeo! I saw you climbing up a rope-ladder into the garden-room when you were supposed to be ill. Juliet Mapp opened the window to you, and you locked her in a passionate embrace. I didn't want to get you into trouble, so I didn't say anything about it, and now you've gone and got her into trouble, you wicked old Romeo, hoots and begorra. I must be godmother, Georgie, and now I'm off to tell Lucia.'

Irene leapt on to her bicycle and disappeared in a cloud of mephitic vapour in the direction of Grebe.

★　★　★

With the restoration of the free circulation of news, it was no wonder that by the afternoon it was universally known that this most interesting addition to the population of Tilling was expected. Neither of the two people most closely concerned spoke of it directly, but indirectly their conduct soon proclaimed it from the house-roofs. Benjy went strutting about with his wife, carrying her market-basket, obviously with the conscious pride of approaching fatherhood, pretty to see; and when he went to play golf, leaving her to do her marketing alone, Elizabeth, wreathed in smiles, explained his absence in hints of which it was impossible to miss the significance.

'I positively drove my Benjy-boy out to the links to-day,' she said to Diva. 'I insisted, though he was very loth to go. But where's the use of his hanging about? Ah, there's quaint Irene: foolish of me, but after her conduct at the elections, it agitates me a little to see her, though I'm sure I forgive her with all my heart. I'll just pop into the grocer's.'

Irene stormed by, and Elizabeth popped out again.

'And you may not have heard yet, dear,' she continued, 'that we want to let our sweet Mallards for six months or a year. Not that I blame anybody but myself for that necessity. Lucia perhaps might have told me that Siriami would not be paying any dividends for a couple of years, but she didn't. That's all.'

'But you were determined to do the

opposite of whatever she advised,' said Diva. 'You told me so.'

'No, you're wrong there,' said Elizabeth, with some vehemence. 'I never said that.'

'But you did,' cried Diva. 'You said that if she bought Siriami, you would sell and versy-visa.'

Instead of passionately denying this, Elizabeth gave a far-away smile like Lucia's music smile over the slow movements of Sonatas.

'We won't argue about it, dear,' she said. 'Have it all your own way.'

This suavity was most uncharacteristic of Elizabeth: was it a small piece of corroborative evidence?

'Anyhow, I'm dreadfully sorry you're in low water,' said Diva. 'Hope you'll get a good let. Wish I could take Mallards myself.'

'A little bigger than you're accustomed to, dear,' said Elizabeth with a touch of the old Eve. 'I don't think you'd be very comfortable in it. If I can't get a long let, I shall have to shut it up and store my furniture, to avoid those monstrous rates, and take a teeny-weeny house somewhere else. For myself I don't seem to mind at all, I shall be happy anywhere, but what really grieves me is that my Benjy must give up his dear garden-room. But as long as we're together, what does it matter, and he's so brave and tender about it . . . Good morning, Mr. Georgie. I've news for you, which I hope you'll think is bad news.'

Georgie had a momentary qualm that this was something sinister about Foljambe, who had been very cross lately: there was no pleasing her.

'I don't know why you should hope I should think it bad news,' he said.

'I shall tease you,' said Elizabeth in a sprightly tone. 'Guess! Somebody going away: that's a hint.'

Georgie knew that if this meant Foljambe was going to leave, it was highly unlikely that she should have told Elizabeth and not him, but it gave him a fresh pang of apprehension.

'Oh, it's so tarsome to be teased,' he said. 'What is it?'

'You're going to lose your neighbours. Benjy and I have got to let Mallards for a long, long time.'

Georgie repressed a sigh of relief.

'Oh, I am sorry: that is bad news,' he said cheerfully. 'Where are you going?'

'Don't know yet. Anywhere. A great wrench, but there's so much to be thankful for. I must be getting home. My boyikins will scold me if I don't rest before lunch.'

Somehow this combination of financial disaster and great expectations raised Elizabeth to a high position of respect and sympathy in the eyes of Tilling. Lucia, Evie and Diva were all childless, and though Susan Wyse had had a daughter by her first marriage, Isabel Poppit was now such a Yahoo, living permanently in an unplumbed shack among the sand-dunes, that she hardly counted as a human being at all. Even if she was one, she was born years before her mother had come to settle here, and thus was no Tillingite. In consequence Elizabeth became a perfect heroine; she was elderly (it was really remarkably appropriate that her name was Elizabeth) and now she was going to wipe the eye of all these childless ladies. Then again her financial straits roused commiseration: it was sad for her to turn out of the house she had lived in for so long and her Aunt Caroline before her. No doubt she had been very imprudent, and somehow the image presented itself of her and Benjy being caught like flies in the great web Lucia had been spinning, in the centre of which she sat, sucking gold out of the spoils entangled there. The image was not accurate, for Lucia had tried to shoo them out of her web, but the general impression remained, and it manifested itself in little acts of homage to Elizabeth at Bridge-parties and social gatherings, in care being taken that she had a comfortable chair, that she was not sitting in draughts, in warm congratulations if she won her rubbers and in sympathy if she lost. She was helped first and largely at dinner, Susan Wyse constantly lent her the Royce for drives in the country, so that she could get plenty of fresh air without undue fatigue, and Evie Bartlett put a fat cushion in her place behind the choir at church. Already she had enjoyed precedence as a bride, but this new precedence quite outshone so conventional a piece of etiquette. Benjy partook of it too in a minor degree, for fatherhood was just as rare in the Tilling circle as motherhood. He could not look down on Georgie's head, for Georgie was the taller, but he straddled before the fire with legs wide apart and looked down on the rest of him and on the entire persons of Mr. Wyse and the Padre. The former must have told his sister, the Contessa Faraglione, who from time to time visited him in Tilling, of the happy event impending, for she sent a message to Elizabeth of so delicate a nature, about her own first confinement, that Mr. Wyse had been totally unable to deliver it himself, and entrusted it to his wife. The Contessa also sent Elizabeth a large jar of Italian honey, notable for its nutritious qualities. As for the Padre, he remembered with shame that he had suggested that a certain sentence should be omitted from Elizabeth's marriage service, which she had insisted should be read, and he made himself familiar with the form for the Churching of Women.

But there were still some who doubted. Quaint Irene was one, in spite of her lewd observations to Georgie, in her coarse way she offered to lay odds that she would have a baby before Elizabeth. Lucia was another. But one morning Georgie, coming out of Mallards Cottage, had seen Dr. Dobbie's car standing at the door of Mallards, and he had positively run down to the High Street to disseminate this valuable piece of indirect evidence, and in particular to tell Lucia. But she was nowhere about, and, as it was a beautiful day, and he was less busy than usual, having finished his piece of *petit point* yesterday, he walked out to Grebe to confront her with it. Just now, being in the Office, she could not be disturbed, as Grosvenor decided that a casual morning call from an old friend could not rank as an urgency, and he sat down to wait for her in the drawing-room. It was impossible to play the piano, for the sound, even with the soft pedal down, would have penetrated into the Great Silence, but he found on the table a fat volume called *Health in the Home*, and saw at once that he could fill up his time very pleasantly with it. He read about shingles and decided that the author could never have come across as bad a case as his own: he was reassured that the slight cough which had troubled him lately was probably not incipient tuberculosis: he made a note of calomel, for he felt pretty sure the Foljambe's moroseness was due to liver, and she might be induced to take a dose. Then he became entirely absorbed in a chapter about mothers. A woman, he read, often got mistaken ideas into her head: she would sometimes think that she was going to have a baby, but would refuse to see a doctor for fear of being told that she was not. Then, hearing Lucia's step on the stairs, he hastily tried to replace the book on the table, but it slipped from his hand and lay open on the carpet, and there was not time to pick it up before Lucia entered. She said not a word, but sank down in a chair, closing her eyes.

'My dear, you're not ill, are you?' said Georgie.

Lucia kept her eyes shut.

'What time is it?' she asked in a hollow voice.

'Getting on for eleven. You are all right, are you?'

Lucia spread out her arms as if measuring some large object.

'Perfectly. But columns of figures, Georgie, and terrific decisions to make, and now reaction has come. I've been telephoning to London. I may be called up any moment. Divert my mind, while I relax. Any news?'

'I came down on purpose to tell you,' said Georgie, 'and perhaps even you will be convinced now. Dr. Dobbie's car was waiting outside Mallards this morning.'

'No!' said Lucia, opening her eyes and becoming extremely brisk and judicial. 'That does look more like business. But still I can't say that I'm convinced. You see, finance makes one look at all possible sides of a situation. Consider. No doubt, it was the doctor's car: I don't dispute that. But Major Benjy may have had an upset. Elizabeth may have fallen downstairs, though I'm sure I hope she hasn't. Her cook may have mumps. Lots of things. No, Georgie, if the putative baby was an industrial share — I put it badly — I wouldn't touch it.'

She pointed at the book on the floor.

'I see what that book is,' she said, 'and I feel sure you've been reading about it. So have I. A rather interesting chapter about the delusions and fancies of middle-aged women lately married. Sometimes, so it said, they do not even believe themselves, but are only acting a kind of charade. Elizabeth must have had great fun, supposing she has been merely acting, getting her Benjy-boy and you and others to believe her, and being made much of.'

Lucia cocked her head thinking she heard the telephone. But it was only a womanly fancy of her own.

'Poor dear,' she said. 'I am afraid her desire to have a baby may have led her to deceive others and perhaps herself, and then of course she liked being petted and exalted and admired. You must all be very kind and oblivious when the day comes that she has to give it up. No more twilight sleep or wanting to buy dolls or having the old green skirt let out — Ah, there's the telephone. Wait for me, will you, for I have something more to say.'

Lucia hurried out, and Georgie, after another glance at the medical book applied his mind to the psychological aspect of the situation. Lucia had doubtless written under the growing ascendency of Elizabeth. She knew about the Contessa's honey, she had seen how Elizabeth was cossetted and helped first and listened to with deference, however abject her utterance, and she could not have liked the secondary place which the sentiment of Tilling assigned to herself. She was a widow of fifty, and Elizabeth in virtue of her approaching motherhood, had really become of the next generation, whose future lies before them. Everyone had let Lucia pass into eclipse. Elizabeth was the great figure, and was the more heroic because she was obliged to let the ancestral home of her Aunt. Then there was the late election: it must have been bitter to Lucia to be at the bottom of the poll and obtain just the same number of votes as Elizabeth. All this explained her incredulity . . . Then once more her step sounded on the stairs.

'All gone well?' asked Georgie.

'*Molto bene.* I convinced my broker that mine was the most likely view. Now about poor Elizabeth. You must all be kind to her, I was saying. There is, I am convinced, an awful anti-climax in front of her. We must help her past it. Then her monetary losses: I really am much distressed about them. But what can you expect when a woman with no financial experience goes wildly gambling in gold mines of which she knows nothing, and thinks she knows better than anybody? Asking for trouble. But I've made a plan, Georgie, which I think will pull her out of the dreadful hole in which she now finds herself. That house of hers, Mallards. Not a bad house. I am going to offer to take it off her hands altogether, to buy the freehold.'

'I think she only wants to let it furnished for a year if she can,' said Georgie, 'otherwise she means to shut it up.'

'Well, listen.'

Lucia ticked off her points with a finger of one hand on the fingers of the other.

'*Uno*. Naturally I can't lease it from her as it is, furnished with mangy tiger-skins, and hip baths for chairs and Polynesian aprons on the walls and a piano that belonged to her grandmother. Impossible.'

'Quite,' said Georgie.

'*Due*. The house wants a thorough doing up from top to bottom. I suspect dry rot. Mice and mildewed wallpaper and dingy paint, I know. And the drains must be overhauled. I don't suppose they've been looked at for centuries. I shall not dream of asking her to put it in order.'

'That sounds very generous so far,' said Georgie.

'That is what it is intended to be. *Tre*. I will take over from her the freehold of Mallards and hand to her the freehold of Grebe with a cheque for two thousand pounds, for I understand that is what she has sunk in her reckless speculations. If she accepts, she will step into this house all in apple-pie order and leave me with one which it will really cost a little fortune to make habitable. But I think I *ought* to do it, Georgie. The law of kindness. *Che pensate?*'

Georgie knew that it had long been the dream of Lucia's life to get Mallards for her own, but the transaction, stated in this manner, wore the aspect of the most disinterested philanthropy. She was evidently persuaded that it was, for she was so touched by the recital of her own generosity that the black bird-like brightness of her eyes was dimmed with moisture.

'We are all here to help each other, Georgie,' she continued, 'and I consider it a Providential privilege to be able to give Elizabeth a hand out of this trouble. There is other trouble in front of her, when she realizes how she has been deceiving others, and, as I say, perhaps herself, and it will make it easier for her if she has no longer this money worry and the prospect of living in some miserable little house. Irene burst into tears when I told her what I was going to do. So emotional.'

Georgie did not cry, for this Providential privilege of helping others, even at so great an expense, would give Lucia just what she wanted most. That consideration dried up, at its source, any real tendency to tears.

'Well, I think she ought to be very grateful to you,' he said.

'No, Georgie, I don't expect that; Elizabeth may not appreciate the benevolence of my intentions, and I shall be the last to point them out. Now let us walk up to the town. The nature of Dr. Dobbie's visit to Mallards will probably be known by now and I have finished with my Office till the arrival of the evening post . . . Do you think she'll take my offer?'

Marketing was over before they got up to the High Street, but Diva made a violent tattoo on her window, and threw it open.

'All a wash-out about Dr. Dobbie,' she called out.

'The cook scalded her hand, that's all. Saw her just now. Lint and oiled silk.'

'Oh, poor thing!' said Lucia. 'What did I tell you, Georgie?'

★   ★   ★

Lucia posted her philanthropic proposal to Elizabeth that very day. In consequence there was a most agitated breakfast duet at Mallards next morning.

'So like her,' cried Elizabeth, when she had read the letter to Benjy with scornful interpolations. 'So very like her. But I know her well enough now to see her meannesses. She has always wanted my house and is taking a low advantage of my misfortunes to try to get it. But she shan't have it. Never! I would sooner burn it down with my own hands.'

Elizabeth crumpled up the letter and threw it into the grate. She crashed her way into a piece of toast and resumed.

'She's an encroacher,' she said, 'and quite unscrupulous. I am more than ever convinced that she put the idea of these libellous dinner-bells into Irene's head.'

Benjy was morose this morning.

'Don't see the connection at all,' he said.

Elizabeth couldn't bother to explain anything so obvious and went on.

'I forgave her that for the sake of peace and quietness, and because I'm a Christian, but this is too much. Grebe indeed! Grab would be the best name for any house she lives in. A wretched villa liable to be swept away by floods, and you and me carried out to sea again on a kitchen table. My answer is no, pass the butter.'

'I shouldn't be too much in a hurry,' said Benjy. 'It's two thousand pounds as well. Even if you got a year's let for Mallards, you'd have to spend a pretty penny in doing it up. Any tenant would insist on that.'

'The house is in perfect repair in every respect,' said Elizabeth.

'That might not be a tenant's view. And you might not get a tenant at all.'

'And the wicked insincerity of her letter,' continued Elizabeth. 'Saying she's sorry I have to turn out of it. Sorry! It's what she's been lying in wait for. I have a good mind not to answer her at all.'

'And I don't see the point of that,' said Benjy. 'If you are determined not to take her offer, why not tell her so at once?'

'You're not very bright this morning, love,' said Elizabeth, who had begun to think.

This spirited denunciation of Lucia's schemings was in fact only a conventional prelude to reflection. Elizabeth went to see her cook; in revenge for Benjy's want of indignation, she ordered him a filthy dinner, and finding that he had left the dining-room, fished Lucia's unscrupulous letter out of the grate, slightly scorched, but happily legible, and read it through again. Then, though she had given him the garden-room for his private sitting-room, she entered, quite forgetting to knock and ask if she might come in, and established herself in her usual seat in the window, where she could observe the movements of society, in order to tune herself back to normal pitch. A lot was happening: Susan's great car got helplessly stuck, as it came out of Porpoise Street, for a furniture van was trying to enter the same street, and couldn't back because there was another car behind it. The longed-for moment therefore had probably arrived, when Susan would have to go marketing on foot. Georgie went by in his van Dyck cape and a new suit (or perhaps dyed), but what was quaint Irene doing? She appeared to be sitting in the air in front of her house on a level with the first storey windows. Field-glasses had to be brought to bear on this: they revealed that she was suspended in a hammock slung from her bedroom window and (clad in pyjamas) was painting the sill in squares of black and crimson. Susan got out of her car and waddled towards the High Street. Georgie stopped and talked to Irene who dropped a paintbrush loaded with crimson on that blue beret of his. All quite satisfactory.

Benjy went to his golf: he had not actually required much driving this morning, and Elizabeth was alone. She had lately started crocheting a little white woollen cap, and tried it on. It curved downwards too sharply, as if designed for a much smaller head than hers, and she pulled a few rows out, and began it again in a flatter arc. A fresh train of musing was set up, and she thought, with strong distaste, of the day when Tilling would begin to wonder whether anything was going to happen, and, subsequently, to know that it wasn't. After all, she had never made any directly misleading statement: she had chosen (it was a free country) to talk about dolls and twilight sleep, and to let out her old green skirt, and Tilling had drawn its own conclusions. 'That dreadful gossipy habit,' she said to herself, 'if there isn't any news they invent it. And I know that they'll blame me for their disappointment. (Again she looked out of the window: Susan's motor had extricated itself, and was on its way to the High Street, and that was a disappointment too.) I must try to think of something to divert their minds when that time comes.'

Her stream of consciousness, eddying round in this depressing backwater, suddenly found an outlet into the main current, and she again read Lucia's toasted letter. It was a very attractive offer; her mouth watered at the thought of two thousand pounds, and though she had expressed to Benjy in unmistakable terms her resolve to reject any proposal so impertinent and unscrupulous, or, perhaps, in a fervour of disdain, not to answer it at all, there was nothing to prevent her accepting it at once, if she chose. A woman in her condition was always apt to change her mind suddenly and violently. (No: that would not do, since she was not a woman in her condition.) And surely here was a very good opportunity of diverting Tilling's attention. Lucia's settling into Mallards and her own move to Grebe would be of the intensest interest to Tilling's corporate mind, and that would be the time to abandon the role of coming motherhood. She would just give it up, just go shopping again with her usual briskness, just take in the green skirt and wear the enlarged woollen cap herself. She need make no explanations for she had said nothing that required them: Tilling, as usual, had done all the talking.

She turned her mind to the terms of Lucia's proposal. The blaze of fury so rightly kindled by the thought of Lucia possessing Mallards was spent, and the thought of that fat capital sum made a warm glow for her among the ashes. As Benjy had said, no tenant for six months or a year would take a house so sorely in need of renovation, and if Lucia was right in supposing that that wretched hole in the ground somewhere in West Africa would not be paying dividends for two years, a tenant for one year, even if she was lucky enough to find one, would only see her half through this impoverished period.

No sensible woman could reject so open a way out of her difficulties.

The mode of accepting this heaven-sent offer required thought. Best, perhaps, just formally to acknowledge the unscrupulous letter, and ask for a few days in which to make up her mind. A little hanging back, a hint conveyed obliquely, say through Diva, that two thousand pounds did not justly represent the difference in values between her lovely Queen Anne house and the villa precariously placed so near the river, a heartbroken wail at the thought of leaving the ancestral home might lead to an increased payment in cash, and that would be pleasant. So, having written her acknowledgment Elizabeth picked up her market-basket and set off for the High Street.

Quaint Irene had finished her window-sill, and was surveying the effect of this brilliant decoration from the other side of the street. In view of the disclosure which must come soon, Elizabeth suddenly made up her mind to forgive her for the dinner-bell outrage for fear she might do something quainter yet: a cradle, for instance, with a doll inside it, left on the doorstep would be very unnerving, and was just the sort of thing Irene might think of. So she said:

'Good morning, love: what a pretty

window-sill. So bright.'

Regardless of Elizabeth's marriage Irene still always addressed her as 'Mapp.'

'Not bad, is it, Mapp,' she said. 'What about my painting the whole of your garden-room in the same style? A hundred pounds down, and I'll begin to-day.'

'That *would* be very cheap,' said Mapp enthusiastically. 'But alas, I fear my days there are numbered.'

'Oh, of course; Lucia's offer. The most angelic thing I ever heard. I knew you'd jump at it.'

'No, dear, not quite inclined to jump,' said Mapp rather injudiciously.

'Oh, I didn't mean literally,' said Irene. 'That would be very rash of you. But isn't it like her, so noble and generous? I cried when she told me.'

'I shall cry when I have to leave my sweet Mallards,' observed Elizabeth. 'If I accept her offer, that is.'

'Then you'll be a crashing old crocodile, Mapp,' said Irene. 'You'll really think yourself damned lucky to get out of that old ruin of yours on such terms. Do you like my pyjamas? I'll give you a suit like them when the happy day — '

'Must be getting on,' interrupted Elizabeth. 'Such a lot to do.'

Feeling slightly battered, but with the glow of two thousand pounds comforting her within, Elizabeth turned into the High Street. Diva, it seemed, had finished her shopping, and was seated on this warm morning at her open window reading the paper. Elizabeth approached quite close unobserved, and with an irresistible spasm of playfulness said 'Bo!'

Diva gave a violent start.

'Oh, it's you, is it?' she said.

'No, dear, somebody quite different,' said Elizabeth skittishly. 'And I'm in such a state of perplexity this morning. I don't know what to do.'

'Benjy eloped with Lucia?' asked Diva. Two could play at being playful.

Elizabeth winced.

'Diva, dear, jokes on certain subjects only hurt me,' she said. '*Tiens! Je vous pardonne.*'

'What's perplexing you then?' asked Diva. 'Come in and talk if you want to, *tiens*. Can't go bellowing bad French into the street.'

Elizabeth came in, refused a low and comfortable chair and took a high one.

'Such an agonizing decision to make,' she said, 'and its coming just now is almost more than I can bear. I got *un petit lettre* from Lucia this morning offering to give me the freehold of Grebe and two thousand pounds in exchange for the freehold of Mallards.'

'I knew she was going to make you some offer,' said Diva. 'Marvellous for you. Where does the perplexity come in? Besides, you were going to let it for a year if you possibly could.'

'Yes, but the thought of never coming back to it. *Mon vieux*, so devoted to his garden-room, where we were engaged. Turning out for ever. And think of the difference between my lovely Queen Anne house and that villa by the side of the road that leads nowhere. The danger of floods. The distance.'

'But Lucia's thought of that,' said Diva, 'and puts the difference down at two thousand pounds. I should have thought one thousand was ample.'

'There are things like atmosphere that can't be represented in terms of money,' said Elizabeth with feeling. 'All the old associations. *Tante* Caroline.'

'Not having known your *Tante Caroline* I can't say what her atmosphere's worth,' said Diva.

'A saint upon earth,' said Elizabeth warmly. 'And Mallards used to be a second home to me long before it was mine.' (Which was a lie.) 'Silly of me, perhaps, but the thought of parting with it is agony. Lucia is terribly anxious to get it, *on m'a dit.*'

185

'She must be if she's offered you such a price for it,' said Diva.

'Diva, dear, we've always been such friends,' said Elizabeth, 'and it's seldom, *n'est ce pas*, that I've asked you for any favour. But I do now. Do you think you could let her know, quite casually, that I don't believe I shall have the heart to leave Mallards? Just that: hardly an allusion to the two thousand pounds.'

Diva considered this.

'Well, I'll ask a favour, too, Elizabeth,' she said, 'and it is that you should determine to drop that silly habit of putting easy French phrases into your conversation. So confusing. Besides everyone sees you're only copying Lucia. So ridiculous. All put on. If you will, I'll do what you ask. Going to tea with her this afternoon.'

'Thank you, sweet. A bargain then, and I'll try to break myself: I'm sure I don't want to confuse anybody. Now I must get to my shopping. Kind Susan is taking me for a drive this afternoon, and then a quiet evening with my Benjy-boy.'

'*Tres agréable*,' said Diva ruthlessly. 'Can't you hear how silly it sounds? Been on my mind a long time to tell you that.'

Lucia was in her office when Diva arrived for tea, and so could not possibly be disturbed. As she was actually having a sound nap, her guests, Georgie and Diva, had to wait until she happened to awake, and then, observing the time, she came out in a great hurry with a pen behind her ear. Diva executed her commission with much tact and casualness, but Lucia seemed to bore into the middle of her head with that penetrating eye. Having pierced her, she then looked dreamily out of the window.

'Dear me, what is that slang word one hears so much in the City?' she said. 'Ah, yes. Bluff. Should you happen to see dear Elizabeth, Diva, would you tell her that I just mentioned to you that my offer does not remain open indefinitely? I shall expect to hear from her in the course of to-morrow. If I hear nothing by then I shall withdraw it.'

'That's the stuff to give her,' said Georgie appreciatively. 'You'll hear fast enough when she knows that.'

But the hours of next day went by, and no communication came from Mallards. The morning post brought a letter from Mammoncash, which required a swift decision, but Lucia felt a sad lack of concentration, and was unable to make up her mind, while this other business remained undetermined. When the afternoon faded into dusk and still there was no answer, she became very anxious, and when, on the top of that, the afternoon post brought nothing her anxiety turned into sheer distraction. She rang up the house agents to ask whether Mrs. Mapp-Flint had received any application for the lease of Mallards for six months or a year, but Messrs. Woolgar and Pipstow, with much regret, refused to disclose the affairs of their client. She rang up Georgie to see if he knew anything, and received the ominous reply that as he was returning home just now, he saw a man, whom he did not recognise, being admitted into Mallards: Lucia in this tension felt convinced that it was somebody come to look over the house. She rang up Diva who had duly and casually delivered the message to Elizabeth at the marketing hour. It was an awful afternoon, and Lucia felt that all the money she had made was dross if she could not get this coveted freehold. Finally after tea (at which she could not eat a morsel) she wrote to Elizabeth turning the pounds into guineas, and gave the note to Cadman to deliver by hand and wait for an answer.

Meantime, ever since lunch, Elizabeth had been sitting at the window of the garden-room, getting on with the conversion of the white crocheted cap into adult size, and casting frequent glances down the street for the arrival of a note from Grebe, to say that

188

Lucia (terrified at the thought that she would not have the heart to quit Mallards) was willing to pay an extra five hundred pounds or so as a stimulant to that failing organ. But no letter came and Elizabeth in turn began to be terrified that the offer would be withdrawn. No sooner had Benjy swallowed a small (not the large) cup of tea on his return from his golf, than she sent him off to Grebe, with a note accepting Lucia's first offer, and bade him bring back the answer.

It was dark by now, and Cadman passing through the Landgate into the town met Major Benjy walking very fast in the direction of Grebe. The notes they both carried must therefore have been delivered practically simultaneously, and Elizabeth, in writing, had consented to accept two thousand pounds, and Lucia, in writing, to call them guineas.

6

This frightful discrepancy in the premium was adjusted by Lucia offering — more than equitably so she thought, and more than meanly thought the other contracting party — to split the difference, and the double move was instantly begun. In order to get into Mallards more speedily, Lucia left Grebe vacant in the space of two days, not forgetting the india-rubber felting in the passage outside the Office, for assuredly there would be another Temple of Silence at Mallards, and stored her furniture until her new house was fit to receive it. Grebe being thus empty, the vans from Mallards poured tiger-skins and Polynesian aprons into it, and into Mallards there poured a regiment of plumbers and painters and cleaners and decorators. Drains were tested, pointings between bricks renewed, floors scraped and ceilings whitewashed, and for the next fortnight other householders in Tilling had the greatest difficulty in getting any repairs done, for there was scarcely a workman who was not engaged on Mallards.

Throughout these hectic weeks Lucia stayed with Georgie at the Cottage, and not even he had ever suspected the sheer horse-power of body and mind which she was capable of developing when really extended. She had breakfasted before the first of her workmen appeared in the morning, and was ready to direct and guide them and to cancel all the orders she had given the day before, till everyone was feverishly occupied, and then she went back to the Cottage to read the letters that had come for her by the first post and skim the morning papers for world-movements. Then Mammoncash got his orders, if he had recommended any change in her investments, and Lucia went back to choose wallpapers, or go down into the big cellars that spread over the entire basement of the house. They had not been used for years, for a cupboard in the pantry had been adequate to hold such alcoholic refreshment as Aunt Caroline and her niece had wished to have on the premises, and bins had disintegrated and laths fallen, and rubbish had been hurled there, until the floor was covered with a foot or more of compacted debris. All this, Lucia decreed, must be excavated, and the floor level laid bare, for both her distaste for living above a rubbish heap, and her passion for restoring Mallards to its original state demanded the clearance. Two navvies with pick-axe and shovel carried up baskets of rubbish through the kitchen where a distracted ironmonger was installing a new boiler. There were rats in this cellar, and Diva very kindly lent Paddy to deal with them, and Paddy very kindly bit a navvy in mistake for a rat. At last the floor level was reached, and Lucia examining it carefully with an electric torch, discovered that there were lines of brickwork lying at an angle to the rest of the floor. The moment she saw them she was convinced that there was a Roman look about them, and secretly suspected that a Roman villa must once have stood here. There was no time to go into that just now: it must be followed up later, but she sent to the London Library for a few standard books on Roman remains in the South of England, and read an article during lunch-time in Georgie's Encyclopaedia about hypocausts.

After such sedentary mornings Lucia dug in the kitchen garden for an hour or two clad in Irene's overalls. Her gardener vainly protested that the spring was not the orthodox season to manure the soil, but it was obvious to Lucia that it required immediate enrichment and it got it. There was a big potato-patch which had evidently been plundered quite lately, for only a few sad stalks remained, and the inference that Elizabeth, before quitting, had dug up all the potatoes and taken them to Grebe was irresistible. The greenhouse, too, was strangely denuded of plants: they must have gone to Grebe as well. But the aspect was admirable for peach trees, and Lucia ordered half-a-dozen to be trained on the wall. Her gardening book recommended that a few bumble-bees should always be domiciled in a peach house for the fertilization of the blossoms, and after a long pursuit her gardener cleverly caught one in his cap. It was transferred with angry buzzings to the peach house and immediately flew out through a broken pane in the roof.

A reviving cup of tea started Lucia off again, and she helped to burn the discoloured paint off the banisters of the stairs which were undoubtedly of oak, and she stayed on at this fascinating job till the sun had set and all the workmen had gone. While dressing for dinner she observed that the ground floor rooms of Mallards that looked on to the street were brilliantly illuminated, as for a party, and realizing that she had left all the electric light burning, she put a cloak over her evening gown and went across to switch them off. A ponderous parcel of books had arrived from the London Library and she promised herself a historical treat in bed that night. She finished dressing and hurried down to dinner, for Georgie hated to be kept waiting for the meals. Lucia had had little conversation all day, and now, as if the dam of a reservoir had burst, the pent waters of vocal intercourse carried all before them.

'Georgino, such an interesting day,' she said, 'but I marvel at the vandalism of the late owner. Drab paint on those beautiful oak banisters, and I feel convinced that I have found the remains of a Roman villa. I conjecture that it runs out towards the kitchen garden. Possibly it may be a temple. My dear, what delicious fish! Did you know that in the time of Elizabeth — not this one — the Court was entirely supplied with fish from Tilling? A convoy of mules took it to London three times a week . . . In a few days more I hope and trust, Mallards will be ready for my furniture, and then you must be at my beck and call all day. Your taste is exquisite: I shall want your sanction for all my dispositions. Shall the garden-room be my office, do you think? But, as you know, I cannot exist without a music-room, and perhaps I had better use that little cupboard of a room off the hall as my office. My ledgers and a telephone is all I want there, but double windows must be put in as it looks on to the street. Then I shall have my books in the garden-room: the Greek dramatists are what I shall chiefly work at this year. My dear, how delicious it would be to give some tableaux in the garden from the Greek tragedians! The return of Agamemnon with Cassandra after the Trojan wars. You must certainly be Agamemnon. Could I not double the parts of Cassandra and Clytemnestra? Or a scene from Aristophanes. I began the *Thesmophoriazusae* a few weeks ago. About the revolt of the Athenian women, from their sequestered and blighted existence. They barricaded themselves into the Acropolis, exactly as the Pankhursts and the suffragettes padlocked themselves to the railings of the House of Commons and the pulpit in Westminster Abbey. I have always maintained that Aristophanes is the most modern of writers, Bernard Shaw, in fact, but with far more wit, more Attic salt. If I might choose a day in all the history of the world to live through, it would be a day in the golden age of Athens. A talk to Socrates in the morning; lunch with Pericles and Aspasia: a matinee at the theatre for a new play by Aristophanes: supper at Plato's Symposium. How it fires the blood!'

Georgie was eating a caramel chocolate and reply was impossible, since the teeth in his upper jaw were firmly glued to those of the lower and care was necessary. He could only nod and make massaging movements with his mouth, and Lucia, like Cassandra, only far more optimistic, was filled with the spirit of prophecy.

'I mean to make Mallards the centre of a new artistic and intellectual life in Tilling,' she said, 'much as the Hurst was, if I may say so without boasting, at our dear little placid Riseholme. My Attic day, I know, cannot be realized, but if there are, as I strongly suspect, the remains of a Roman temple or villa stretching out into the kitchen garden, we shall have a whiff of classical ages again. I shall lay bare the place, even if it means scrapping the asparagus bed. Very likely I shall find a tesselated pavement or two. Then we are so near London, every now and then I shall have a string quartet down, or get somebody to lecture on an archæological subject, if I am right about my Roman villa. I am getting rather rich, Georgie, I don't mind telling you, and I shall spend most of my gains on the welfare and enlightenment of Tilling. I do not regard the money I spent in buying Mallards a selfish outlay. It was equipment: I must have some central house with a room like the garden-room where I can hold my gatherings and symposia and so forth, and a garden for rest and refreshment and meditation. *Non e bella vista?*'

Georgie had rid himself of the last viscous strings of the caramel by the aid of a mouthful of hot coffee which softened them.

'My dear, what big plans you have,' he said. 'I always — ' but the torrent foamed on.

'*Caro*, you know well that I have never cared for small interests and paltry successes. The broad sweep of the brush, Georgie: the great scale! Indeed it will be a change in the life-history of Mallards — I think I shall call it Mallards House — to have something going on there beyond those perennial spyings from the garden-room window to see who goes to the dentist. And I mean to take part in the Civic, the municipal government of the place: that too, is no less than a duty. Dear Irene's very ill-judged exhibition at the election to the Town Council, deprived me, I feel sure, of hundreds of votes, though she meant so well. It jarred, it was not in harmony with the lofty aims I was hoping to represent. I *am* the friend of the poor, but a public pantomime was not the way to convince the electors of that. I shall be the friend of the rich, too. Those nice Wyses, for instance, their intellectual horizons are terribly bounded, and dear Diva hasn't got any horizons at all. I seem to see a general uplift, Georgie, an intellectual and artistic curiosity, such as that out of which all renaissances came. Poor Elizabeth! Naturally, I have no programme at present: it is not time

197

for that yet. Well, there's just the outline of my plans. Now let us have an hour of music.'

'I'm sure you're tired,' said Georgie.

'Never fresher. I consider it is a disgrace to be tired. I was, I remember, after our last day's canvassing, and was much ashamed of myself. And how charming it is to be spending tranquil quiet evenings with you again. When you decided on a permanent beard after your shingles, and went to your own house again, the evenings seemed quite lonely sometimes. Now let us play something that will really test us.'

Lucia's fingers were a little rusty from want of practice and she had a few minutes of rapid scales and exercises. Then followed an hour of duets, and she looked over some samples of chintzes.

That night Georgie was wakened from his sleep by the thump of some heavy object on the floor of the adjoining bedroom. Lucia, so he learned from her next morning, had dropped into a doze as she was reading in bed one of those ponderous books from the London Library about Roman remains in the South of England, and it had slid on to the floor.

Thanks to the incessant spur and scourge of Lucia's presence, which prevented any of her workmen having a slack moment throughout the day, the house was ready incredibly soon for the reception of her furniture, and Cadman had been settled into a new garage and cottage near by, so that Foljambe's journeys between her home and Georgie's were much abbreviated. There was a short interlude during which fires blazed and hot water pipes rumbled in every room in Mallards for the drying of newly hung paper and of paint. Lucia chafed at this inaction, for there was nothing for her to do but carry coal and poke the fires, and then a second period of feverish activity set in. The vans of her stored furniture disgorged at the door and Georgie was continually on duty so that Lucia might consult his exquisite taste and follow her own.

'Yes, that bureau would look charming in the little parlour upstairs,' she would say. 'Charming! How right you are! But somehow I seem to see it in the garden-room. I think I must try it there first.'

In fact Lucia saw almost everything in the garden-room, till a materialistic foreman told her that it would hold no more unless she meant it to be a lumber-room, in which case another table or two might be stacked there. She hurried out and found it was difficult to get into the room at all, and the piano was yet to come. Back came a procession of objects which were gradually dispersed among other rooms which hitherto had remained empty. Minor delays were caused by boxes of linen being carried out to the garden-room because she was sure they contained books, and boxes of books being put in the cellar because she was equally certain that they contained wine.

But by mid-April everything was ready for the house-warming lunch. All Tilling was bidden with the exception of quaint Irene, for she had another little disturbance with Elizabeth, and Lucia thought that their proximity was not a risk that should be taken on an occasion designed to be festive, for there were quite enough danger zones without that. Elizabeth at first was inclined to refuse her invitation: it would be too much of a heart-break to see her ancestral home in the hands of an alien, but she soon perceived that it would be a worse heart-break not to be able to comment bitterly on the vulgarity or the ostentation or the general uncomfortableness or whatever she settled should be the type of outrage which Lucia had committed in its hallowed precincts, and she steeled herself to accept. She had to steel herself also to something else, which it was no longer any use putting off; the revelation must be made, and, as in the case of Georgie's beard everybody had better know together. Get it over.

Elizabeth had fashioned a very striking costume for the occasion. One of Benjy's tiger-skins was clearly not sufficiently strong to stand the wear and tear of being trodden on, but parts of it were excellent still, and she had cut some strips out of it which she hoped were sound and with which she trimmed the edge of the green skirt which had been exciting such interest in Tilling, and the collar of the coat which went with it. On her head she wore a white woollen crochetted cap, just finished: a decoration of artificial campanulas, rendering its resemblance to the cap of a hydrocephalous baby less noticeable.

Elizabeth drew in her breath, wincing with a stab of mental anguish when she saw the dear old dingy panels in the hall, once adorned with her water-colour sketches, gleaming with garish white paint, and she and Benjy followed Grosvenor out to the garden-room. The spacious cupboard in the wall once concealed behind a false bookcase of shelves ranged with leather simulacra of book backs, 'Elegant Extracts,' and 'Poems' and 'Commentaries,' had been converted into a real bookcase, and Lucia's library of standard and classical works filled it from top to bottom. A glass chandelier hung from the ceiling, Persian rugs had supplanted the tiger-skins and the walls were of dappled blue.

Lucia welcomed them.

'So glad you could come,' she said. 'Dear Elizabeth, what lovely fur! Tiger, surely.'

'So glad you like it,' said Elizabeth. 'And sweet of you to ask us. So here I am in my dear garden-room again. Quite a change.'

She gave Benjy's hand a sympathetic squeeze, for he must be feeling the desecration of his room, and in came the Padre and Evie, who after some mouselike squeals of rapture began to talk very fast.

'What a beautiful room!' she said. 'I shouldn't have known it again, would you, Kenneth? How de do, Elizabeth. Bits of Major Benjy's tiger-skins, isn't it? Why that used to be the cupboard where you had been hoarding all sorts of things to eat in case the coal strike went on, and one day the door flew open and all the corned beef and dried apricots came bumping out. I remember it as if it was yesterday.'

Lucia hastened to interrupt that embarrassing reminiscence.

'Dear Elizabeth, pray don't stand,' she said. 'There's a chair in the window by the curtain, just where you used to sit.'

'Thanks, dear,' said Elizabeth, continuing slowly to revolve, and take in the full horror of the scene. 'I should like just to look round. So clean, so fresh.'

Diva trundled in. Elizabeth's tiger-trimmings at once caught her eye, but as Elizabeth had not noticed her cropped hair the other day, she looked at them hard and was totally blind to them.

'You've made the room lovely, Lucia,' she said. 'I never saw such an improvement, did you, Elizabeth? What a library, Lucia! Why that used to be a cupboard behind a false bookcase. Of course, I remember — '

'And such a big chandelier,' interrupted Elizabeth, fearful of another recitation of that frightful incident. 'I should find it a little dazzling, but then my eyes are wonderful.'

'Mr. and Mrs. Wyse,' said Grosvenor at the door.

'Grosvenor, sherry at once,' whispered Lucia, feeling the tension. 'Nice of you to come, Susan. *Buon giorno, Signor Sapiente.*'

Elizabeth, remembering her promise to Diva, just checked herself from saying '*Bon jour, Monsieur Sage,*' and Mr. Wyse kissed Lucia's hand, Italian-fashion, as a proper reply to this elegant salutation, and put up his eyeglass.

'Genius!' he said. 'Artistic genius! Never did I appreciate the beautiful proportions of this room before; it was smothered — ah, Mrs. Mapp-Flint! Such a pleasure, and a lovely costume if I may say so. That poem of Blake's:

'Tiger, tiger, burning bright.' I am writing to my sister Amelia to-day, and I must crave your permission to tell her about it. How she scolds me if I do not describe to her the latest fashions of the ladies of Tilling.'

'A glass of sherry, dear Elizabeth,' said Lucia.

'No, dear, not a drop, thanks. Poison to me,' said Elizabeth fiercely.

Georgie arrived last. He, of course, had assisted at the transformation of the garden-room, but naturally he added his voice to the chorus of congratulation which Elizabeth found so trying.

'My dear, how beautiful you've got the room!' he said. 'You'd have made a fortune over house-decorating. When I think what it was like — oh, good morning, Mrs. Major Benjy. What a charming frock, and how ingenious. It's bits of the tiger that used to be the hearthrug here. I always admired it so much.'

But none of these compliments soothed Elizabeth's savagery, for the universal admiration of the garden-room was poisoning her worse than sherry. Then lunch was announced, and it was with difficulty she was persuaded to lead the way, so used was she to follow other ladies as hostess, into the dining-room. Then, urged to proceed, she went down the steps with astonishing alacrity, but paused in the hall as if uncertain where to go next.

'All these changes,' she said. 'Quite bewildering. Perhaps Lucia has turned another room into the dining-room.'

'No, ma'am, the same room,' said Grosvenor.

More shocks. There was a refectory table where her own round table had been, and a bust of Beethoven on the chimney-piece. The walls were of apple-green, and instead of being profusely hung with Elizabeth's best water-colours, there was nothing on them but a sconce or two for electric light. She determined to eat not more than one mouthful of any dish that might be offered her, and conceal the rest below her knife and fork. She sat down, stubbing her toes against the rail that ran round the table, and gave a little squeal of anguish.

'So stupid of me,' she said. 'I'm not accustomed to this sort of table. Ah, I see. I must put my feet over the little railing. That will be quite comfortable.'

Lobster *à la Riseholme* was handed round, and a meditative silence followed in its wake, for who could help dwelling for a moment on the memory of how Elizabeth, unable to obtain the recipe by honourable means, stole it from Lucia's kitchen? She took a mouthful, and then, according to plan, hid the rest of it under her fork and fish-knife. But her mouth began to water for this irresistible delicacy, and she surreptitiously gobbled up the rest, and then with a wistful smile looked round the desecrated room.

'An admirable shade of green,' said Mr. Wyse, bowing to the walls. 'Susan, we must memorize this for the time when we do up our little *salle à manger*.'

'Begorra, it's the true Oirish colour,' said the Padre. 'I canna mind me what was the way of it before.'

'I can tell you, dear Padre,' said Elizabeth eagerly. 'Biscuit-colour, such a favourite tint of mine, and some of my little paintings on the walls. Quite plain and homely. Benjy, dear, how naughty you are: hock always punishes you.'

'Dear lady,' said Mr. Wyse, 'surely not such nectar as we are now enjoying. How I should like to know the vintage. Delicious!'

Elizabeth turned to Georgie.

'You must be very careful of these treacherous spring days, Mr. Georgie,' she said. 'Shingles are terribly liable to return, and the second attack is always much worse than the first. People often lose their eyesight altogether.'

'That's encouraging,' said Georgie.

Luckily Elizabeth thought that she had now sufficiently impressed on everybody what a searing experience it was to her to re-visit her ancestral home, and see the melancholy changes that had been wrought on it, and under the spell of the nectar her extreme acidity mellowed. The nectar served another purpose also: it bucked her up for the anti-maternal revelation which she had determined to make that very day. She walked very briskly about the garden after lunch. She tripped across the lawn to the *giardino segreto*: she made a swift tour of the kitchen garden under her own steam, untowed by Benjy, and perceived that the ladies were regarding her with a faintly puzzled air: they were beginning to see what she meant them to see. Then with Diva she lightly descended the steps into the green-house and, diverted from her main purpose for the moment, felt herself bound to say a few words about Lucia's renovations in general, and the peach trees in particular.

'Poor things, they'll come to nothing,' she said. 'I could have told dear hostess that, if she had asked me. You might as well plant cedars of Lebanon. And the dining-room, Diva! The colour of green apples, enough to give anybody indigestion before you begin! The glaring white paint in the hall! The garden-room! I feel that the most, and so does poor Benjy. I was prepared for something pretty frightful, but not as bad as this!'

'Don't agree,' said Diva. 'It's all beautiful. Should hardly have known it again. You'd got accustomed to see the house all dingy, Elizabeth, and smothered in cobwebs and your own water-colours and muck — '

That was sufficient rudeness for Elizabeth to turn her back on Diva, but it was for a further purpose that she whisked round and positively twinkled up those steep steps again. Diva gasped. For weeks now Elizabeth had leant on Benjy if there were steps to mount, and had walked with a slow and dignified gait, and all of a sudden she had resumed her nimble and rapid movement. And then the light broke. Diva felt she would burst unless she at once poured her interpretation of these phenomena into some feminine ear, and she hurried out of the greenhouse nearly tripping up on the steps that Elizabeth had so lightly ascended.

The rest of the party had gathered again in the garden-room, and by some feminine intuition Diva perceived in the eyes of the other women the knowledge which had just dawned on her. Presently the Mapp-Flints said good-bye, and Mr. Wyse, who, with the obtuseness of a man, had noticed nothing, was pressing Elizabeth to take the Royce and go for a drive. Then came the first-hand authentic disclosure.

'So good of you,' said she, 'but Benjy and I have promised ourselves a long walk. Lovely party, Lucia: some day you must come and see your old house. Just looked at your peach trees: I hope you'll have quantities of fruit. Come along, Benjy, or there won't be time for our tramp. Good-bye, sweet garden-room.'

They went out, and instantly there took place a species of manœuvre which partook of the nature of a conjuring trick and a conspiracy. Evie whispered something to her Padre, and he found that he had some urgent district-visiting to do: Susan had a quiet word with her husband, and he recollected that he must get off his letter to Contessa Amelia Faraglione by the next post and Lucia told Georgie that if he could come back in half-an-hour she would be at leisure to try that new duet. The four ladies therefore were left, and Evie and Diva, as soon as the door of the garden-room was shut, broke into a crisp, unrehearsed dialogue of alternate sentences, like a couple of clergymen intoning the Commination service.

'She's given it up,' chanted Diva. 'She

209

nipped up those steep steps from the greenhouse, as if it was on the flat.'

'But such a sell, isn't it,' cried Evie. 'It *would* have been exciting. Ought we to say anything about it to her? She must feel terribly disappointed — '

'Not a bit,' said Diva. 'I don't believe she ever believed it. Wanted us to believe it: that's all. Most deceitful.'

'And Kenneth had been going through the Churching of Women.'

'And she had no end of drives in your motor, Susan. False pretences, I call it. You'd never have lent her it at all, unless — '

'And all that nutritious honey from the Contessa.'

'And I think she's taken in the old green skirt again, but the strips of tiger-skin make it hard to be certain.'

'And I'm sure she was crocheting a baby-cap in white wool, and she must have pulled a lot of it out and begun again. She was wearing it.'

'And while I think of it,' said Diva in parenthesis, 'there'll be a fine mess of tiger hairs on your dining-room carpet, Lucia. I saw clouds of them fly when she banged her foot.'

Susan Wyse had not had any chance at present of joining in this vindictive chant.

Sometimes she had opened her mouth to speak, but one of the others had been quicker. At this point, as Diva and Evie were both a little out of breath, she managed to contribute.

'I don't grudge her her drives,' she said, 'but I do feel strongly about that honey. It was very special honey. My sister-in-law, the Contessa, took it daily when she was expecting her baby, and it weighed eleven pounds.'

'Eleven pounds of honey? O dear me, that is a lot!' said Evie.

'No, the baby — '

The chant broke out afresh.

'And so rude about the sherry,' said Diva, 'saying it was poison.'

'And pretending not to know where the dining-room was.'

'And saying that the colour of the walls gave her indigestion like green apples. She's enough to give anybody indigestion herself.'

The torrent spent itself: Lucia had been sitting with eyes half-closed and eyebrows drawn together as if trying to recollect something, and then took down a volume from her bookshelves of classical literature and rapidly turned over the pages. She appeared to find what she wanted, for she read on in silence a moment, and then replaced the book with a faraway sigh.

'I was saying to Georgie the other day,' she said, 'how marvellously modern Aristophanes was. I seemed to remember a scene in one of his plays — the *Thesmophoriazusae* — where a somewhat similar situation occurred. A woman, a dear, kind creature really, of middle-age or a little more, had persuaded her friends (or thought she had) that she was going to have a baby. Such Attic wit — there is nothing in English like it. I won't quote the Greek to you, but the conclusion was that it was only a 'wind-egg.' Delicious phrase, really untranslatable, but that is what it comes to. Shan't we all leave it at that? Poor dear Elizabeth! Just a wind-egg. So concise.'

She gave a little puff with her pursed lips, as if blowing the wind-egg away.

Rather awed by this superhuman magnanimity the conductors of the Commination service dispersed, and Lucia went into the dining-room to see if there was any serious deposit of tiger-hairs on her new carpet beside Elizabeth's place. Certainly there were some, though not quite the clouds of which Diva had spoken. Probably then that new pretty decoration would not be often seen again since it was moulting so badly. 'Everything seems to go wrong with the poor soul,' thought Lucia in a spasm of most pleasurable compassion, 'owing to her deplorable lack of foresight. She bought Siriami without ascertaining whether it paid dividends: she tried to make us all believe that she was going to have a baby without ascertaining whether there was the smallest reason to suppose she would, and with just the same blind recklessness she trimmed the old green skirt with tiger without observing how heavily it would moult when she moved.'

She returned to the garden-room for a few minutes' intensive practice of the duet she and Georgie would read through when he came back, and seating herself at the piano she noticed a smell as of escaping gas. Yet it could not be coal gas, for there was none laid on now to the garden-room, the great chandelier and other lamps being lit by electricity. She wondered whether this smell was paint not quite dry yet, for during the renovation of the house her keen perception had noticed all kinds of smells incident to decoration: there was the smell of pear-drops in one room, and that was varnish: there was the smell of advanced corruption in another, and that was the best size: there was the smell of elephants in the cellar and that was rats. So she thought no more about it, practised for a quarter of an hour, and then hurried away from the piano when she saw Georgie coming down the street, so that he should not find her poaching in the unseen suite by Mozart.

Georgie was reproachful.

'It was tarsome of you,' he said, 'to send me away when I longed to hear what you all thought about Elizabeth. I knew what it meant when I saw how she skipped and pranced and had taken in the old green skirt again — '

'Georgie, I never noticed that,' said Lucia. 'Are you sure?'

'Perfectly certain, and how she was going for a tramp with Benjy. The baby's off. I wonder if Benjy was an accomplice — '

'Dear Georgie!' remonstrated Lucia.

Georgie blushed at the idea that he could have meant anything so indelicate.

'Accomplice to the general deception was what I was going to say when you interrupted. I think we've all been insulted. We ought to mark our displeasure.'

Lucia had no intention of repeating her withering comment about the wind-egg. It was sure to get round to him.

'Why be indignant with the poor thing?' she said. 'She has been found out and that's quite sufficient punishment. As to her making herself so odious at lunch and doing her best, without any success, to spoil my little party, that was certainly malicious. But about the other, Georgie, let us remember what a horrid job she had to do. I foresaw that, you may remember, and expressed my wish that, when it came, we should all be kind to her. She must have skipped and pranced, as you put it, with an aching heart, and certainly with aching legs. As for poor Major Benjy, I'm sure he was putty in her hands, and did just what she told him. How terribly a year's marriage has aged him, has it not?'

'I should have been dead long ago,' said Georgie.

Lucia looked round the room.

'My dear, I'm so happy to be back in this house,' she said, 'and to know it's my own, that I would forgive Elizabeth almost anything. Now let us have an hour's harmony.'

They went to the piano where, most carelessly, Lucia had left on the music-rack the duet they were to read through for the first time. But Georgie did not notice it. He began to sniff.

'Isn't there a rather horrid smell of gas?' he asked.

'I thought I smelled something,' said Lucia, successfully whisking off the duet. 'But the foreman of the gasworks is in the house now, attending to the stove in the kitchen. I'll get him to come and smell too.'

Lucia sent the message by Grosvenor, and an exceedingly cheerful young man bounded into the room. He smelt, too, and burst into a merry laugh.

'No, ma'am, that's not *my* sort of gas,' he said gaily. 'That'll be sewer gas, that will. That's the business of the town surveyor and he's my brother. I'll ring him up at once and get him to come and see to it.'

'Please do,' said Lucia.

'He'll nip up in a minute to oblige Mrs. Lucas,' said the gasman. 'Dear me, how we all laughed at Miss Irene's procession, if you'll excuse my mentioning it. But this is business now, not pleasure. Horrid smell that. It won't do at all.'

Lucia and Georgie moved away from the immediate vicinity of the sewer, and presently with a rap on the door, a second young man entered exactly like the first.

'A pleasure to come and see into your little trouble, ma'am,' he said. 'In the window my brother said. Ah, now I've got it.'

He laughed very heartily.

'No, no,' he said. 'Georgie's made a blooming error — beg your pardon, sir, I mean my brother — Let's have him in.'

In came Georgie of the gasworks.

'You've got something wrong with your nosepiece, Georgie,' said the sewer man.

216

'That's coal gas, that is.'

'Get along, Percy!' said Georgie. 'Sewers. Your job, my lad.'

Lucia assumed her most dignified manner.

'Your immediate business, gentlemen,' she said, 'is to ascertain whether I am living (i) in a gas pipe or (ii) in a main drain.'

Shouts of laughter.

'Well, there's a neat way to put it,' said Percy appreciatively. 'We'll tackle it for you, ma'am. We must have a joint investigation, Georgie, till we've located it. It must be percolating through the soil and coming up through the floor. You send along two of your fellows in the morning, and I'll send two of the Corporation men, and we'll dig till we find out. Bet you a shilling it's coal gas.'

'I'll take you. Sewers,' said Georgie.

'But I can't live in a room that's full of either,' said Lucia. 'One may explode and the other may poison me.'

'Don't you worry about that, ma'am,' said Georgie. 'I'll guarantee you against an explosion, if it's my variety of gas. Not near up to inflammatory point.'

'And I've workmen, ma'am,' said Percy, 'who spend their days revelling in a main drain, you may say, and live to ninety. We'll start to dig in the road outside in the morning, Georgie and me, for that's where it

217

must come from. No one quite knows where the drains are in this old part of the town, but we'll get on to their scent if it's sewers, and then tally-ho. Good afternoon, ma'am. All O.K.'

At an early hour next morning the combined exploration began. Up came the pavement outside the garden-room and the cobbles of the street, and deeper all day grew the chasm, while the disturbed earth reeked even more strongly of the yet unidentified smell. The news of what was in progress reached the High Street at the marketing hour, and the most discouraging parallels to this crisis were easily found. Diva had an uncle who had died in the night from asphyxiation owing to a leak of coal gas, and Evie, not to be outdone in family tragedies, had an aunt, who, when getting into a new house (ominous), noticed a 'faint' smell in the dining-room, and died of blood-poisoning in record time. But Diva put eucalyptus on her handkerchief and Evie camphor and both hurried up to the scene of the excavation. To Elizabeth this excitement was a god-send, for she had been nervous as to her reception in the High Street after yesterday's revelation, but found that everyone was entirely absorbed in the new topic. Personally she was afraid (though hoping she might prove to be wrong) that the clearing out of the cellars at Mallards might somehow have tapped a reservoir of a far deadlier quality of vapour than either coal gas or sewer gas. Benjy, having breathed the polluted air of the garden-room yesterday, thought it wise not to go near the plague-spot at all, but after gargling with a strong solution of carbolic, fled to the links, with his throat burning very uncomfortably, to spend the day in the aseptic sea air. Georgie (not Percy's gay brother) luckily remembered that he had bought a gas-mask during the war, in case the Germans dropped pernicious bombs on Riseholme, and Foljambe found it and cleared out the cobwebs. He adjusted it (tarsome for the beard) and watched the digging from a little distance, looking like an elephant whose trunk had been cut off very short. The Padre came in the character of an expert, for he could tell sewer gas from coal gas, begorra, with a single sniff, but he had scarcely taken a proper sniff when the church clock struck eleven, and he had to hurry away to read matins. Irene, smoking a pipe, set up her easel on the edge of the pit and painted a fine impressionist sketch of navvies working in a crater. Then, when the dinner-hour arrived, the two gay brothers, Gas and Drains, leaped like Quintus Curtius into the chasm and shovelled feverishly till their workmen returned, in order that no time should be lost in arriving at a solution and the settlement of their bet.

As the excavation deepened Lucia with a garden-spud, raked carefully among the baskets of earth which were brought up, and soon had a small heap of fragments of pottery, which she carried into Mallards. Georgie was completely puzzled at this odd conduct, and, making himself understood with difficulty through the gas-mask, asked her what she was doing.

Lucia looked round to make sure she would not be overheard.

'Roman pottery without a doubt,' she whispered. 'I am sure they will presently come across some remains of my Roman villa — '

A burst of cheering came from the bowels of the earth. One of the gas workmen with a vigorous stroke of his pick at the side of the pit close to the garden-room brought down a slide of earth, and exposed the mouth of a tiled aperture some nine inches square.

'Drains and sewers it is,' he cried, 'and out we go,' and he and his comrade downed tools and clambered out of the pit, leaving the town surveyor's men to attend to the job now demonstrated to be theirs.

The two gay brethren instantly jumped into the excavation. The aperture certainly did look like a drain, but just as certainly there was nothing coming down it. Percy put his nose into it, and inhaled deeply as a Yogi, drawing a long breath through his nostrils.

'Clean as a whistle, Georgie,' he said, 'and sweet as a sugar-plum. Drains it may have been, old man, but not in the sense of our bet. We were looking for something active and stinkful — '

'But drains it is, Per,' said Georgie.

A broken tile had fallen from the side of it, and Percy picked it up.

'There's been no sewage passing along that for a sight of years,' he said. 'Perhaps it was never a drain at all.'

Into Lucia's mind there flashed an illuminating hypocaustic idea.

'Please give me that tile,' she called out.

'Certainly, ma'am,' said Percy, reaching up with it, 'and have a sniff at it yourself. Nothing there to make your garden-room stink. You might lay that on your pillow — '

Percy's sentence was interrupted by a second cheer from his two men who had gone on working, and they also downed tools.

''Ere's the gas pipe at last,' cried one. 'Get going at your work again, gas brigade!'

'And lumme, don't it stink,' said the other.

'Leaking fit to blow up the whole neighbourhood. Soil's full of it.'

They clambered out of the excavation, and stood with the gas workers to await further orders.

'Have a sniff at that, Georgie,' said Per encouragingly, 'and then hand me a bob. That's something like a smell, that is. Put that on your pillow and you'll sleep so as you'll never wake again.'

Georgie, though crestfallen, retained his sense of fairness, and made no attempt to deny that the smell that now spread freely from the disengaged pipe was the same as that which filled the garden-room.

'Seems like it,' he said, 'and there's your bob, not but what the other was a drain. We'll find the leak and have it put to rights now.'

'And then I hope you'll fill up that great hole,' said Lucia.

'No time to-day, ma'am,' said Georgie. 'I'll see if I can spare a couple of men tomorrow, or next day at the latest.'

Lucia's Georgie, standing on the threshold of Mallards, suddenly observed that the excavation extended right across the street, and that he was quite cut off from the Cottage. He pulled off his gas-mask.

'But, look, how am I to get home?' he asked in a voice of acute lamentation. 'I can't climb down into that pit and up on the other side.'

Great laughter from the brethren.

'Well, sir, that is awkward,' said Per. 'I'm afraid you'll have to nip round by the High Street and up the next turning to get to your little place. But it will be all right, come the day after to-morrow.'

Lucia carried her tile reverently into the house, and beckoned to Georgie.

'That square-tiled opening confirms all I conjectured about the lines of foundation in the cellar,' she said. 'Those wonderful Romans used to have furnaces underneath the floors of their houses and their temples — I've been reading about it — and the hot air was conveyed in tiled flues through the walls to heat them. Undoubtedly this was a hot-air flue and not a drain at all.'

'That would be interesting,' said Georgie. 'But the pipe seemed to run through the earth, not through a wall. At least there was no sign of a wall that I saw.'

'The wall may have perished at that point,' said Lucia after only a moment's thought. 'I shall certainly find it further on in the garden, where I must begin digging at once. But not a word to anybody yet. Without doubt, Georgie, a Roman villa stood here or perhaps a temple. I should be inclined to say a temple.

On the top of the hill, you know: just where they always put temples.'

Dusk had fallen before the leak in the gas pipe was repaired, and a rope was put up round the excavation and hung with red lanterns. Had the pit been less deep, or the sides of it less precipitous, Lucia would have climbed down into it and continued her study of the hot-air flue. She took the tile to her bathroom and scrubbed it clean. Close to the broken edge of it there were stamped the letters S.P.

She dined alone that night and went back to the garden-room from which the last odours of gas had vanished. She searched in vain in her books from the London Library for any mention of Tilling having once been a Roman town, but its absence made the discovery more important, as likely to prove a new chapter in the history of Roman Britain. Eagerly she turned over the pages: there were illustrations of pottery which fortified her conviction that her fragments were of Roman origin: there was a picture of a Roman tile as used in hot-air flues which was positively identical with her specimen. Then what could S.P. stand for? She ploughed through a list of inscriptions found in the South of England and suddenly gave a great crow of delight. There was one headed S.P.Q.R., which being interpreted meant *Senatus Populusque Romanus,* 'the Senate and the People of Rome.' Her instinct had been right: a private villa would never have borne those imperial letters; they were reserved for state-erected buildings, such as temples . . . It said so in her book.

7

For the next few days Lucia was never once seen in the streets of Tilling, for all day she supervised the excavations in her garden. To the great indignation of her gardener, she hired two unemployed labourers at very high wages in view of the importance of their work, and set them to dig a trench across the potato-patch which Elizabeth had despoiled and the corner of the asparagus bed, so that she must again strike the line of the hot-air flue, which had been so providentially discovered at the corner of the garden-room. Great was her triumph when she hit it once more, though it was a pity to find that it still ran through the earth, and not, as she had hoped through the buried remains of a wall. But the soil was rich in relics, it abounded in pieces of pottery on the same type as those she had decided were Roman, and there were many pretty fragments of iridescent, oxydised glass, and a few bones which she hoped might turn out to be those of red deer which at the time of the Roman occupation were common in Kent and Sussex. Her big table in the garden-room was cleared of its books and writing apparatus, and loaded with cardboard trays of glass and pottery. She scarcely entered the Office at all, and but skimmed through the communications from Mammon-cash.

Georgie dined with her on the evening of the joyful day when she had come across the hot-air flue again. There was a slightly earthy odour in the garden-room where after dinner they pored over fragments of pottery, and vainly endeavoured to make pieces fit together.

'It's most important, Georgie,' she said, 'as you will readily understand, to keep note of the levels at which objects are discovered. Those in Tray D come from four feet down in the corner of the asparagus bed: that is the lowest level we have reached at present, and they, of course, are the earliest.'

'Oh, and look at Tray A,' said Georgie. 'All those pieces of clay tobacco pipes. I didn't know the Romans smoked. Did they?'

Lucia gave a slightly superior laugh.

'*Caro*, of course they didn't,' she said. 'Tray A: yes, I thought so. Tray A is from a much higher level, let me see, yes, a foot below the surface of the ground. We may put it down therefore as being subsequent to Queen Elizabeth when tobacco was intro-duced. At a guess I should say those pipes were Cromwellian. A Cromwellian look, I fancy. I am rather inclined to take a complete tile from the continuation of the air flue which I laid bare this morning, and see if it is marked in full S.P.Q.R. The tile from the street, you remember, was broken and had only S.P. on it. Yet is it a Vandalism to meddle at all with such a fine specimen of a flue evidently *in situ*?'

'I think I should do it,' said Georgie, 'you can put it back when you've found the letters.'

'I will then. To-morrow I expect my trench to get down to floor level. There may be a tesselated pavement like that found at Richborough. I shall have to unearth it all, even if I have to dig up the entire kitchen garden. And if it goes under the garden-room, I shall have to underpin it, I think they call it. Fancy all this having come out of a smell of gas!'

'Yes, that was a bit of luck,' said Georgie stifling a yawn over Tray A, where he was vainly trying to make a complete pipe out of the fragments.

Lucia put on the kind, the indulgent smile suitable to occasions when Georgie did not fully appreciate her wisdom or her brilliance.

'Scarcely fair to call it entirely luck,' she said, 'for you must remember that when the cellar was dug out I told you plainly that I should find Roman remains in the garden. That was before the gas smelt.'

'I'd forgotten that,' said Georgie. 'To be sure you did.'

'Thank you, dear. And to-morrow morning, if you are strolling and shopping in the High Street, I think you might let it be known that I am excavating in the garden and that the results, so far, are most promising. Roman remains: you might go as far as that. But I do not want a crowd of sightseers yet: they will only impede the work. I shall admit nobody at present.'

★ ★ ★

Foljambe had very delicately told Georgie that there was a slight defect in the plumbing system at Mallards Cottage, and accordingly he went down to the High Street next day to see about this. It was pleasant to be the bearer of such exciting news about Roman remains, and he announced it to Diva through the window and presently met Elizabeth. She had detached the tiger-skin border from the familiar green skirt.

'Hope the smell of gas or drains or both has quite gone away now, Mr. Georgie,' she said. 'I'm told it was enough to stifle anybody.

Odd that I never had any trouble in my time nor Aunt Caroline in hers. Lucia none the worse?'

'Not a bit. And no smell left,' said Georgie.

'So glad! Most dangerous it must have been. Any news?'

'Yes: she's very busy digging up the kitchen garden — '

'What? My beautiful garden?' cried Elizabeth shrilly. 'Ah, I forgot. Yes?'

'And she's finding most interesting Roman remains. A villa, she thinks, or more probably a temple.'

'Indeed! I must go up and have a peep at them.'

'She's not showing them to anybody just yet,' said Georgie. 'She's deep down in the asparagus bed. Pottery. Glass. Air flues.'

'Well, that is news! Quite an archæologist, and nobody ever suspected it,' observed Elizabeth smiling her widest. 'Padre, dear Lucia has found a Roman temple in my asparagus bed.'

'Ye dinna say! I'll rin up, bedad.'

'No use,' said Elizabeth. 'Not to be shown to anybody yet.'

Georgie passed on to the plumbers. 'Spencer & Son' was the name of the firm, and there was the proud legend in the window that it had been established in Tilling in 1820 and undertook all kinds of work connected with plumbing and drains. Mr. Spencer promised to send a reliable workman up at once to Mallards Cottage.

The news disseminated by Georgie quickly spread from end to end of the High Street, and reached the ears of an enterprising young gentleman who wrote paragraphs of local news for the *Hastings Chronicle*. This should make a thrilling item, and he called at Mallards just as Lucia was coming in from her morning's digging, and begged to be allowed to communicate any particulars she could give him to the paper. There seemed no harm in telling him what she had allowed Georgie to reveal to Tilling (in fact she liked the idea) and told him briefly that she had good reason to hope that she was on the track of a Roman villa, or, more probably, a temple. It was too late for the news to appear in this week's issue, but it would appear next week, and he would send her a copy. Lucia lunched in a great hurry and returned to the asparagus bed.

Soon after Georgie appeared to help. Lucia was standing in the trench with half of her figure below ground level, like Erda in Wagner's justly famous opera. If only Georgie had not dyed his beard, he might have been Wotan.

'*Ben arrivato,*' she called to him in the Italian translation. 'I'm on the point of taking out a tile from my hot-air flue. I am glad you are here as a witness, and it will be interesting for you. This looks rather a loose one. Now.'

She pulled it out and turned it over.

'Georgie,' she cried. 'Here's the whole of the stamped letters of which I had only two.'

'Oh, how exciting,' said Georgie. 'I do hope there's a Q.R. as well as the S.P.'

Lucia rubbed the dirt off the inscription and then replaced the tile.

'What is the name of that plumber in the High Street established a century ago?' she asked in a perfectly calm voice.

Georgie guessed what she had found.

'My dear, how tarsome!' he said. 'I'm afraid it *is* Spencer.'

Lucia got nimbly out of the trench, and wiped her muddy boots against the box edging of the path.

'Georgie, that is a valuable piece of evidence,' she said. 'No doubt this is an old drain. I confess I was wrong about it. Let us date it, tentatively, *circa* 1830. Now we know more about the actual levels. First we have the Cromwellian stratum: tobacco pipes. Below again — what is that?'

There were two workmen in the trench, the one with a pick, the other shovelling the earth into a basket to dump it on to the far corner of the potato-patch uprooted by Elizabeth. Georgie was glad of this diversion (whatever it might be) for it struck him that the stratum which Lucia had assigned to Cromwell was far above the air flue stratum, once pronounced to be Roman, but now dated *circa* 1830 . . . The digger had paused with his pickaxe poised in the air.

'Lovely bit of glass here, ma'am,' he said. 'I nearly went crash into it!'

Lucia jumped back into the trench and became Erda again. It was a narrow escape indeed. The man's next blow must almost certainly have shattered a large and iridescent piece of glass, which gleamed in the mould. Tenderly and carefully, taking off her gloves, Lucia loosened it.

'Georgie!' she said in a voice faint and ringing with emotion, 'take it from me in both hands with the utmost caution. A wonderful piece of glass, with an inscription stamped on it.'

'Not Spencer again, I hope,' said Georgie.

Lucia passed it to him from the trench, and he received it in his cupped hands.

'Don't move till I get out and take it from you,' said she. 'Not another stroke for the present,' she called to her workman.

There was a tap for the garden-hose close

by. Lucia let the water drip very gently, drop by drop, on to the trove. It was brilliantly iridescent, of a rich greenish colour below the oxydized surface, and of curved shape. Evidently it was a piece of some glass vessel, ewer or bottle. Tilting it this way and that to catch the light she read the letters stamped on it.

'A.P.O.L.' she announced.

'It's like crosswords,' said Georgie. 'All I can think of is 'Apology'.'

Lucia sat down on a neighbouring bench, panting with excitement but radiant with triumph.

'Do you remember how I said that I suspected I should find the remains of a Roman temple?' she asked.

'Yes: or a villa,' said Georgie.

'I thought a temple more probable, and said so. Look at it, Georgie. Some sacrificial vessel — there's a hint for you — some flask for libations dedicated to a God. What God?'

'Apollo!' cried Georgie. 'My dear, how perfectly wonderful! I don't see what else it could be. That makes up for all the Spencers. And it's the lowest level of all, so that's all right anyhow.'

Reverently holding this (quite large) piece of the sacrificial vessel in her joined hands, Lucia conveyed it to the garden-room, dried

234

the water off it with blotting-paper, and put it in a tray by itself, since the objects in Tray D, once indubitably Roman, had been found to be Spenserian.

'All important to find the rest of it,' she said. 'We must search with the utmost care. Let us go back and plan what is to be done. I think I had better lock the door of the garden-room.'

The whole system of digging was revised. Instead of the earth at the bottom of the trench being loosened with strong blows of the pick, Lucia, starting at the point where this fragment of a sacrificial vessel was found, herself dug with a trowel, so that no random stroke should crash into the missing pieces: when she was giddy with blood to the head from this stooping position, Georgie took her place. Then there was the possibility that missing pieces might have been already shovelled out of the trench, so the two workmen were set to turn over the mound of earth already excavated with microscopic diligence.

'It would be unpardonable of me,' said Lucia, 'if I missed finding the remaining portions, for they must be here, Georgie. I'm so giddy: take the trowel.'

'Something like a coin, ma'am,' sang out one of the workmen on the dump. 'Or it may be a button.'

Lucia vaulted out of the trench with amazing agility.

'A coin without doubt,' she said. 'Much weathered, alas, but we may be able to decipher it. Georgie, would you kindly put it — you have the key of the garden-room — in the same tray as the sacrificial vessel?'

For the rest of the afternoon the search was rewarded by no further discovery. Towards sunset a great bank of cloud arose in the west, and all night long, the heavens streamed with torrential rain. The deluge disintegrated the dump, and the soil was swept over the newly-planted lettuces, and on to the newly gravelled garden-path. The water drained down into the trench from the surface of the asparagus bed, and next day work was impossible, for there was a foot of water in it, and still the rain continued. Driven to more mercenary pursuits, Lucia spent a restless morning in the office, considering the latest advice from Mammoncash. He was strongly of opinion that the rise in the Industrial market had gone far enough: he counselled her to take her profits, of which he enclosed a most satisfactory list, and again recommended gilt-edged stock. Prices there had dwindled a good deal since the Industrial boom began, and the next week or two ought to see a rise. Lucia gazed at the picture of

Dame Catherine Winterglass for inspiration, and then rang up Mammoncash (trunk-call) and assented. In her enthusiasm for archæological discoveries, all this seemed tedious business: it required a great effort to concentrate on so sordid an aim as money-making, when further pieces of sacrificial vessels (or vessel) from a temple of Apollo must be lurking in the asparagus bed. But the rain continued and at present they were inaccessible below a foot or more of opaque water enriched with the manure she had dug into the surrounding plots.

Several days elapsed before digging could be resumed, and Tilling rang with the most original reports about Lucia's discoveries. She herself was very cautious in her admissions, for before the complete 'Spencer' tile was unearthed, she had, on the evidence of the broken 'S.P.' tile, let it be known that she had found Roman remains, part of a villa or a temple, in the asparagus bed, and now this evidence was not quite so conclusive as it had been. The Apolline sacrificial vessel, it is true, had confirmed her original theory, but she must wait for more finds, walls or tesselated pavement, before it was advisable to admit sightseers to the digging, or make any fresh announcement. Georgie was pledged to secrecy, all the gardener knew was that she had spoiled his asparagus bed, and as for the coin (for coin it was and no button) the most minute scrutiny could not reveal any sort of image or superscription on its corroded surface: it might belong to the age of Melchizedeck or Hadrian or Queen Victoria. So since Tilling could learn nothing from official quarters, it took the obvious course, sanctified by tradition, of inventing discoveries for itself: a statue was hinted at and a Roman altar. All this was most fortunate for Elizabeth, for the prevailing excitement about the ancient population of Tilling following on the gas and sewer affair, had rendered completely obsolete its sense of having been cheated when it was clear that she was not about to add to the modern population, and her appearance in the High Street alert and active as usual ceased to rouse any sort of comment. To make matters square between the late and the present owner of Mallards, it was only right that, just as Lucia had never believed in Elizabeth's baby, so now Elizabeth was entirely incredulous about Lucia's temple.

Elizabeth, on one of these days of April tempest when digging was suspended, came up from Grebe for her morning's marketing in her raincloak and Russian boots. The approach of a violent shower had driven her to take shelter in Diva's house, who could scarcely refuse her admittance, but did not want her at all. She put down her market-basket, which for the best of reasons smelt of fish, where Paddy could not get at it.

'Such a struggle to walk up from Grebe in this gale,' she said. 'Diva, you could hardly believe the monstrous state of neglect into which the kitchen garden there has fallen. Not a vegetable. A sad change for me after my lovely garden at Mallards where I never had to buy even a bit of parsley. But beggars can't be choosers, and far be it from me to complain.'

'Well, you took every potato out of the ground at Mallards before you left,' said Diva. 'That will make a nice start for you.'

'I said I didn't complain, dear,' said Elizabeth sharply. 'And how is the Roman Forum getting on? Any new temples? Too killing! I don't believe a single word about it. Probably poor Lucia has discovered the rubbish-heap of odds and ends I threw away when I left my beloved old home for ever.'

'Did you bury them in the ground where the potatoes had been?' asked Diva, intensely irritated at this harping on the old home.

Elizabeth, as was only dignified, disregarded this harping on potatoes.

'I'm thinking of digging up two or three old apple-trees at Grebe which can't have borne fruit for the last hundred years,' she said, 'and telling everybody that I've found the Ark of the Covenant or some Shakespeare Folios among their roots. Nobody shall see them, of course. Lucia finds it difficult to grow old gracefully: that's why she surrounds herself with mysteries, as I said to Benjy the other day. At that age nobody takes any further interest in her for herself, and so she invents Roman Forums to kindle it again. Must be in the limelight. And the fortune she's supposed to have made, the office, the trunk-calls to London. More mystery. I doubt if she's made or lost more than half-a-crown.'

'Now that's jealousy,' said Diva. 'Just because you lost a lot of money yourself, and can't bear that she should have made any. You might just as well say that I didn't make any.'

'Diva, I ask you. *Did* you make any?' said Elizabeth, suddenly giving tongue to a suspicion that had long been a terrible weight on her mind.

'Yes. I did,' said Diva with great distinctness, turning a rich crimson as she spoke. 'And if you want to know how much, I tell you it's none of your business.'

'*Chérie* — I mean Diva,' said Elizabeth very earnestly, 'I warn you for your good, you're becoming a *leetle* mysterious, too. Don't let it grow on you. Let us be open and frank with each other always. No one would be more delighted than me if Lucia turns out to have found the Parthenon in the gooseberry bushes, but why doesn't she let us see anything? It is these hints and mysteries which I deprecate. And the way she talks about finance, as if she was a millionaire. Pending further evidence, I say 'Bunkum' all round.'

The superb impudence of Elizabeth of all women giving warnings against being mysterious and kindling waning interest by hinting at groundless pretensions, so dumbfounded Diva that she sat with open mouth staring at her. She did not trust herself to speak for fear she might say, not more than she meant but less. It was better to say nothing than not be adequate and she changed the subject.

'How's the tiger-skirt?' she asked. 'And collar.'

Elizabeth rather mistakenly thought that she had quelled Diva over this question of middle-aged mysteriousness. She did not want to rub it in, and adopted the new subject with great amiability.

'Sweet of you to ask, dear, about my new little frock,' she said. 'Everybody complimented me on it, except you, and I was a little hurt. But I think — so does Benjy — that it's a wee bit smart for our homely Tilling. How I hate anybody making themselves conspicuous.'

Diva could trust herself to speak on this

subject without fear of saying too little.

'Now Elizabeth,' she said, 'you asked me as a friend to be open and frank with you, and so I tell you that that's not true. The hair was coming off your new little frock — it was the old green skirt anyway — in handfuls. That day you lunched with Lucia and hit your foot against the table-rail it flew about. Grosvenor had to sweep the carpet afterwards. I might as well trim my skirt with strips of my doormat and then say it was too smart for Tilling. You'd have done far better to have buried that mangy tiger-skin and the eye I knocked out of it with the rest of your accumulations in the potato-patch. I should be afraid of getting eczema if I wore a thing like that, and I don't suppose that at this minute there's a single hair left on it. There!'

It was Elizabeth's turn to be dumbfounded at the vehemence of these remarks. She breathed through her nose and screwed her face up into amazing contortions.

'I never thought to have heard such words from you,' she said.

'And I never thought to be told that strips from a mangy tiger-skin were too smart to wear in Tilling,' retorted Diva. 'And pray, Elizabeth, don't make a face as if you were going to cry. Do you good to hear the truth. You think everybody else is being mysterious and getting into deceitful ways just because you're doing so yourself. All these weeks you've been given honey and driven in Susan's Royce and nobody's contradicted you because — oh, well, you know what I mean, so leave it at that.'

Elizabeth whisked up her market-basket and the door banged. Diva opened the window to get rid of that horrid smell of haddock.

'I'm not a bit sorry,' she said to herself. 'I hope it may do her good. It's done me good, anyhow.'

★   ★   ★

The weather cleared, and visiting the flooded trench one evening Lucia saw that the water had soaked away and that digging could be resumed. Accordingly she sent word to her two workmen to start their soil-shifting again at ten next morning. But when, awaking at seven, she found the sun pouring into her room from a cloudless sky, she could not resist going out to begin operations alone. It was a sparkling day, thrushes were scudding about the lawn listening with cocked heads for the underground stir of worms and then rapturously excavating for their breakfast: excavation, indeed, seemed like some beautiful law of Nature which all must obey.

243

Moreover she wanted to get on with her discoveries as quickly as possible, for to be quite frank with herself, the unfortunate business of the Spencer tile had completely exploded, sky-high, all her evidence, and in view of what she had already told the reporter from the *Hastings Chronicle*, it would give a feeling of security to get some more. To-day was Friday, the *Hastings Chronicle* came out on Saturday, and, with the earth soft for digging, with the example of the thrushes on the lawn and the intoxicating tonic of the April day, she had a strong presentiment that she would find the rest of that sacred bottle with the complete dedication to Apollo in time to ring up the *Hastings Chronicle* with this splendid intelligence before it went to press.

Trowel in hand Lucia jumped lightly into the trench. Digging with a trowel was slow work, but much safer than with pick and shovel, for she could instantly stop when it encountered any hard underground resistance which might prove to be a fragment of what she sought. Sometimes it was a pebble that arrested her stroke, sometimes a piece of pottery, and once her agonised heart leapt into her mouth when the blade of her instrument encountered and crashed into some brittle substance. But it was only a snail-shell: it proved to be a big brown one and she remembered a correspondence in the paper about the edible snails which the Romans introduced into Britain, so she put it carefully aside. The clock struck nine and Grosvenor stepping cautiously on the mud which the rain had swept on to the gravel-path came out to know when she would want breakfast. Lucia didn't know herself, but would ring when she was ready.

Grosvenor had scarcely gone back again to the house, when once more Lucia's trowel touched something which she sensed to be brittle, and she stopped her stroke before any crash followed, and dug round the obstruction with extreme caution. She scraped the mould from above it, and with a catch in her breath disclosed a beautiful piece of glass, iridescent on the surface, and of a rich green in substance. She clambered out of the trench and took it to the garden tap. Under the drip of the water there appeared stamped letters of the same type as the APOL on the original fragment: the first four were LINA, and there were several more, still caked with a harder incrustation, to follow. She hurried to the garden-room, and laid the two pieces together. They fitted exquisitely, and the 'Apol' on the first ran straight on into the 'Lina' of the second.

'Apollina,' murmured Lucia. In spite of her Latin studies and her hunts through pages of Roman inscriptions, the name 'Apollina' (perhaps a feminine derivative from Apollo) was unfamiliar to her. Yet it held the suggestion of some name which she could not at once recall. Apollina . . . a glass vessel. Then a hideous surmise loomed up in her mind, and with brutal roughness regardless of the lovely iridescent surface of the glass, she rubbed the caked earth off the three remaining letters, and the complete legend 'Apollinaris' was revealed.

She sat heavily down and looked the catastrophe in the face. Then she took a telegraph form, and after a brief concentration addressed it to the editor of the *Hastings Chronicle*, and wrote: 'Am obliged to abandon my Roman excavations for the time. Stop. Please cancel my interview with your correspondent as any announcement would be premature. Emmeline Lucas, Mallards House, Tilling.'

She went into the house and rang for Grosvenor.

'I want this sent at once,' she said.

Grosvenor looked with great disfavour at Lucia's shoes. They were caked with mud which dropped off in lumps on to the carpet.

'Yes, ma'am,' she said. 'And hadn't you

246

better take off your shoes on the door mat? If you have breakfast in them you'll make an awful mess on your dining-room carpet. I'll bring you some indoor shoes and then you can put the others on again if you're going on digging after breakfast.'

'I shan't be digging again,' said Lucia.

'Glad to hear it, ma'am.'

Lucia breakfasted, deep in meditation. Her excavations were at an end, and her one desire was that Tilling should forget them as soon as possible, even as, in the excitement over them, it had forgotten about Elizabeth's false pretences. Oblivion must cover the memory of them, and obliterate their traces. Not even Georgie should know of the frightful tragedy that had occurred until all vestiges of it had been disposed of; but he was coming across at ten to help her, and he must be put off, with every appearance of cheerfulness so that he should suspect nothing. She rang him up, and her voice was as brisk and sprightly as ever.

'Dood morning, Georgino,' she said. 'No excavazione to-day.'

'Oh, I'm sorry,' said Georgie. 'I was looking forward to finding more glass vessel.'

'Me sorry, too,' said Lucia. 'Dwefful busy to-day, Georgie. We dine to-morrow, don't we, *alla casa dei sapienti.*'

'Where?' asked Georgie, completely puzzled.

'At the Wyses,' said Lucia.

She went out to the garden-room. Bitter work was before her but she did not flinch. She carried out, one after the other, trays A, B, C and D, to the scene of her digging, and cast their contents into the trench. The two pieces of glass that together formed a nearly complete Apollinaris bottle gleamed in the air as they fell, and the undecipherable coin clinked as it struck them. Back she went to the garden-room and returned to the London Library every volume that had any bearing on the Roman occupation of Britain. At ten o'clock her two workmen appeared and they were employed for the rest of the day in shovelling back into the trench every spadeful of earth which they had dug out of it. Their instructions were to stamp it well down.

Lucia had been too late to stop her brief communication to the reporter of the *Hastings Chronicle* from going to press, and next morning when she came down to breakfast she found a marked copy of it ('see page 2' in blue pencil). She turned to it and with a curdling of her blood read what this bright young man had made out of the few words she had given him.

'All lovers of art and archæology will be thrilled to hear of the discoveries that Mrs.

Lucas has made in the beautiful grounds of her Queen Anne mansion at Tilling. The *châtelaine* of Mallards House most graciously received me there a few days ago, and in her exquisite *salon* which overlooks the quaint old-world street gave me, over 'the cup that cheers but not inebriates,' a brilliant little *résumé* of her operations up to date and of her hopes for the future. Mrs. Lucas, as I need not remind my readers, is the acknowledged leader of the most exclusive social circles in Tilling, a first-rate pianist, and an accomplished scholar in languages, dead and alive.

"'I have long,' she said, 'been studying that most interesting and profoundly significant epoch in history, namely the Roman occupation of Britain, and it has long been my daydream to be privileged to add to our knowledge of it. That day-dream, I may venture to say, bids fair to become a waking reality.'

"'What made you first think that there might be Roman remains hidden in the soil of Tilling?' I asked.

'She shook a playful but warning finger at me. (Mrs. Lucas's hands are such as a sculptor dreams of but seldom sees.)

"'Now I'm not going to let you into my whole secret yet,' she said. 'All I can tell you is that when, a little while ago, the street outside my house was dug up to locate some naughty leaking gas pipe, I, watching the digging closely, saw something unearthed that to me was indisputable evidence that under my *jardin* lay the remains of a Roman villa or temple. I had suspected it before: I had often said to myself that this hill of Tilling, commanding so wide a stretch of country, was exactly the place which those wonderful old Romans would have chosen for building one of their *castra* or forts. My intuition has already been justified, and, I feel sure will soon be rewarded by even richer discoveries. More I cannot at present tell you, for I am determined not to be premature. Wait a little while yet, and I think, yes, I think you will be astonished at the results . . . ' '

Grosvenor came in.

'Trunk-call from London, ma'am,' she said. 'Central News Agency.'

Lucia, sick with apprehension, tottered to the office.

'Mrs. Lucas?' asked a buzzing voice.

'Yes.'

'Central News Agency. We've just heard by 'phone from Hastings of your discovery of Roman remains at Tilling,' it said. 'We're sending down a special representative this morning to inspect your excavations and write — '

250

'Not the slightest use,' interrupted Lucia. 'My excavations have not yet reached the stage when I can permit any account of them to appear in the press.'

'But the London Sunday papers are most anxious to secure some material about them to-morrow, and Professor Arbuthnot of the British Museum, whom we have just rung up is willing to supply them. He will motor down and be at Tilling — '

Lucia turned cold with horror.

'I am very sorry,' she said firmly, 'but it is quite impossible for me to let Professor Arbuthnot inspect my excavations at this stage, or to permit any further announcement concerning them.'

She rang off, she waited a moment, and, being totally unable to bear the strain of the situation alone, rang up Georgie. There was no Italian or baby-talk to-day.

'Georgie, I must see you at once,' she said.

'My dear, anything wrong about the excavations?' asked the intuitive Georgie.

'Yes, something frightful. I'll be with you in one minute.'

'I've only just begun my break — ' said Georgie and heard the receiver replaced.

With the nightmare notion in her mind of some sleuth-hound of an archæologist calling while she was out and finding no excavation at all, Lucia laid it on Grosvenor to admit nobody to the house under any pretext, and hatless, with the *Hastings Chronicle* in her hand, she scudded up the road to Mallards Cottage. As she crossed the street she heard from the direction of Irene's house a prolonged and clamorous ringing of a dinner-bell, but there was no time now even to conjecture what that meant.

Georgie was breakfasting in his blue dressing-gown. He had been touching up his hair and beard with the contents of the bottle that always stood in a locked cupboard in his bedroom. His hair was not dry yet, and it was most inconvenient that she should want to see him so immediately. But the anxiety in her telephone-voice was unmistakable, and very likely she would not notice his hair.

'All quite awful, Georgie,' she said, noticing nothing at all. 'Now first I must tell you that I found the rest of the Apollo-vessel yesterday, and it was an Apollinaris bottle.'

'My dear, how tarsome,' said Georgie sympathetically.

'Tragic rather than tiresome,' said Lucia. 'First the Spencer-tile and then the Apollinaris bottle. Nothing Roman left, and I filled up the trench yesterday. *Finito!* O Georgie, how I should have loved a Roman temple in my garden! Think of the prestige! Archæologists

252

and garden parties with little lectures! It is cruel. And then as if the extinction of all I hoped for wasn't enough there came the most frightful complications. Listen to the *Hastings Chronicle* of this morning.'

She read the monstrous fabrication through in a tragic monotone.

'Such fibs, such inventions!' she cried. 'I never knew what a vile trade journalism was! I did see a young man last week — I can't even remember his name or what he looked like — for two minutes, not more, and told him just what I said you might tell Tilling. It wasn't in the garden-room and I didn't give him tea, because it was just before lunch, standing in the hall, and I never shook a playful forefinger at him or talked about day-dreams or naughty gas pipes, and I never called the garden *jardin*, though I may have said *giardino*. And I had hardly finished reading this tissue of lies just now, when the Central News rang me up and wanted to send down Professor Arbuthnot of the British Museum to see my excavations. Georgie, how I should have loved it if there had been anything to show him! I stopped that — the Sunday London papers wanted news too — but what am I to do about this revolting *Chronicle*?'

Georgie glanced through the paper again.

'I don't think I should bother much,' he said. 'The *châtelaine* of Mallards, you know, leader of exclusive circles, lovely hands, pianist and scholar: all very complimentary. What a rage Elizabeth will be in. She'll burst.'

'Very possibly,' said Lucia. 'But don't you see how this drags me down to her level? That's so awful. We've all been despising her for deceiving us and trying to make us think she was to have a baby, and now here am I no better than her, trying to make you all think I had discovered a Roman temple. And I did believe it much more than she ever believed the other. I did indeed, Georgie, and now it's all in print which makes it ever so much worse. Her baby was never in print.'

Georgie had absently passed his fingers through his beard, to assist thought, and perceived a vivid walnut stain on them. He put his hand below the tablecloth.

'I never thought of that,' he said. 'It is rather a pity. But think how very soon we forgot about Elizabeth. Why it was almost the next day after she gave up going to be a mother and took in the old green skirt again that you got on to your discoveries, and nobody gave a single thought to her baby any more. Can't we give them all something new to jabber about?'

Georgie had got up from the table and with

254

his walnut hand still concealed strayed to the open window and looked out.

'If that isn't Elizabeth at the door of Mallards!' he said. 'She's got a paper in her hand: *Hastings Chronicle*, I bet. Grosvenor's opened the door, but not very wide. Elizabeth's arguing — '

'Georgie, she mustn't get in,' cried the agonized Lucia. 'She'll pop out into the garden, and see there's no excavation at all.'

'She's still arguing,' said Georgie in the manner of Brangaene warning Isolde. 'She's on the top step now . . . Oh, it's all right. Grosvenor's shut the door in her face. I could hear it, too. She's standing on the top step, thinking. Oh, my God, she's coming here, just as she did before, when she was canvassing. But there'll be time to tell Foljambe not to let her in.'

Georgie hurried away on this errand, and Lucia flattened herself against the wall so that she could not be seen from the street. Presently the door-bell tinkled, and Foljambe's voice was heard firmly reiterating, 'No, ma'am, he's not at home . . . No ma'am, he's not in . . . No, ma'am, he's out, and I can't say when he'll be in. Out.'

The door closed, and next moment Elizabeth's fell face appeared at the open window. A suspiciously-minded person might have thought that she wanted to peep into Georgie's sitting-room to verify (or disprove) Foljambe's assertions, and Elizabeth, who could read suspicious minds like an open book, made haste to dispel so odious a supposition. She gave a slight scream at seeing him so close to her and in such an elegant costume.

'Dear Mr. Georgie,' she said. 'I beg your pardon, but your good Foljambe was so certain you were out, and I, seeing the window was open, I — I just meant to pop this copy of the *Hastings Chronicle* in. I knew how much you'd like to see it. Lovely things about sweet Lucia, *châtelaine* of Mallards and Queen of Tilling and such a wonderful archæologist. Full of surprises for us. How little one knows on the spot!'

Georgie, returning from warning Foljambe, had left the door ajar, and in consequence Lucia, flattening herself like a shadow against the wall between it and the window, was in a strong draught. The swift and tingling approach of a sneeze darted through her nose and it crashed forth.

'Thanks very much,' said Georgie in a loud voice to Elizabeth, hoping in a confused manner by talking loud to drown what had already resounded through the room. Instantly Elizabeth thrust her head a little further through the window and got a satisfactory glimpse of

Lucia's skirt. That was enough: Lucia was there and she withdrew her head from its strained position.

'We're all agog about her discoveries,' she said. 'Such an excitement! You've seen them, of course.'

'Rather!' said Georgie with enthusiasm. 'Beautiful Roman tiles and glass and pottery. Exquisite!'

Elizabeth's face fell: she had hoped otherwise.

'Must be trotting along,' she said. 'We meet at dinner, don't we, at Susan Wyse's. Her Majesty is coming, I believe.'

'Oh, I didn't know she was in Tilling,' said Georgie. 'Is she staying with you?'

'Naughty! I only meant the Queen of Tilling.'

'Oh, I see,' said Georgie. '*Au reservoir.*'

★   ★   ★

Lucia came out of her very unsuccessful lair.

'Do you think she saw me, Georgie?' she asked. 'It might have been Foljambe as far as the sneeze went.'

'Certainly she saw you. Not a doubt of it,' said Georgie rather pleased at this compromising role which had been provided for him. 'And now Elizabeth will tell everybody that you and I were breakfasting in my dressing-gown — you see what I mean — and that you hid when she looked in. I don't know what she mightn't make of that.'

Lucia considered this a moment, weighing her moral against her archæological reputation.

'It's all for the best,' she said decidedly. 'It will divert her horrid mind from the excavations. And did you ever hear such acidity in a human voice as when she said 'Queen of Tilling'? A dozen lemons, well squeezed, were saccharine compared to it. But, my dear, it was most clever and most loyal of you to say you had seen my exquisite Roman tiles and glass. I appreciate that immensely.'

'I thought it was pretty good,' said he. 'She didn't like that.'

'*Caro*, it was admirable, and you'll stick to it, won't you? Now the first thing I shall do is to go to the newsagents and buy up all their copies of the *Hastings Chronicle*. It may be useful to cut off her supplies . . . Oh, Georgie, your hand. Have you hurt it? Iodine?'

'Just a little sprain,' said Georgie. 'Nothing to bother about.'

Lucia picked up her hat at Mallards, and hurried down to the High Street. It was rather a shock to see a news-board outside the paper-shop with prominent in the contents of the current number of the *Hastings Chronicle*, and a stronger shock to find that all the copies had been sold.

'Went like hot cakes, ma'am,' said the proprietor, 'on the news of your excavations, and I've just telephoned a repeat order.'

'Most gratifying,' said Lucia, looking the reverse of gratified . . . There was Diva haggling at the butcher's as she passed, and Diva ran out, leaving Pat to guard her basket.

'Morning,' she said. 'Seen Elizabeth?'

Lucia thought of replying 'No, but she's seen me,' but that would entail lengthy explanations, and it was better first to hear what Diva had to say, for evidently there was news.

'No, dear,' she said. 'I've only just come down from Mallards. Why?'

Diva whistled to Pat, who, guarding her basket, was growling ferociously at anyone who came near it.

'Mad with rage,' she said. '*Hastings Chronicle*. Seen it?'

Lucia concentrated for a moment, in an effort of recollection.

'Ah, that little paragraph about my

excavations,' said she lightly. 'I did glance at it. Rather exaggerated, rather decorated, but you know what journalists are.'

'Not an idea,' said Diva, 'but I know what Elizabeth is. She told me she was going to expose you. Said she was convinced you'd not found anything at all. Challenging you. Of course what really riled her was that bit about you being leader of social circles, etcetera. From me she went on to tell Irene, and then to call on you and ask you point-blank whether your digging wasn't all a fake, and then she was going on to Georgie . . . Oh, there's Irene.'

Diva called shrilly to her, and she pounded up to them on her bicycle on which was hung a paint-box, a stool and an immense canvas.

'Beloved!' she said to Lucia. 'Mapp's been to see me. She told me she was quite sure you hadn't found any Roman remains. So I told her she was a liar. Just like that. She went gabbling on, so I rang my dinner-bell close to her face until she could not bear it any more and fled. Nobody can bear a dinner-bell for long if it's rung like that: all nerve specialists will tell you so. We had almost a row, in fact.'

'Darling, you're a true friend,' cried Lucia, much moved.

'Of course I am. What else do you expect me to be? I shall bring my bell to the Wyses' this evening, in case she begins again. Good-bye, adored. I'm going out to a farm on the marsh to paint a cow with its calf. If Mapp annoys you any more I shall give the cow her face, though it's bad luck on the cow, and send it to our summer exhibition. It will pleasantly remind her of what never happened to her.'

Diva looked after her approvingly as she snorted up the High Street.

'That's the right way to handle Elizabeth, when all's said and done,' she remarked. 'Quaint Irene understands her better than anybody. Think how kind we all were to her, especially you, when she was exposed. You just said 'Wind-egg.' Never mentioned it again. Most ungrateful of Elizabeth, I think. What are you going to do about it? Why not show her a few of your finds, just to prove what a liar she is?'

Lucia thought desperately a moment, and then a warm, pitying smile dawned on her face.

'My dear, it's really beneath me,' she said, 'to take any notice of what she told you and Irene and no doubt others as well. I'm only sorry for that unhappy jealous nature of hers. Incurable, I'm afraid: chronic, and I'm sure she suffers dreadfully from it in her better moments. As for my little excavations, I'm abandoning them for a time.'

'That's a pity!' said Diva. 'Should have thought it was just the time to go on with them. Why?'

'Too much publicity,' said Lucia earnestly. 'You know how I hate that. They were only meant to be a modest little amateur effort, but what with all that *réclame* in the *Hastings Chronicle*, and the Central News this morning telling me that Professor Arbuthnot of the British Museum, who, I understand is the final authority on Roman archæology, longing to come down to see them — '

'No! from the British Museum?' cried Diva. 'I shall tell Elizabeth that. When is he coming?'

'I've refused. Too much fuss. And then my arousing all this jealousy and ill-feeling in — well, in another quarter, is quite intolerable to me. Perhaps I shall continue my work later on, but very quietly. Georgie, by the way, has seen my little finds, such as they are, and thinks them exquisite. But I stifle in this atmosphere of envy and malice. Poor Elizabeth! Good-bye, dear, we meet this evening at the Wyses', do we not?'

Lucia walked pensively back to Mallards, not displeased with herself. Irene's dinner-bell and her own lofty attitude would probably scotch Elizabeth for the present, and with Georgie as a deep-dyed accomplice and Diva as an ardent sympathiser, there was not much to fear from her. The *Hastings Chronicle* next week would no doubt announce that she had abandoned her excavations for the present, and Elizabeth might make exactly what she chose out of that. Breezy unconsciousness of any low libels and machinations was decidedly the right ticket.

Lucia quickened her pace. There had flashed into her mind the memory of a basket of odds and ends which she had brought from Grebe, but which she had not yet unpacked. There was a box of Venetian beads among them, a small ebony elephant, a silver photograph frame or two, some polished agates, and surely she seemed to recollect some pieces of pottery. She had no very distinct remembrance of them, but when she got home she unearthed (more excavation) this basket of dubious treasures from a cupboard below the stairs, and found in her repository of objects suitable for a jumble sale, a broken bowl and a saucer (patera) of red stamped pottery. Her intensive study of Roman remains in Britain easily enabled her to recognise them as being of 'Samian ware,' not uncommonly found on sites of Roman settlements in this island. Thoughtfully she dusted them, and carried them out to the garden-room. They were pretty, they looked attractive casually but prominently disposed on the top of the piano. Georgie must be reminded how much he had admired them when they were found . . .

8

With social blood pressure so high, with such embryos of plots and counterplots darkly developing, with, generally, an atmosphere so charged with electricity, Susan Wyse's party to-night was likely (to change the metaphor once more) to prove a scene of carnage. These stimulating expectations were amply fulfilled.

The numbers to begin with were unpropitious. It must always remain uncertain whether Susan had asked the Padre and Evie to dine that night, for though she maintained ever afterwards that she had asked them for the day after, he was equally willing to swear in Scotch, Irish and English that it was for to-night. Everyone, therefore, when eight people were assembled, thought that the party was complete, and that two tables of Bridge would keep it safely occupied after dinner. Then when the door opened (it was to be hoped) for the announcement that dinner was ready, it proved to have been opened to admit these two further guests, and God knew what would happen about Bridge. Susan shook hands with them in a dismayed and distracted manner, and slipped out of the room, as anyone could guess, to hold an agitated conference with her cook and her butler, Figgis, who said he had done his best to convince them that they were not expected, but without success. Starvation corner therefore was likely to be a Lenten situation, served with drumsticks and not enough soup to cover the bottom of the plate. Very embarrassing for poor Susan, and there was a general feeling that nobody must be sarcastic at her wearing the cross of a Member of the British Empire, which she had unwisely pinned to the front of her ample bosom, or say they had never been told that Orders would be worn. In that ten minutes of waiting, several eggs of discord (would that they had only been wind-eggs!) had been laid and there seemed a very good chance of some of them hatching.

In the main it was Elizabeth who was responsible for this clutch of eggs, for she set about laying them at once. She had a strong suspicion that the stain on Georgie's fingers, which he had been unable to get rid of, was not iodine but hair-dye, and asked him how he had managed to sprain those fingers all together: such bad luck. Then she turned to Lucia and enquired anxiously how her cold was: she hoped she had been having no further sneezing fits, for prolonged sneezing was so exhausting. She saw Georgie and

Lucia exchange a guilty glance and again turned to him: 'We must make a plot, Mr. Georgie,' she said, 'to compel our precious Lucia to take more care of herself. All that standing about in the wet and cold over her wonderful excavations.'

By this time Irene had sensed that these apparent dew-drops were globules of corrosive acid, though she did not know their precise nature, and joined the group.

'Such a lovely morning I spent, Mapp,' she said with an intonation that Elizabeth felt was very like her own. 'I've been painting a cow with its dear little calf. Wasn't it lovely for the cow to have a sweet baby like that?'

During this wait for dinner Major Benjy, screened from his wife by the Padre and Diva managed to secure three glasses of sherry and two cocktails. Then Susan returned followed by Figgis, having told him not to hand either to her husband or her that oyster-savoury which she adored, since there were not enough oysters, and to be careful about helpings. But an abundance of wine must flow in order to drown any solid deficiencies, and she had substituted champagne for hock, and added brandy to go with the chestnut ice *à la Capri*. They went into dinner: Lucia sat on Mr. Wyse's right and Elizabeth on his left in starvation corner. On her other side was

Georgie, and Benjy sat next Susan Wyse on the same side of the table as his wife and entirely out of the range of her observation.

Elizabeth, a little cowed by Irene's artless story, found nothing to complain of in starvation corner, as far as soup went: indeed Figgis's rationing had been so severe on earlier recipients that she got a positive lake of it. She was pleased at having a man on each side of her, her host on her right, and Georgie on her left, whereas Lucia had quaint Irene on her right. Turbot came next; about that Figgis was not to blame, for people helped themselves, and they were all so inconsiderate that, when it came to Elizabeth's turn, there was little left but spine and a quantity of shining black mackintosh, and as for her first glass of champagne, it was merely foam. By this time, too, she was beginning to get uneasy about Benjy. He was talking in a fat contented voice, which she seldom heard at home, and neither by leaning back nor by leaning forward could she get any really informatory glimpse of him or his wine-glasses. She heard his gobbling laugh at the end of one of his own stories, and Susan said, 'Oh fie, Major, I shall tell of you.' That was not reassuring.

Elizabeth stifled her uneasiness and turned to her host.

'Delicious turbot, Mr. Wyse,' she said. 'So good. And did you see the *Hastings Chronicle* this morning about the great Roman discoveries of the *châtelaine* of Mallards. Made me feel quite a Dowager.'

Mr. Wyse had clearly foreseen the deadly feelings that might be aroused by that article, and had made up his mind to be extremely polite to everybody, whatever they were to each other. He held up a deprecating hand.

'You will not be able to persuade your friends of that,' he said. 'I protest against your applying the word Dowager to yourself. It has the taint of age about it. The ladies of Tilling remain young for ever, as my sister Amelia so constantly writes to me.'

Elizabeth tipped up her champagne-glass, so that he could scarcely help observing that there was really nothing in it.

'Sweet of the dear Contessa,' she said. 'But in my humble little Grebe, I feel quite a country mouse, so far away from all that's going on. Hardly Tilling at all: my Benjy-boy tells me I must call the house 'Mouse-trap.''

Irene was still alert for attacks on Lucia.

'How about calling it Cat and Mouse trap, Mapp?' she enquired across the table.

'Why, dear?' said Elizabeth with terrifying suavity.

Lucia instantly engaged quaint Irene's

attention, or something even more quaint might have followed, and Mr. Wyse made signals to Figgis and pointed towards Elizabeth's wineglass. Figgis thinking that he was only calling his notice to wine-glasses in general filled up Major Benjy's which happened to be empty, and began carving the chicken. The maid handed the plates and Lucia got some nice slices off the breast. Elizabeth receiving no answer from Irene, wheeled round to Georgie.

'What a day it will be when we are all allowed to see the great Roman remains,' she said.

'Won't it?' said Georgie.

A dead silence fell on the table except for Benjy's jovial voice.

'A saucy little customer she was. They used to call her the Pride of Poona. I've still got her photograph somewhere, by Jove.'

Rockets of conversation, a regular bouquet of them, shot up all round the table.

'And was Poona where you killed those lovely tigers, Major?' asked Susan. 'What a pretty costume Elizabeth made of the best bits. So ingenious. Figgis, the champagne.'

'Irene dear,' said Lucia in her most earnest voice, 'I think you must manage our summer picture-exhibition this year. My hands are so full. Do persuade her to, Mr. Wyse.'

Mr. Wyse bowed right and left particularly to Elizabeth.

'I see on all sides of me such brilliant artists and such competent managers — ' he began.

'Oh, pray not me!' said Elizabeth. 'I'm quite out of touch with modern art.'

'Well, there's room for old masters and mistresses, Mapp,' said Irene encouragingly. 'Never say die.'

Lucia had just finished her nice slice of breast when a well-developed drumstick, probably from the leg on which the chicken habitually roosted, was placed before Elizabeth. Black roots of plucked feathers were dotted about in the yellow skin.

'Oh, far too much for me,' she said. 'Just a teeny slice after my lovely turbot.'

Her plate was brought back with a piece of the drumstick cut off. Chestnut ice with brandy followed, and the famous oyster savoury, and then dessert, with a *compote* of figs in honey.

'A little Easter gift from my sister Amelia,' explained Mr. Wyse to Elizabeth. 'A domestic product of which the recipe is an heirloom of the mistress of Castello Faraglione. I think Amelia had the privilege of sending you a spoonful or two of the Faraglione honey not so long ago.'

The most malicious brain could not have devised two more appalling *gaffes* than this pretty speech contained. There was that unfortunate mention of the word 'recipe' again, and everyone thought of lobster, and who could help recalling the reason why Contessa Amelia had sent Elizabeth the jar of nutritious honey? The pause of stupefaction was succeeded by a fresh gabble of conversation, and a spurt of irrepressible laughter from quaint Irene.

Dinner was now over: Susan collected ladies' eyes, and shepherded them out of the room, while the Padre held the door open and addressed some bright and gallant little remark in three languages to each. In spite of her injunction to her husband that the gentlemen mustn't be long, or there would be no time for Bridge, it was impossible to obey, for Major Benjy had a great number of very amusing stories to tell, each of which suggested another to him. He forgot the point of some, and it might have been as well if he had forgotten the point of others, but they were all men together, he said, and it was a sad heart that never rejoiced. Also he forgot once or twice to send the port on when it came to him, and filled up his glass again when he had finished his story.

'Most entertaining,' said Mr. Wyse frigidly

272

as the clock struck ten. 'A long time since I have laughed so much. You are a regular storehouse of amusing anecdotes, Major. But Susan will scold me unless we join the ladies.'

'Never do to keep the lil' fairies waiting,' said Benjy. 'Well, thanks, just a spot of sherry. Capital good dinner I've had. A married man doesn't often get much of a dinner at home, by Jove, at least I don't, though that's to go no further. Ha, ha! Discretion.'

Then arose the very delicate question of the composition of the Bridge tables. Vainly did Mr. Wyse (faintly echoed by Susan) explain that they would both much sooner look on, for everybody else, with the same curious absence of conviction in their voices, said that they would infinitely prefer to do the same. That was so palpably false that without more ado cards were cut, the two highest to sit out for the first rubber. Lucia drew a king, and Elizabeth drew a knave, and it seemed for a little that they would have to sit out together, which would have been quite frightful, but then Benjy luckily cut a Queen. A small sitting-room, opening from the drawing-room would enable them to chat without disturbing the players, and Major Benjy gallantly declared that he would sooner have a talk with her than win two grand slams.

Benjy's sense of exuberant health and happiness was beginning to be overshadowed, as if the edge of a coming eclipse had nicked the full orb of the sun — perhaps the last glass or two of port had been an error in an otherwise judicious dinner — but he was still very bright and loquacious and suffused.

''Pon my word, a delightful little dinner,' he said, as he closed the door into the little sitting-room. 'Good talk, good friends, a glass of jolly good wine and a rubber to follow. What more can a man ask, I ask you, and Echo answers 'Cern'ly not.' And I've not had a pow-wow with you for a long time, Signora, as old Camelia Faradiddleone would say.'

Lucia saw that he had had about enough wine, but after many evenings with Elizabeth who wouldn't?

'No, I've been quite a hermit lately,' she said. 'So busy with my little jobs — oh, take care of your cigar, Major Benjy: it's burning the edge of the table.'

'Dear me, yes, monstrous stupid of me: where there's smoke there's fire! We've been busy, too, settling in. How do you think Liz is looking?'

'Very well, exceedingly well,' said Lucia enthusiastically. 'All her old energy, all her delightful activity seem to have returned. At one time — '

Major Benjy looked round to see that the door was closed and nodded his head with extreme solemnity.

'Quite, quite. Olive-branches. Very true,' he said. 'Marvellous woman, ain't she, the way she's put it all behind her. Felt it very much at the time, for she's mos' sensitive. Highly strung. Concert pitch. Liable to ups and downs. For instance, there was a paragraph in the Hastings paper this morning that upset Liz so much that she whirled about like a spinning top, butting into the tables and chairs. 'Take it quietly, Lisbeth Mapp-Flint,' I told her. Beneath you to notice it, or should I go over and punch the Editor's head?'

'Do you happen to be referring to the paragraph about me and my little excavations?' asked Lucia.

'God bless me, if I hadn't forgotten what it was about,' cried Benjy. 'You're right, Msslucas, the very first time. That's what it was about, if I may say so without prejudice. I only remembered there was something that annoyed Lisbeth Mapp-Flint, and that was enough for Major B, late of His Majesty's India forces, God bless him, too. If something annoys my wife, it annoys me, too, that's what I say. A husband's duty, Msslucas, is always to stand between her and any annoyances, what? Too many annoyances lately and often my

275

heart's bled for her. Then it was a sad trial parting with her old home which she'd known ever since her aunt was a lil' girl, or since they were lil' girls together, if not before. Then that was a bad business about the Town Council and those dinner-bells. A dirty business I might call it, if there wasn't a lady present, though that mustn't go any further. Not cricket, hie. All adds up, you know, in the mind of a very sensitive woman. Twice two and four, if you see what I mean.'

Benjy sank down lower in his chair, and after two attempts to relight his cigar, gave it up, and the eclipse spread a little further.

'I'm not quite easy in my mind about Lisbeth,' he said, 'an' that's why it's such a privilege to be able to have quiet talk with you like this. There's no more sympathetic woman in Tilling, I tell my missus, than Msslucas. A thousand pities that you and she don't always see eye to eye about this or that, whether it's dinner bells or it might be Roman antiquities or changing houses. First it's one thing and then it's another, and then it's something else. Anxious work.'

'I don't think there's the slightest cause for you to be anxious, Major Benjy,' said Lucia.

Benjy thumped the table with one hand, then drew his chair a little closer to hers, and laid the other hand on her knee.

'That reminds me what I wanted to talk to you about,' he said. 'Grebe, you know, our lil' place Grebe. Far better house in my opinion than poor ole Auntie's. I give you my word on that, and Major B's word's as good's his bond, if not better. Smelt of dry rot, did Auntie's house, and the paint peeling off the walls same as an orange. But 'Lisbeth liked it, Msslucas. It suited 'Lisbeth down to the ground. You give the old lady a curtain to sit behind an' something puzzling going on in the street outside, and she'll be azappy as a Queen till the cows come home, if not longer. She misses that at our lil' place, Grebe, and it goes to my heart, Msslucas.'

He was rather more tipsy, thought Lucia than she had supposed, but he was much better here, maundering quietly along than coming under Elizabeth's eye, for her sake as well as his, for she had had a horrid evening with nothing but foam to drink and mackintosh and muscular drumstick to eat, to the accompaniment of all those frightful *gaffes* about cat-traps and recipes and nutritious honey and hints about Benjy's recollections of the Pride of Poona, poor woman. Lucia sincerely hoped that the rubbers now in progress would be long, so that he might get a little steadier before he had to make a public appearance again.

'It gives 'Lisbeth the hump, does Grebe,' he went on in a melancholy voice. 'No little side-shows going on outside. Nothing but sheep and sea-gulls to squint at from behind a curtain at our lil' place. Scarcely worth getting behind a curtain at all, it isn't, and it's a sad come-down for her. I lie awake thinking of it, and I'll tell you what, Msslucas, though it mustn't go any further. Mum's the word, like what we had at dinner. I believe, though I couldn't say for certain, that she'd be willing to let you have Grebe, if you offered her thousan' pounds premium, and go back to Auntie's herself. Worth thinking about, or lemme see, do I mean that she'd give you thousan' pounds premium? Split the difference. Why, here's 'Lisbeth herself! There's a curious thing!'

Elizabeth stood in the doorway, and took him in from head to foot in a single glance, as he withdrew his hand from Lucia's knee as if it had been a live coal, and, hoisting himself with some difficulty out of his chair, brushed an inch of cigar-ash off his waistcoat.

'We're going home, Benjy,' she said. 'Come along.'

'But I want to have rubber of Bridge, Liz,' said he. 'Msslucas and I've been waiting for our lil' rubber of Bridge.'

Elizabeth continued to be as unconscious

of Lucia as if they were standing for the Town Council again.

'You've had enough pleasure for one evening, Benjy,' said she, 'and enough — '

Lucia, crushing a natural even a laudable desire to hear what should follow, slipped quietly from the room and closed the door. Outside a rubber was still going on at one table, and at the other the Padre, Georgie and Diva were leaning forward discussing something in low tones.

'But she *had* quitted her card,' said Diva. 'And the whole rubber was only ninepence, and she's not paid me. Those hectoring ways of hers — '

'Diva, dear,' said Lucia, seating herself in the vacant chair. 'Let's cut for deal at once and go on as if nothing had happened. You and me. Laddies against lassies, Padre.'

They were still considering their hands when the door into the inner room opened again, and Elizabeth swept into the room followed by Benjy.

'Pray don't let anyone get up,' she said. 'Such a lovely evening, dear Susan! Such a lovely party! No, Mr. Wyse, I insist. My Benjy tells me it's time for me to go home. So late. We shall walk and enjoy the beautiful stars. Do us both good. Goloshes outside in the hall. Everything.'

Mr. Wyse got up and pressed the bell.

'But, my dear lady, no hurry, so early,' he said. 'A sandwich surely, a tunny sandwich, a little lemonade, a drop of whisky. Figgis: Whisky, sandwiches, goloshes!'

Benjy suddenly raised the red banner of revolt. He stood quite firmly in the middle of the room, with his hand on the back of the Padre's chair.

'There's been a lil' mistake,' he said. 'I want my lil' rubber of Bridge. Fair play's a jewel. I want my tummy sandwich and mouthful whisky and soda. I want — '

'Benjy, I'm waiting for you,' said Elizabeth.

He looked this way and that but encountered no glance of encouragement. Then he made a smart military salute to the general company and marched from the room stepping carefully but impeccably, as if treading a tight rope stretched over an abyss, and shut the door into the hall with swift decision.

'Puir wee mannie,' said the Padre. 'Three no trumps, Mistress Plaistow.'

'She *had* quitted the card,' said Diva still fuming. 'I saw the light between it and her fingers. Oh, is it me? Three spades, I mean four.'

9

Lucia and Georgie were seated side by side on the bench of the organ in Tilling church. The May sunshine streamed on to them through the stained glass of a south window, vividly colouring them with patches of the brightest hues, so that they looked like objects daringly camouflaged in war-time against enemy aircraft, for nobody could have dreamed that those brilliant Joseph-coats could contain human beings. The lights cast upon Lucia's face and white dress reached her through a picture of Elijah going up to heaven in a fiery chariot. The heat from this vehicle would presumably have prevented the prophet from feeling cold in interstellar space, for he wore only an emerald-green bathing-dress which left exposed his superbly virile arms and legs, and his snowy locks streamed in the wind. The horses were flame-coloured, the chariot was red-hot, and high above it in an ultramarine sky hung an orange sun which seemed to be the object of the expedition. Georgie came under the influence of the Witch of Endor. She was wrapt in an *eau de nil* mantle, which made his auburn beard look livid. Saul in a purple cloak, and

Samuel in a black dressing-gown made sombre stains on his fawn-coloured suit.

The organ was in process of rebuilding. A quantity of fresh stops were being added to it, and an electric blowing apparatus had been installed. Lucia clicked on the switch which set the bellows working, and opened a copy of the Moonlight Sonata.

'It sounds quite marvellous on the organ, Georgie,' she said. 'I was trying it over yesterday. What I want you to do is to play the pedals. Just those slow base notes: pom, pom. Quite easy.'

Georgie put a foot on the pedals. Nothing happened.

'Oh, I haven't pulled out any pedal stop,' said Lucia. By mistake she pulled out the *tuba*, and as the pedals happened to be coupled to the solo organ a blast of baritone fury yelled through the church. 'My fault,' she said, 'entirely my fault, but what a magnificent noise! One of my new stops.'

She uncoupled the pedals and substituted the *bourdon:* Elijah and the Witch of Endor rattled in their leaded frames.

'That's perfect!' she said. 'Now with one hand I shall play the triplets on the swell, and the solo tune with the other on the *vox humana*! Oh, that *tuba* again! I thought I'd put it in.'

The plaintive throaty bleating of the *vox humana* was enervatingly lovely, and Lucia's America-cloth eyes grew veiled with moisture.

'So heart-broken,' she intoned, her syllables keeping time with the air. 'A lovely contralto tone. Like Clara Butt, is it not? The passionate despair of it. Fresh courage coming. So noble. No, Georgie, you must take care not to put your foot on two adjacent pedals at once. Now, listen! Do you hear that lovely crescendo? That I do by just opening the swell very gradually. Isn't it a wonderful effect? . . . I am surprised that no one has ever thought of setting this Sonata for the organ . . . Go on pulling out stops on the great organ — yes, to your left there — in case I want them. One always has to look ahead in organ playing. Arrange your palette, so to speak. No, I shan't want them . . . It dies away, softer and softer . . . Hold on that bass C sharp till I say now . . . Now.'

They both gave the usual slow movement sigh. Then the volume of Beethoven tumbled on to the great organ on which Georgie had pulled out all the stops, and the open diapasons received it with a shout of rapture. Lucia slipped from the bench to pick it up. On the floor round about was an assemblage of small pipes.

'I think this lot is the *cor anglais*,' she said.

'I am putting in a beautiful *cor anglais*.'

She picked up one of the pipes, and blew through it.

'A lovely tone,' she said. 'It reminds one of the last act of *Tristan*, does it not, where the shepherd-boy goes on playing the *cor anglais* for ever and ever.'

Georgie picked up a pipe belonging to the *flute*. It happened to be a major third above Lucia's *cor anglais*, and they blew on them together with a very charming effect. They tried two others, but these happened to be a semitone apart, and the result was not so harmonious. Then they hastily put them down, for a party of tourists, being shown round the church by the Padre, came in at the north door. He was talking very strong Scots this morning, with snatches of early English in compliment to the architecture.

'The orrgan, ye see, is being renovated,' he said. ''Twill be a bonny instrument, I ken. Good morrow to ye, Mistress Lucas.'

Then, as she and Georgie passed him on their way out, he added in an audible aside:

'The leddy whose munificence has given it to the church. Eh, a grand benefaction. A thousand pounds and mair, what wi' lutes and psaltery, and a' the whustles.'

★   ★   ★

'I often go and have a little practice on my organ during the workmen's dinner-hour,' said Lucia as they stepped out into the hot sunshine. 'The organ, Georgie, I find is a far simpler instrument on which to get your effects than the piano. The stops supply expression: you just pull them out or push them in. That *vox humana*, for instance, with what ease one gets the singing tone, that's so difficult on the piano.'

'You've picked it up wonderfully quickly,' said Georgie. 'I thought you had a beautiful touch. And when will your organ be finished?'

'In a month or less, I hope. We must have a service of dedication and a recital: the Padre, I know, will carry out my wishes about that. Georgie, I think I shall open the recital myself. I am sure that Tilling would wish it. I should play some little piece, and then make way for the organist. I might do worse than give them that first movement of the 'Moonlight.''

'I'm sure Tilling would be much disappointed if you didn't,' said Georgie warmly. 'May I play the pedals for you?'

'I was going to suggest that, and help me with the stops. I have progressed, I know, and I'm glad you like my touch, but I hardly think I could manage the whole complicated business alone yet. *Festina lente*. Let us practice in the dinner-hour every day. If I give the 'Moonlight' it must be exquisitely performed. I must shew them what can be done with it when the orchestral colour of the organ is added.'

'I promise to work hard,' said Georgie. 'And I do think, as the Padre said to the tourists just now, that it's a most munificent gift.'

'Oh, did he say that?' asked Lucia who had heard perfectly. 'That was why they all turned round and looked at me. But, as you know, it was always my intention to devote a great part, anyhow, of what I made on the Stock Exchange to the needs of our dear Tilling.'

'Very generous, all the same,' repeated Georgie.

'No, dear; simple duty. That's how I see it ... Now what have I got to do this afternoon? That tea-party for the school-children: a hundred and twenty are coming. Tea in the garden in the shade, and then games and races. You'll be helping me all the time, won't you? Only four o'clock till seven.'

'Oh dear: I'm not very good with children,' said Georgie. 'Children are so sticky, particularly after tea, and I won't run a race with anybody.'

'You shan't run a race. But you'll help to start them, won't you, and find their mothers

286

for them and that sort of thing. I know I can depend on you, and children always adore you. Let me see: do I dine with you to-night or you with me?'

'You with me. And then to-morrow's your great dinner-party. I tell you I'm rather nervous, for there are so many things we mustn't talk about, that there's scarcely a safe subject. It'll be the first complete party anyone's had since that frightful evening at the Wyses'.'

'It was clearly my duty to respond to Diva's appeal,' said Lucia, 'and all we've got to do is to make a great deal of poor Elizabeth. She's had a horrid time, most humiliating, Georgie, and what makes it worse for her is that it was so much her own fault. Four o'clock then, dear, this afternoon, or perhaps a little before.'

★　★　★

Lucia let herself into her house, musing at considerable length on the frightful things that had happened since that night at the Wyses' to which Georgie had alluded, when Elizabeth and Benjy had set out in their goloshes, to walk back to Grebe. That was an unwise step, for the fresh night air had made Benjy much worse, and the curate returning home on the other side of the High Street after a meeting of the Band of Hope (such a contrast) had witnessed dreadful goings-on. Benjy had stood in the middle of the road, compelling a motor to pull up with a shriek of brakes, and asked to see the driver's license, insisting that he was a policeman in plain clothes on point duty. When that was settled in a most sympathetic manner by a real policeman, Benjy informed him that Msslucas was a regular stunner, and began singing 'You are Queen of my heart to-night.' At that point the curate, pained but violently interested, reluctantly let himself into his house, and there was no information to be had with regard to the rest of their walk home to Grebe. Then the sad tale was resumed, for Withers told Foljambe (who told Georgie who told Lucia) that Major Mapp-Flint on arrival had, no doubt humorously, suggested getting his gun and shooting the remaining tiger-skins in the hall, but that Mrs. Mapp-Flint wouldn't hear of it and was not amused. 'Rather the reverse,' said Withers . . . Bed.

The curate felt bound to tell his spiritual superior about the scene in the High Street and Evie told Diva, so that by the time Elizabeth came up with her market-basket next morning, this sad sequel to the Wyses' dinner party was known everywhere. She propitiated Diva by paying her the ninepence which had been in dispute, and went so far as to apologise to her for her apparent curtness at the bridge-table last night. Then, having secured a favourable hearing, she told Diva how she had found Benjy sitting close to Lucia with his hand on her knee. 'He had had more to drink than he should,' she said, 'but never would he have done that unless she had encouraged him. That's her nature, I'm afraid: she can't leave men alone. She's no better than the Pride of Poona!'

So, when Diva met Lucia half an hour afterwards, she could not resist being distinctly 'arch' about her long tête-à-tête with Benjy during the first rubber. Lucia, not appreciating this archness, had answered not a word, but turned her back and went into Twistevant's. Diva hadn't meant any harm, but this truculent conduct (combined with her dropping that ninepence down a grating in the gutter) made her see red, and she instantly told Irene that Lucia had been flirting with Benjy. Irene had tersely replied, 'You foul-minded old widow.'

Then as comment spread, Susan Wyse was blamed for having allowed Benjy (knowing his weakness) to drink so much champagne, and Mr. Wyse was blamed for being so liberal with his port. This was quite unfounded: it was Benjy who had been so liberal with his port. The Wyses adopted a lofty attitude: they simply were not accustomed to their guests drinking too much, and must bear that possibility in mind for the future: Figgis must be told. Society therefore once again, as on the occasion of the municipal elections, was rent. The Wyses were aloof, Elizabeth and Diva would not speak to Lucia, nor Diva to Irene, and Benjy would not speak to anybody because he was in bed with a severe bilious attack.

This haycock of inflammatory material would in the ordinary course of things soon have got dispersed or wet through or trodden into the ground, according to the Tilling use of disposing of past disturbances in order to leave the ground clear for future ones, but for the unexpected arrival of the Contessa Faraglione who came on a flying visit of two nights to her brother. He and Susan were still adopting their tiresome lofty, un-Tillingish attitude, and told her nothing at all exhaustive about Benjy's inebriation, Lucia's excavations, Elizabeth's disappointment and other matters of first-rate importance, and in the present state of tension thought it better not to convoke any assembly of Tilling Society in Amelia's honour. But she met

Elizabeth in the High Street who was very explicit about Roman antiquities, and she met Lucia, who was in a terrible fright lest she should begin talking Italian, and learned a little more, and she went to tea with Diva, who was quite the best chronicler in Tilling, and who poured into her madly interested ear a neat *résumé* of all previous rows, and had just got down to the present convulsion when the Padre popped in, and he and Diva began expounding it in alternate sentences after the manner of a Greek tragedy. Faradiddlione sat, as if hypnotised, alert and wide-eyed while this was going on, but when told of Elizabeth's surmise that Lucia had encouraged Benjy to make love to her, she most disconcertingly burst into peals of laughter. Muffins went the wrong way, she choked, she clapped her hands, her eyes streamed, and it was long before she could master herself for coherent speech.

'But you are all adorable,' she cried. 'There is no place like Tilling, and I shall come and live here for ever when my Cecco dies and I am dowager. My poor brother (such a prig!) and fat Susan were most discreet: they told me no more than that your great Benjy — he was my flirt here before, was he not, the man like a pink walrus — that he had a bilious attack, but of his tipsiness and of all those *gaffes* at dinner and of that scene of passion in the back drawing-room not a word. Thr-r-rilling! Imagine the scene. Your tipsy walrus. Your proud Lucia in her Roman blue stockings. She is a Duse, all cold alabaster without and burning with volcanic passion within. Next door is Mapp quarrelling about ninepence. What did the guilty ones do? I would have given anything to have been behind the curtain. Did they kiss? Did they embrace? Can you picture them? And then the entry of Mapp with her ninepence still in her pocket.'

'It's only fair to say that she paid me next morning,' said Diva scrupulously.

'Oh, stop me laughing,' cried Faradiddlione. 'Mapp enters. 'Come home, Benjy,' and then 'Queen of my Heart' all down the High Street. The rage of the Mapp! If she could not have a baby she must invent for her husband a mistress. Who shall say it is not true, though? When his bilious attack is better will they meet in the garden at Mallards? He is Lothario of the tiger-skins. Why should it not be true? My Cecco has had a mistress for years — such a good-natured pretty woman — and why not your Major? *Basta!* I must be calm.'

This flippant and deplorably immoral view of the crisis had an inflammatory rather than a cooling effect. If Tilling was anything, it was intensely serious, and not to be taken seriously by this lascivious Countess made it far more serious. So, after a few days during which social intercourse was completely paralysed, Lucia determined to change the currents of thought by digging a new channel for them. She had long been considering which should be the first of those benefactions to Tilling which would raise her on a pinnacle of public preeminence and expunge the memory of that slight fiasco at the late municipal elections, and now she decided on the renovation and amplification of the organ on which she and Georgie had been practising this morning. The time was well chosen, for surely those extensive rents in the social fabric would be repaired by the universal homage rendered her for her munificence, and nothing more would be heard of Roman antiquities and dinner-bells and drunkenness and those odious and unfounded aspersions on the really untarnishable chastity of her own character. All would be forgotten.

Accordingly next Sunday morning the Padre had announced from the pulpit in accents trembling with emotion that through the generosity of a donor who preferred to remain anonymous the congregation's psalms and hymns of praise would soon be accompanied by a noble new relay of trumpets and shawms. Then, as nobody seemed to guess (as Lucia had hoped) who the anonymous donor was, she had easily been persuaded to let this thin veil of anonymity be withdrawn. But even then there was not such a tumultuous outpouring of gratitude and admiration as to sweep away all the hatchets that still lay perilously about: in fact Elizabeth who brought the news to Diva considered the gift a very ostentatious and misleading gesture.

'It's throwing dust in our eyes,' she observed with singular acidity. 'It's drawing a red herring across her Roman excavations and her abominable forwardness with Benjy on that terrible evening. As for the gift itself, I consider it far from generous. With the fortune she has made in gold-mines and rails and all the rest of it, she doesn't feel the cost of it one atom. What I call generosity is to deprive yourself — '

'Now you're not being consistent, Elizabeth,' said Diva. 'You told me yourself that you didn't believe she had made more than half-a-crown.'

'No, I never said that, dear,' affirmed Elizabeth. 'You must be thinking of someone else you were gossiping with.'

'No, I mustn't,' said Diva. 'You did say it. And even if you hadn't, it would be very paltry of you to belittle her gift just because she was rich. But you're always carping and picking holes, and sowing discord.'

'I?' said Elizabeth, not believing her ears.

'Yes, you. Go back to that terrible evening as you call it. You've talked about nothing else since: you've been keeping the wound open. I don't deny that it was very humiliating for you to see Major Benjy exceed like that, and of course no woman would have liked her husband to go bawling out 'Queen of my Heart' all the way home about some other woman. But I've been thinking it over. I don't believe Lucia made up to him any more than I did. We should all be settling down again happily if it wasn't for you, instead of being at loggerheads with each other. Strawberries will be in next week, and not one of us dares ask the rest to our usual summer Bridge parties for fear of there being more ructions.'

'Nonsense, dear,' said Elizabeth. 'As far as I am concerned it isn't a question of not daring at all, though of course I wouldn't be so rude as to contradict you about your own moral cowardice. It's simply that I prefer not to see anything of people like Lucia or Susan who on that night was neither more nor less than a barmaid encouraging Benjy to drink, until they've expressed regret for their conduct.'

'If it comes to expressions of regret,' retorted Diva, 'I think Major Benjy had better show the way and you follow. How you can call yourself a Christian at all is beyond me.'

'Benjy has expressed himself very properly to me,' said Elizabeth, 'so there's the end of that. As for my expressing regret I can't conceive what you wish me to express regret for. Painful though I should find it to be excommunicated by you, dear, I shall have to bear it. Or would you like me to apologise to Irene for all the wicked things she said to me that night?'

'Well I daren't ask our usual party,' said Diva, 'however brave you are. You may call it moral cowardice, but it's simply common sense. Lucia would refuse with some excuse that would be an insult to my intelligence, and Mr. Georgie would certainly stick to her. So would Irene; besides she called me a foul-minded old widow. The Wyses won't begin, and I agree it wouldn't be any use your trying. The only person who's got the power or position or whatever you like to call it, to bring us all together again is Lucia herself. Don't look down your nose, Elizabeth, because it's true. I've a good mind to apologise to her for my bit of silly chaff about Major Benjy, and to ask her to do something for us.'

'I hope, dear,' said Elizabeth rising, 'that you won't encourage her to think that Benjy and I will come to her house. That would only lead to disappointment.'

'By the way, how is he?' said Diva. 'I forgot to ask.'

'So I noticed, dear. He's better, thanks. Gone to play golf again to-day.'

★ ★ ★

Diva put her pride in her pocket and went up to Mallards that very afternoon and said that she was very sorry that a word of hers spoken really in jest, should have given offence to Lucia. Lucia, as might have been expected from her lofty and irritating ways, looked at her smiling and a little puzzled, with her head on one side.

'Dear Diva, what do you mean?' she said. 'How can you have offended me?'

'What I said about Benjy and you,' said Diva. 'Just outside Twistevant's. Very stupid of me, but just chaff.'

'My wretched memory,' said Lucia. 'I've no recollection of it at all. I think you must have dreamed it. But so nice to see you, and tell me all the news. Heaps of pleasant little parties? I've been so busy with my new organ and so on, that I'm quite out of the movement.'

'There's not been a single party since that

dinner at Susan's,' said Diva.

'You don't say so! And how is Major Benjy? I think somebody told me he had caught a chill that night, when he walked home. People who have lived much in the tropics are liable to them: he must take more care of himself.'

They had strolled out into the garden, awaiting tea, and looked into the greenhouse where the peach trees were covered with setting fruit. Lucia looked wistfully at the potato and asparagus beds.

'More treasures to be unearthed some time, I hope,' she said with really unparalleled nerve. 'But at present my hands are so full: my organ, my little investments, Georgie just dines quietly with me or I with him, and we make music or read. Happy busy days!'

Really she was quite maddening, thought Diva, pretending like this to be totally unaware of the earthquake which had laid in ruins the social life of Tilling. On she went.

'Otherwise I've seen no one but Irene, and just a glimpse of dear Contessa Faraglione, and we had a refreshing chat in Italian. I found I was terribly rusty. She told me that it was just a flying visit.'

'Yes, she's gone,' said Diva.

'Such a pity: I should have liked to get up an evening with *un po' di musica* for her,' said Lucia, who had heard from Georgie, who had it from the Padre, all about her monstrously immoral views and her maniac laughter. 'Ah, tea ready, Grosvenor? Tell me more Tilling news, Diva.'

'But there isn't any,' said Diva, 'and there won't be unless you do something for us.'

'I?' asked Lucia. 'Little hermit I?'

Diva could have smacked her for her lofty unconsciousness, but in view of her mission had to check that genial impulse.

'Yes, you, of course,' she said. 'We've all been quarrelling. Never knew anything so acute. We shall never get together again, unless you come to the rescue.'

Lucia sighed.

'Dear Diva, how you all work me, and come to me when there's trouble. But I'm very obedient. Tell me what you want me to do. Give one of my simple little parties, *al fresco*, here some evening?'

'Oh, *do!*' said Diva.

'Nothing easier. I'm afraid I've been terribly remiss, thinking of nothing but my busy fragrant life. Very naughty of me. And if, as you say, it will help to patch up some of your funny little disagreements between yourselves, of which I know nothing at all, so much the better. Let's settle a night at once. My engagement-book, Grosvenor.'

Grosvenor brought it her. There were no

evening engagements at all in the future, and slightly tipping it up, so that Diva could not see the fair white pages, she turned over a leaf or two.

'This week, impossible, I'm afraid,' she said, with a noble disregard of her own admission that she and Georgie dined quietly together every night. 'But how about Wednesday next week? Let me think — yes, that's all right. And whom am I to ask? All our little circle?'

'Oh do!' said Diva. 'Start us again. Break the ice. Put out the fire. They'll all come.'

Diva was right: even Elizabeth who had warned her that such an invitation would only lead to disappointment accepted with pleasure, and Lucia made the most tactful arrangements for this *agapé*. Grosvenor was instructed to start every dish at Mrs. Mapp-Flint, and to offer barley-water as well as wine to all the guests. They assembled before dinner in the garden-room, and there, on the top of the piano, compelling notice, were the bowl and saucer of Samian ware. Mr. Wyse, with his keen perception for the beautiful, instantly enquired what they were.

'Just some fragments of Roman pottery,' said Lucia casually. 'So glad you admire them. They are pretty, but, alas, the bowl as you see is incomplete.'

Evie gave a squeal of satisfaction: she had always believed in Lucia's excavations.

'Oh, look, Kenneth,' she said to her husband. 'Fancy finding those lovely things in an empty potato-patch.'

'Begorra, Mistress Lucia,' said he, "twas worth digging up a whole garden entoirely.'

Elizabeth cast a despairing glance at this convincing evidence, and dinner was announced.

Conversation was a little difficult at first; for there were so many dangerous topics to avoid that to carry it on was like crossing a quaking bog and jumping from one firm tussock to another over soft and mossy places. But Elizabeth's wintriness thawed, when she found that not only was she placed on Georgie's right hand who was acting as host, but that every dish was started with her, and she even asked Irene if she had been painting any of her sweet pictures lately. Dubious topics and those allied to them were quite avoided, and before the end of dinner, if Lucia had proposed that they should sing 'Auld Lang Syne,' there would not have been a silent voice. Bridge, of so friendly a kind that it was almost insipid, followed, and it was past midnight before anyone could suppose that it was half-past ten. Then most cordial partings took place in the hall: Susan was loaded with her furs, Diva dropped a shilling and was distracted. Benjy found a clandestine opportunity to drink a strong whisky and soda, Irene clung passionately to Lucia, as if she would never finish saying good night, the Royce sawed to and fro before it could turn and set forth on its journey of one hundred yards, and the serene orbs of heaven twinkled benignly over a peaceful Tilling. This happy result (all but the stars) was Lucia's achievement: she had gone skimming up the pinnacle of social pre-eminence till she was almost among the stars herself.

10

Naturally nobody was foolish enough to expect that such idyllic harmony would be of long duration, for in this highly alert and critical society, with Elizabeth lynx-eyed to see what was done amiss, and Lucia, as was soon obvious, so intolerably conscious of the unique service she had done Tilling in having reconciled all those 'funny little quarrels' of which she pretended to be quite unaware, discord was sure to develop before long; but at any rate tea-parties for Bridge were in full swing by the time strawberries were really cheap, and before they were over came the ceremony of the dedication of Lucia's organ.

She had said from the first that her whole function (and that a privilege) was to have made this little contribution to the beauty of the church services: that was all, and she began and ended there. But in a quiet talk with the Padre she suggested that the day of its dedication might be made to coincide with the annual confirmation of the young folk of the parish. The Bishop, perhaps, when his laying on of hands was done, would come to lunch at Mallards and take part in the other ceremony in the afternoon. The Padre thought that an excellent notion, and in due course the Bishop accepted Lucia's invitation and would be happy (D.V.) to dedicate the organ and give a short address.

Lucia had got her start: now like a great liner she cast off her tugs and began to move out under her own steam. There was another quiet talk in the garden-room.

'You know how I hate all fuss, dear Padre,' she said, 'but I do think, don't you, that Tilling would wish for a little pomp and ceremony. An idea occurred to me: the Mayor and Corporation perhaps might like to escort the Bishop in procession from here to the church after lunch. If that is their wish, I should not dream of opposing it. Maces, scarlet robes; there would be picturesqueness about it which would be suitable on such an occasion. Of course I couldn't suggest it myself, but, as Vicar, you might ascertain what they felt.'

' 'Twould be a gran' sight,' said the Padre, quite distinctly seeing himself in the procession.

'I think Tilling would appreciate it,' said Lucia thoughtfully. 'Then about the service: one does not want it *too* long. A few prayers, a Psalm, such as 'I was glad when they said unto me': a lesson, and then, don't you think, as we shall be dedicating my organ, some anthem in praise of music? I had thought of that last chorus in Parry's setting of Milton's Ode on St. Cecilia's Day, 'Blest Pair of Syrens'. Of course my organ would accompany the psalm and the anthem, but, as I seem to see it, unofficially incognito. After that, the Bishop's address: so sweet of him to suggest that.'

'Very menseful of him,' said the Padre.

'Then,' said Lucia, waving the Samian bowl, 'then there would follow the dedication of my organ, and its *official* appearance. An organ recital — not long — by our admirable organist to show the paces, the powers of the new instrument. Its scope. The *tuba*, the *vox humana* and the *cor anglais:* just a few of the new stops. Afterwards, I shall have a party in the garden here. It might give pleasure to those who have never seen it. Our dear Elizabeth, as you know, did not entertain much.'

The Mayor and Corporation welcomed the idea of attending the dedication of the new organ in state, and of coming to Mallards just before the service and conducting the Bishop in procession to the church. So that was settled, and Lucia, now full steam ahead, got to work on the organist. She told him, very diffidently, that her friends thought it would

305

be most appropriate if, before his official recital (how she was looking forward to it!), she herself, as donor, just ran her hands, so to speak, over the keys. Mr. Georgie Pillson, who was really a wonderful performer on the pedals, would help her, and it so happened that she had just finished arranging the first movement of Beethoven's 'Moonlight Sonata' for the organ. She was personally very unwilling to play at all, and in spite of all this pressure she had refused to promise to do so. But now as he added his voice to the general feeling she felt she must overcome her hesitation. It mustn't be mentioned at all: she wanted it to come as a little surprise to everybody. *Then* would follow the real, the skilled recital by him. She hoped he would then give them Falberg's famous 'Storm at Sea,' that marvellous tone-poem with thunder on the pedals, and lightning on the *Diocton*, and the choir of voices singing on the *vox humana* as the storm subsided. Terribly difficult, of course, but she knew he would play it superbly, and she sent him round a copy of that remarkable composition.

The day arrived, a hot and glorious morning, just as if Lucia had ordered it. The lunch at Mallards for the Bishop was very *intime:* just the Padre and his wife and the Bishop and his chaplain. Not even Georgie was asked, who, as a matter of fact, was in such a state of nerves over his approaching performance of the pedal part of the 'Moonlight' that he could not have eaten a morsel, and took several aspirin tablets instead. But Lucia had issued invitations broadcast for the garden party afterwards, to the church choir, the Mayor and Corporation, and all her friends to meet the Bishop. R.S.V.P.; and there was not a single refusal. Tea for sixty.

The procession to church was magnificent, the sun poured down on maces and scarlet robes and on the Bishop, profusely perspiring, in his cope and mitre. Lucia had considered whether she should take part in the procession herself, but her hatred of putting herself forward in any way had caused her to abandon the idea of even walking behind the Bishop, and she followed at such a distance that not even those most critical of her conduct could possibly have accused her of belonging to the pageant, herself rather nervous, and playing triplets in the air to get her fingers supple. She took her seat close to the organ beside Georgie, so that they could slip into their places on the organ-bench while the Bishop was returning from the pulpit after his sermon. A tremendous bank of cloud had risen in the north, promising storm: it was lucky that it had held off till now, for umbrellas would certainly have spoiled the splendour of the procession.

The choir gave a beautiful rendering of the last chorus in 'Blest Pair of Sirens,' and the Bishop a beautiful address. He made a very charming allusion to the patroness of organs, St. Cecilia, and immediately afterwards spoke of the donor 'your distinguished citizeness' almost as if Lucia and that sainted musician were one. A slight stir went through the pews containing her more intimate friends: they had not thought of her like that, and Elizabeth murmured 'St. Lucecilia' to herself for future use. During the address the church grew exceedingly dark, and the gloom was momentarily shattered by several vivid flashes of lightning followed by the mutter of thunder. Then standing opposite the organ, pastoral staff in hand, the Bishop solemnly dedicated it, and, as he went back to his seat in the Chancel, Lucia and Georgie, like another blest pair of sirens, slid on to the organ-seat, unobserved in the gathering gloom, and were screened from sight by the curtain behind it. There was a momentary pause, the electric light in the church was switched on, and the first piece of the organ recital began. Though Lucia's friends had not heard it for some time, it was familiar to them, and Diva and Elizabeth looked at each other, puzzled at first, but soon picking up the scent, as it were, of old associations. The scent grew hotter, and each inwardly visualized the picture of Lucia sitting at her piano with her face in profile against a dark curtain, and her fingers dripping with slow triplets: surely this was the same piece. Sacred edifice or not, these frightful suspicions had to be settled, and Elizabeth quietly rose and stood on tiptoe. She saw, quite distinctly, the top of Georgie's head and of Lucia's remarkable new hat. She sat down again, and in a hissing whisper said to Diva, 'So we've all been asked to come to church to hear Lucia and Mr. Georgie practise.' . . . Diva only shook her head sadly. On the slow movement went, its monotonous course relieved just once by a frightful squeal from the great organ as Georgie, turning over, put his finger on one of the top notes, and wailed itself away. The blest pair of sirens tiptoed round the curtain again, thereby completely disclosing themselves and sank into their seats.

Then to show off the scope of the organ there followed Falberg's famous tone-poem, 'Storm at Sea.' The ship evidently was having a beautiful calm voyage but then the wind began to whistle on swiftly ascending chromatic scales, thunder muttered on the pedals, and the *Diocton* contributed some flashes of forked lightning. Louder grew the thunder, more vivid the lightning as the storm waxed fiercer. Then came a perfectly appalling crash, and the Bishop, who was perhaps dozing a little after his labours and his lunch, started in his seat and put his mitre straight. Diva clutched at Elizabeth, Evie gave a mouse-like squeal of admiring dismay, for never had anybody heard so powerful an instrument. Bang, it went again and then it dawned on the more perceptive that Nature herself was assisting at the dedication of Lucia's organ with two claps of thunder immediately overhead at precisely the right moment. Lucia herself sat with her music-face on, gazing dreamily at the vaulting of the church, as if her organ was doing it all. Then the storm at sea (organ solo without Nature) died away and a chorus presumably of sailors and passengers *(vox humana)* sang a soft chorale of thanksgiving. Diva gave a swift suspicious glance at the choir to make sure this was not another trick, but this time it was the organ. Calm broad chords, like sunshine on the sea, succeeded the chorale, and Elizabeth writhing in impotent jealousy called Diva's attention to the serene shafts of real sunshine that were now streaming through

Elijah going up to heaven and the witch of Endor.

Indeed it was scarcely fair. Not content with supplying that stupendous *obbligato* to the storm at sea, Nature had now caused the sun to burst brilliantly forth again, in order to make Lucia's garden party as great a success as her organ, unless by chance the grass was too wet for it. But during the solemn melody which succeeded, the sun continued to shine resplendently, and the lawn at Mallards was scarcely damp. There was Lucia receiving her guests and their compliments: the Mayor in his scarlet robe and chain of office was talking to her as Elizabeth stepped into what she still thought of as her own garden.

'Magnificent instrument, Mrs. Lucas,' he was saying. 'That storm at sea was very grand.'

Elizabeth was afraid that he thought the organ had done it all, but she could hardly tell him his mistake.

'Dear Lucia,' she said. 'How I enjoyed that sweet old tune you've so often played to us. Some of your new stops a little harsh in tone, don't you think? No doubt they will mellow. Oh, how sadly burned up my dear garden is looking!'

Lucia turned to the Mayor again.

'So glad you think my little gift will add to

the beauty of our services,' she said. 'You must tell me, Mr. Mayor, what next — Dear Diva, so pleased to see you. You liked my organ?'

'Yes, and wasn't the real thunderstorm a bit of luck?' said Diva. 'Did Mr. Georgie play the pedals in the Beethoven? I heard him turn over.'

Lucia swerved again.

'Good of you to look in, Major Benjy,' she said. 'You'll find tea in the marquee, and other drinks in the *giardino segreto*.'

That was clever: Benjy ambled off in an absent-minded way towards the place of other drinks, and Elizabeth, whom Lucia wanted to get rid of, ambled after him, and towed him towards the less alcoholic marquee. Lucia went on ennobling herself to the Mayor.

'The unemployed,' she said. 'They are much and often on my mind. And the hospital. I'm told it is in sad need of new equipments. Really it will be a privilege to do something more before very long for our dear Tilling. You must spare me half-an-hour sometime and talk to me about its needs.'

Lucia gave her most silvery laugh.

'Dear me, what a snub I got over the election to the Town Council,' she said. 'But nothing discourages me, Mr. Mayor . . . Now

I think all my guests have come, so let us go and have a cup of tea. I am quite ashamed of my lawn to-day, but not long ago I had an entertainment for the school-children and games and races, and they kicked it up sadly, dear mites.'

As they walked towards the marquee, the Mayor seemed to Lucia to have a slight bias (like a bowl); towards the *giardino segreto* and she tactfully adapted herself to this change of direction. There were many varieties of sumptuous intoxicants, cocktails and sherry and whisky and hock-cup. Grosvenor was serving, but just now she had a flinty face, for a member of the Corporation had been addressing her as 'Miss', as if she was a barmaid. Then Major Benjy joined Grosvenor's group, having given Elizabeth the slip while she was talking to the Bishop, and drank a couple of cocktails in a great hurry before she noticed his disappearance. Lucia was specially attentive to members of the Corporation, making, however, a few slight errors, such as recommending her greengrocer the strawberries she had bought from him, and her wine merchant his own sherry, for that was bringing shop into private life. Then Elizabeth appeared with the Bishop in the doorway of the *giardino segreto*, and with a wistful face she pointed out to him this favourite spot in her ancestral home: but she caught sight of Benjy at the bar and her wistfulness vanished, for she had found something of her own again. Firmly she convoyed him to the less alcoholic garden, and Lucia took the Bishop, who was interested in Roman antiquities, to see the pieces of Samian ware in the garden-room and the scene of her late excavations. 'Too sad,' she said, 'to have had to fill up my trenches again, but digging was terribly expensive, and the organ must come first.'

A group was posed for a photograph: Lucia stood between the Mayor and the Bishop, and afterwards she was more than affable to the reporter for the *Hastings Chronicle*, whose account of her excavations had already made such a stir in Tilling. She gave him hock-cup and strawberries, and sitting with him in a corner of the garden, let him take down all she said in shorthand. Yes: it was she who had played the opening piece at the recital (the first movement of the sonata in C sharp minor by Beethoven, usually called the 'Moonlight'). She had arranged it herself for the organ ('Another glass of hock-cup, Mr. Meriton?') and hoped that he did not think it a vandalism to adapt the Master. The Bishop had lunched with her, and had been delighted with her little Queen Anne house and thought very highly of her Roman antiquities. Her future movements this summer? Ah, she could not tell him for certain. She would like to get a short holiday, but they worked her very hard in Tilling. She had been having a little chat with the Mayor about some schemes for the future, but it would be premature to divulge them yet . . . Elizabeth standing near and straining her ears, heard most of this frightful conversation and was petrified with disgust. The next number of the *Hastings Chronicle* would be even more sickening than the excavation number. She could bear it no longer and went home with Benjy, ordering a copy in advance on her way.

The number, when it appeared justified her gloomiest anticipations. The Bishop's address about the munificent citizeness was given very fully, and there was as well a whole column almost entirely about Lucia. With qualms of nausea Elizabeth read about Mrs. Lucas's beautiful family home that dated from the reign of Queen Anne, its panelled parlours, its garden-room containing its positively Bodleian library and rare specimens of Samian ware which she had found in the excavations in her old-world garden. About the lawn with the scars imprinted on its velvet surface by the happy heels of the school-children whom she had entertained for an afternoon of tea and frolics. About the Office with its ledgers and strip of noiseless indiarubber by the door, where the *châtelaine* of Mallards conducted her financial operations. About the secret garden (Mrs. Lucas who spoke Italian with the same ease and purity as English referred to it as '*mio giardino segreto*') in which she meditated every morning. About the splendour of the procession from Mallards to the church with the Mayor and the maces and the mitre and the cope of the Lord Bishop, who had lunched privately with Mrs. Lucas. About the masterly arrangement for the organ of the first movement of Beethoven's 'Moonlight Sonata', made by Mrs. Lucas, and her superb performance of the same. About her princely entertainment of the local magnates. About her hat and her hock-cup.

'I wonder how much she paid for that,' said Elizabeth, tossing the foul sheet across to Benjy as they sat at breakfast. It fell on his poached egg, in which he had just made a major incision, and smeared yolk on the clean table-cloth. She took up the *Daily Mirror*, and there was the picture of Lucia standing between the Mayor and the Bishop. She took up the *Financial Gazette*, and Siriami had slumped another shilling.

It was not only Elizabeth who was ill-pleased with this sycophantic column. Georgie had ordered a copy, which he first skimmed swiftly for the name of Mr. G. Pillson: a more careful reading of it showed him that there was not the smallest allusion to his having played the pedals in the 'Moonlight.' Rather mean of Lucia; she certainly ought to have mentioned that, for, indeed, without the pedals it would have been a very thin performance. 'I don't mind for myself,' thought Georgie, 'for what good does it do me to have my name in a squalid provincial rag, but I'm afraid she's getting grabby. She wants to have it all. She wants to be on the top with nobody else in sight. Her masterly arrangement of the 'Moonlight'! Rubbish! She just played the triplets with one hand and the air with the other, while I did the bass on the pedals. And her family house! It's been in her family (only she hasn't got one) since April. Her Italian, too! And the Samian ware from her excavations! That's a whopper. All she got from her excavations was three-quarters of an Apollinaris bottle. If she had asked my advice, I should have told her that it was wiser to let sleeping dogs lie!' . . . So instead of popping into Mallards and congratulating her on her marvellous press, Georgie went straight down to the High Street in a condition known as dudgeon. He saw the back of Lucia's head in the Office, and almost hoped she would disregard Mammoncash's advice and make some unwise investment.

There was a little group of friends at the corner, Diva and Elizabeth and Evie. They all hailed him: it was as if they were waiting for him, as indeed they were.

'Have you read it, Mr. Georgie?' asked Diva. (There was no need to specify what.)

'Her family home,' interrupted Elizabeth musingly. 'And this is my family market-basket. It came into my family when I bought it the day before yesterday and it's one of my most cherished heirlooms. Did you *ever*, Mr. Georgie? It's worse than her article about the Roman forum, in the potato-bed.'

'And scarcely a word about Kenneth,' interrupted Evie. 'I always thought he was Vicar of Tilling — '

'No, dear, we live and learn when we come up against the *châtelaine* of Mallards,' said Elizabeth.

'After all, you and the Padre went to lunch, Evie,' said Diva who never let resentment entirely obliterate her sense of fairness. 'But I think it's so mean of her not to say that Mr. Georgie played the pedals for her. I enjoyed

318

them much more than the triplets.'

'What I can't understand is that she never mentioned the real thunderstorm,' said Elizabeth. 'I expected her to say she'd ordered it. Surely she did, didn't she? Such a beauty, too: she might well be prouder of it than of her hat.'

Georgie's dudgeon began to evaporate in these withering blasts of satire. They were ungrateful. Only a few weeks ago Lucia had welded together the fragments of Tilling society, which had been smashed up in the first instance by the tipsiness of Benjy. Nobody could have done it except her, strawberry time would have gone by without those luscious and inexpensive teas and now they were all biting the hand that had caused them to be fed. It was bright green jealousy, just because none of them had ever had a line in any paper about their exploits, let alone a column. And who, after all, had spent a thousand pounds on an organ for Tilling, and got a Bishop to dedicate it, and ordered a thunderstorm, and asked them all to a garden party afterwards? They snatched at the benefits of their patroness, and then complained that they were being patronised. Of course her superior airs and her fibs could be maddening sometimes, but even if she did let a reporter think that she spoke Italian as naturally as English and had

319

dug up Samian ware in her garden, it was 'pretty Fanny's way,' and they must put up with it. His really legitimate grievance about his beautiful pedalling vanished.

'Well, I thought it was a wonderful day,' he said. 'She's more on a pinnacle than ever. Oh, look: here she comes.'

Indeed she did, tripping gaily down the hill with a telegraph form in her hand.

'*Buon giorno a tutti*,' she said. 'Such a nuisance: my telephone is out of order and I must go to the post-office. A curious situation in dollars and francs. I've been puzzling over it.'

Stony faces and forced smiles met her. She tumbled to it at once, the clever creature.

'And how good of you all to have rallied round me,' she said, 'and have made our little *festa* such a success. I was so anxious about it, but I needn't have been with so many dear loyal friends to back me up. The Bishop was enchanted with Mallards, Elizabeth: of course I told him that I was only an interloper. And what sweet things he said to me about the Padre, Evie.'

Lucia racked her brain to invent something nice which he said about Diva. So, though Pat hadn't been at the party, how immensely the Bishop admired her beautiful dog!

'And how about a little Bridge this

afternoon?' she asked. 'Shan't invite you, Georgino: just a woman's four. Yes and yes and yes? Capital! It's so hot that we might play in the shelter in Elizabeth's secret garden. Four o'clock then. Georgie, come to the stationer's with me. I want you to help me choose a book. My dear, your pedalling yesterday! How enthusiastic the organist was about it. *Au reservoir*, everybody.

'Georgie, I must get a great big scrap-book,' she went on, 'to paste my press notices into. They multiply so. That paragraph the other day about my *excavazioni*, and to-day a whole column, and the photograph in the *Daily Mirror*. It would be amusing perhaps, years hence, to turn over the pages and recall the past. I must get a handsome looking book, morocco, I think. How pleased all Tilling seems to be about yesterday.'

11

The holiday season came round with August, and, as usual, the householders of the Tilling social circle let their own houses, and went to live in smaller ones, thereby not only getting a change of environment, but making, instead of spending, money on their holiday, for they received a higher rent for the houses they quitted than they paid for the houses they took. The Mapp-Flints were the first to move: Elizabeth inserted an advertisement in the *Times* in order to save those monstrous fees of house agents and instantly got an enquiry from a most desirable tenant, no less than the widow of a Baronet. In view of her rank, Elizabeth asked for and obtained a higher rent than she had ever netted at Mallards, and, as on her honeymoon, she took a very small bungalow near the sea, deficient in plumbing, but otherwise highly salubrious, and as she touchingly remarked 'so near the golf links for my Benjy-boy. He will be as happy as the day is long.' She was happy, too, for the rent she received for Grebe was five times what (after a little bargaining) she paid for this shack which would be so perfect for her Benjy-boy.

Her new tenant was interesting: she had forty-seven canaries, each in its own cage, and the noise of their pretty chirping could be heard if the wind was favourable a full quarter of a mile from the house. It was ascertained that she personally cleaned out all their cages every morning, which accounted for her not being seen in Tilling till after lunch. She then rode into the town on a tricycle and bought rape seed and groundsel in prodigious quantities. She had no dealings with the butcher, so it was speedily known, and thus was probably a vegetarian; and Diva, prowling round Grebe one Friday morning, saw her clad in a burnous, kneeling on a carpet in the garden and prostrating herself in an eastward position. It might therefore be inferred that she was a Mahommedan as well.

This was all very satisfactory, a titled lady, of such marked idiosyncrasies, was evidently a very promising addition to Tilling society, and Diva, not wishing to interrupt her devotions, went quietly away, greatly impressed, and called next day, meaning to follow up this formality with an invitation to a vegetarian lunch. But even as she waited at the front door a window directly above was thrown open, and a shrill voice shouted 'Not at home. Ever.' So Diva took the tram out to the golf links, and told Elizabeth that her tenant was certainly a lunatic. Elizabeth was much disturbed, and spent an hour every afternoon for the next three days in hiding behind the hornbeam hedge at Grebe, spying upon her. Lucia thought that Diva's odd appearance might have accounted for this chilling reception and called herself. Certainly nobody shouted at her, but nobody answered the bell and, after a while, pieces of groundsel rained down on her, probably from the same upper window . . . The Padre let the Vicarage for August and September, and took a bungalow close to the Mapp-Flints. He and Major Benjy played golf during the day and the four played hectic Bridge in the evening.

Diva at present had not succeeded in letting her house, even at a very modest rental, and so she remained in the High Street. One evening horrid fumes of smoke laden with soot came into her bathroom where she was refreshing herself before dinner, and she found that they came down the chimney from the kitchen of the house next door. The leakage in the flue was localized, and it appeared that Diva was responsible for it, since, for motives of economy, which seemed sound at the time, she had caused the overflow pipe from her cistern to be passed through it. The owner of the house next door most obligingly promised not to use his range till Diva had the damage to the flue repaired, but made shift with his gas-ring, since he was genuinely anxious not to suffocate her when she was washing. But Diva could not bring herself to spend nine pounds (a frightful sum) on the necessary work on the chimney, and for the next ten days took no further steps.

Then Irene found a tenant for her house, and took that of Diva's neighbour. He explained to her that just at present, until Mrs. Plaistow repaired a faulty flue, the kitchen range could not be used, and suggested that Irene might put a little pressure on her, since this state of things had gone on for nearly a fortnight, and his repeated reminders had had no effect. So Irene put pressure, and on the very evening of the day she moved in, she and Lucy lit an enormous fire in her range, though the evening was hot, and waited to see what effect that would have. Diva happened to be again in her bath, musing over the terrible expense she would be put to: nine pounds meant the saving of five shillings a week for the best part of a year. These gloomy meditations were interrupted by volumes of acrid smoke pouring through the leak, and she sprang out of her bath, convinced that the house was on fire, and without drying herself she threw on her dressing-gown. She had left the bath-room door open: thick vapours followed her downstairs. She hastily dressed and with her servant and Paddy wildly barking at her heels flew into the High Street and hammered on Irene's door.

Irene, flushed with stoking, came upstairs.

'So I've smoked you out,' she said. 'Serve you right.'

'I believe my house is on fire,' cried Diva. 'Never saw such smoke in my life.'

'Call the fire-engine then,' said Irene. 'Goodbye: I must put some more damp wood on. And mind, I'll keep that fire burning day and night, if I don't get a wink of sleep, till you've had that flue repaired.'

'Please, please,' cried Diva in agony. 'No more damp wood, I beg. I promise. It shall be done to-morrow.'

'Well, apologise for being such a damned nuisance,' said Irene. 'You've made me and Lucy roast ourselves over the fire. Not to mention the expense of the firing.'

'Yes. I apologise. Anything!' wailed Diva. 'And I shall have to re-paper my bathroom. Kippered.'

'Your own fault. Did you imagine I was going to live on a gas-ring, because you wouldn't have your chimney repaired?'

Then Diva got a tenant in spite of the

kippered bathroom, and moved to a dilapidated hovel close beside the railway line, which she got for half the rent which she received for her house. Passing trains shook its crazy walls and their whistlings woke her at five in the morning, but its cheapness gilded these inconveniences, and she declared it was delightful to be awakened betimes on these August days. The Wyses went out to Capri to spend a month with the Faragliones, and so now the whole of the Tilling circle, with the exception of Georgie and Lucia, were having change and holiday to the great advantage of their purses. They alone remained in their adjoining abodes and saw almost as much of each other as during those weeks when Georgie was having shingles and growing his beard in hiding at Grebe. Lucia gave her mornings to finance and the masterpieces of the Greek tragedians, and in this piping weather recuperated herself with a siesta after lunch. Then in the evening coolness they motored and sketched or walked over the field-paths of the marsh, dined together and had orgies of Mozartino. All the time (even during her siesta) Lucia's head was as full of plans as an egg of meat, and she treated Georgie to spoonfuls of it. They were approaching the town on one such evening from the south. The new road, now finished, curved round the bottom of the hill on which the town stood: above it was a bare bank with tufts of coarse grass rising to the line of the ancient wall.

Lucia stood with her head on one side regarding it.

'An ugly patch,' she said. 'It offends the eye, Georgie. It is not in harmony with the mellow brick of the wall. It should be planted. I seem to see it covered with almond trees; those late flowering ones. Pink blossom, a foam of pink blossom for *la bella Primavera*. I estimate that it would require at least fifty young trees. I shall certainly offer to give them to the town and see to them being put in.'

'That would look lovely,' said Georgie.

'It shall look lovely. Another thing. I'm going to stop my financial career for the present. I shall sell out my tobacco shares — realize them is the phrase we use — on which I have made large profits. I pointed out to my broker, that, in my opinion, tobaccos were high enough, and he sees the soundness of that.'

Georgie silently interpreted this swanky statement. It meant, of course, that Mammoncash had recommended their sale; but there was no need to express this. He murmured agreement.

'Also I must rid myself of this continual strain,' Lucia went on. 'I am ashamed of myself, but I find it absorbs me too much: it keeps me on the stretch to be always watching the markets and estimating the effect of political disturbances. The Polish corridor, Hitler, Geneva, the new American president. I shall close my ledgers.'

They climbed in silence up the steep steps by the Norman tower. They were in considerable need of repair, and Lucia, contemplating the grey bastion in front, stumbled badly over an uneven paving-stone.

'These ought to be looked to,' she said. 'I must make a note of that.'

'Are you going to have them repaired?' asked Georgie humorously.

'Quite possibly. You see, I've made a great deal of money, Georgie. I've made eight thousand pounds — '

'My dear, what a sum. I'd no notion.'

'Naturally one does not talk about it,' said Lucia loftily. 'But there it is, and I shall certainly spend a great deal of it, keeping some for myself — the labourer is worthy of his hire-on Tilling. I want — how can I put it — to be a fairy godmother to the dear little place. For instance, I expect the plans for my new operating-theatre at the hospital in a day or two. That I regard as necessary. I have told the Mayor that I shall provide it, and he will announce my gift to the Governors when they meet next week. He is terribly keen that I should accept a place on the Board: really he's always worrying me about it. I think I shall allow him to nominate me. My election, he says, will be a mere formality, and will give great pleasure.'

Georgie agreed. He felt he was getting an insight into Lucia's schemes, for it was impossible not to remember that after her gift of the organ she reluctantly consented to be a member of the Church Council.

'And do you know, Georgie,' she went on, 'they elected me only to-day to be President of the Tilling Cricket Club. Fancy! Twenty pounds did that — I mean I was only too glad to give them the heavy roller which they want very much, and I was never more astonished in my life than when those two nice young fellows, the foreman of the gas works and the town surveyor — '

'Oh yes, Georgie and Per,' said he, 'who laughed so much over the smell in the garden-room, and started you on your Roman — '

'Those were their names,' said Lucia. 'They came to see me and begged me to allow them to nominate me as their President, and I was elected unanimously to-day. I promised to appear at a cricket match they have to-morrow against a team they called the Zingari. I hope they did not see me shudder, for as you know it should be 'I Zingari': the Italian for 'gipsies.' And the whole of their cricket ground wants levelling and relaying. I shall walk over it with them, and look into it for myself.'

'I didn't know you took any interest in any game,' said Georgie.

'Georgino, how you misjudge me! I've always held, always, that games and sport are among the strongest and most elevating influences in English life. Think of Lord's, and all those places where they play football, and the Lonsdale belt for boxing, and Wimbledon. Think of the crowds here, for that matter, at cricket and football matches on early closing days. Half the townspeople of Tilling are watching them: Tilling takes an immense interest in sport. They all tell me that people will much appreciate my becoming their President. You must come with me to-morrow to the match.'

'But I don't know a bat from a ball,' said Georgie.

'Nor do I, but we shall soon learn. I want to enter into every side of life here. We are too narrow in our interests. We must get a larger outlook, Georgie, a wider sympathy. I understand they play football on the cricket ground in the winter.'

'Football's a sealed book to me,' said Georgie, 'and I don't intend to unseal it.'

They had come back to Mallards, and Lucia standing on the doorstep looked over the cobbled street with its mellow brick houses.

'*Bella piccolo città!*' she exclaimed. 'Dinner at eight here, isn't it, and bring some *musica*. How I enjoy our little domestic evenings.'

'Domestic': just the word 'domestic' stuck in Georgie's mind as he touched up his beard, and did a little sewing while it dried, before he dressed for dinner. It nested in his head, like a woodpecker, and gave notice of its presence there by a series of loud taps at frequent intervals. No doubt Lucia was only referring to their usual practice of dining together and playing the piano afterwards, or sitting (even more domestically) as they often did, each reading a book in easy silence with casual remarks. Such a mode of spending the evening was infinitely pleasanter and more sensible than that they should sit, she at Mallards and he at the Cottage, over solitary meals and play long solos on their pianos instead of those adventurous duets. No doubt she had meant nothing more than that by the word.

★ ★ ★

The party from the bungalows, the Mapp-Flints and the Padre and his wife, came into Tilling next day to see the cricket match. They mingled with the crowd and sat on public benches, and Elizabeth observed with much uneasiness how Lucia and Georgie were conducted by the town surveyor to reserved deck-chairs by the pavilion: she was afraid that meant something sinister. Lucia had put a touch of sun-burn rouge on her face, in order to convey the impression that she often spent a summer day watching cricket, and she soon learned the difference between bats and balls: but she should have studied the game a little more before she asked Per, when three overs had been bowled and no wicket had fallen, who was getting the best of it. A few minutes later a Tilling wicket fell and Per went in. He immediately skied a ball in the direction of long on, and Lucia clapped her hands wildly. 'Oh, look, Georgie,' she said. 'What a beautiful curve the ball is describing! And so high. Lovely . . . What? Has he finished already?'

Tilling was out for eighty-seven runs, and between the inningses, Lucia, in the hat which the *Hastings Chronicle* had already described, was escorted out to look at the pitch by the merry brothers. She had learned so much about cricket in the last hour that her experienced eye saw at once that the greater part of the field ought to be levelled and the turf relaid. Nobody took any particular notice of Georgie, so while Lucia was inspecting the pitch he slunk away and lunched at home. She, as President of the Tilling Club, lunched with the two teams in the pavilion, and found several opportunities of pronouncing the word Zingari properly.

The bungalow-party having let their houses picnicked on sandwiches and indulged in gloomy conjecture as to what Lucia's sudden appearance in sporting circles signified. Then Benjy walked up to the Club nominally to see if there were any letters for him and actually to have liquid refreshment to assuage the thirst caused by the briny substances which Elizabeth had provided for lunch, and brought back the sickening intelligence that Lucia had been elected President of the Tilling Cricket Club.

'I'm not in the least surprised,' said Elizabeth. 'I suspected something of the sort. Nor shall I be surprised if she plays football for Tilling in the winter. Shorts, and a jersey of Tilling colours. Probably that hat.'

Satire, it was felt, had said its last word.

The *Hastings Chronicle* on the next Saturday was a very painful document. It contained a large-print paragraph on its middle page headed 'Munificent Gift by Mrs. Lucas of Mallards House, Tilling.' Those who felt equal to reading further then learnt that she had most graciously consented to become President of the Tilling Cricket Club, and had offered, at the Annual General Meeting of the Club, held after the XI's match against the Zingari, to have the cricket field levelled and relaid. She had personally inspected it (so said Mrs. Lucas in her Presidential address) and was convinced that Tilling would never be able to do itself justice at the King of Games till this was done. She therefore considered it a privilege, as President of the Club, in which she had always taken so deep an interest, to undertake this work (loud and prolonged applause) . . . This splendid gift would benefit footballers as well as cricketers since they used the same ground, and the Committee of the football club, having ascertained Mrs. Lucas's feelings on the subject, had unanimously elected her as President.

The very next week there were more of these frightful revelations. Again there was that headline, 'Munificent Gift, etc!' This time it was the Tilling Hospital. At a meeting of the Governors the Mayor announced that Mrs. Lucas (already known as the Friend of the Poor) had offered to build a new operating-theatre, and to furnish it with the most modern

335

equipment according to the plan and schedule which he now laid before them —

Elizabeth was reading this aloud to Benjy, as they lunched in the verandah of their bungalow, in an indignant voice. At this point she covered up with her hand the remainder of the paragraph.

'Mark my words, Benjy,' she said. 'I prophesy that what happened next was that the Governors accepted this gift with the deepest gratitude and did themselves the honour of inviting her to a seat on the Board.'

It was all too true, and Elizabeth finished the stewed plums in silence. She rose to make coffee.

'The *Hastings Chronicle* ought to keep 'Munificent Gift by Mrs. Lucas of Mallards House, Tilling,' permanently set up in type,' she observed. 'And 'House' is new. In my day and Aunt Caroline's before me, 'Mallards' was grand enough. It will be 'Mallards Palace' before she's finished with it.'

★ ★ ★

But with this last atrocity, the plague of munificences was stayed for the present. August cooled down into September, and September disgraced itself at the season of its spring tides by brewing a terrific southwest gale. The sea heaped up by the continued press of the wind broke through the shingle bank on the coast and flooded the low land behind, where some of the bungalows stood. That inhabited by the Padre and Evie was built on a slight elevation and escaped being inundated, but the Mapp-Flints were swamped. Nearly a foot of water covered the rooms on the ground floor, and until it subsided, the house was uninhabitable unless you treated it like a palazzo on the Grand Canal at Venice, and had a gondola moored to the banisters of the stairs. News of the disaster was brought to Tilling by the Padre when he bicycled in to take Mattins on Sunday morning. He met Lucia at the church door, and in a few vivid sentences described how the unfortunate couple had waded ashore. They had breakfasted with him and Evie and would lunch and sup there, but then they would have to wade back again to sleep, since he had no spare room. A sad holiday experience: and he hurried off to the vestry to robe.

The beauty of her organ wrought upon Lucia, for she had asked the organist to play Falberg's 'Storm at Sea' as a voluntary at the end of the service, and, as she listened, the inexorable might of Nature, of which the Mapp-Flints were victims, impressed itself on her. Moreover she really enjoyed dispensing benefits with a bountiful hand on the worthy and unworthy alike, and by the time the melodious storm was over she had made up her mind to give board and lodging to the refugees until the salt water had ebbed from their ground-floor rooms. Grebe was still let and resonant with forty-seven canaries, and she must shelter them, as Noah took back the dove sent out over the waste of waters, in the Ark of their old home . . . She joined softly in the chorale of passengers and sailors, and left the church with Georgie.

'I shall telephone to them at once, Georgie,' she said, 'and offer to take them in at Mallards House. The car shall fetch them after lunch.'

'I wouldn't,' said Georgie. 'Why shouldn't they go to an hotel?'

'*Caro*, simply because they wouldn't go,' said Lucia. 'They would continue to wade to their beds and sponge on the Padre. Besides if their bungalow collapsed — it is chiefly made of laths tied together with pieces of string and pebbles from the shore — and buried them in the ruins, I should truly regret it. Also I welcome the opportunity of doing a kindness to poor Elizabeth. Mallards House will always be at the service of the needy. I imagine it will only be for a day or two. You must promise to lunch and dine with me,

338

won't you, as long as they are with me, for I don't think I could bear them alone.'

Lucia adopted the seignorial manner suitable to the donor of organs and operating-theatres. She instructed Grosvenor to telephone in the most cordial terms to Mrs. Mapp-Flint, and wrote out what she should say. Mrs. Lucas could not come to the telephone herself at that moment, but she sent her sympathy, and insisted on their making Mallards House their home, till the bungalow was habitable again: she thought she could make them quite comfortable in her little house. Elizabeth of course accepted her hospitality though it was odd that she had not telephoned herself. So Lucia made arrangements for the reception of her guests. She did not intend to give up her bedroom and dressing-room which they had occupied before, since it would be necessary to bring another bed in, and it would be very inconvenient to turn out herself. Besides, so it happily occurred to her, it would arouse very poignant emotion if they found themselves in their old nuptial chamber. Elizabeth should have the pleasant room looking over the garden, and Benjy the one at the end of the passage, and the little sitting-room next Elizabeth's should be devoted to their exclusive use. That would be princely hospitality, and thus the garden-room, where she always sat, would not be invaded during the day. After tea, they might play Bridge there, and of course use it after dinner for more Bridge or music. Then it was time to send Cadman with the motor to fetch them, and Lucia furnished it with a thick fur rug and a hot water-bottle in case they had caught cold with their wadings. She put a Sunday paper in their sitting-room, and strewed a few books about to give it an inhabited air, and went out as usual for her walk, for it would be more in the seigniorial style if Grosvenor settled them in, and she herself casually returned about tea-time, certain that everything would have been done for their comfort.

This sumptuous *insouciance* a little miscarried, for though Grosvenor had duly conducted the visitors to their own private sitting-room, they made a quiet little pilgrimage through the house while she was unpacking for them, peeped into the Office, and were sitting in the garden-room when Lucia returned.

'So sorry to be out when you arrived, dear Elizabeth,' she said, 'but I knew Grosvenor would make you at home.'

Elizabeth sprang up from her old seat in the window. (What a bitter joy it was to survey from there again.)

340

'Dear Lucia,' she cried. 'Too good of you to take in the poor homeless ones. Putting you out dreadfully, I'm afraid.'

'Not an atom. *Tutto molto facile*. And there's the parlour upstairs ready for you, which I hope Grosvenor showed you.'

'Indeed she did,' said Elizabeth effusively. 'Deliciously cosy. So kind.'

'And what a horrid experience you must have had,' said Lucia. Tea will be ready: let us go in.'

'A waste of waters,' said Elizabeth impressively, 'and a foot deep in the dining-room. We had to have a boat to take our luggage away. It reminded Benjy of the worst floods on the Jumna.'

''Pon my word, it did,' said Benjy, 'and I shouldn't wonder if there's more to come. The wind keeps up, and there's the highest of the spring tides to-night. Total immersion of the Padre, perhaps. Ha! Ha! Baptism of those of Riper Years.'

'Naughty!' said Elizabeth. Certainly the Padre had been winning at Bridge all this week, but that hardly excused levity over things sacramental, and besides he had given them lunch and breakfast. Lucia also thought his joke in poor taste and called attention to her dahlias. She had cut a new flower-bed, where there had once stood a very repulsive

341

weeping-ash, which had been planted by Aunt Caroline, and which, to Elizabeth's pretty fancy, had always seemed to mourn for her. She suddenly felt its removal very poignantly, and not trusting herself to speak about that, called attention to the lovely red admiral butterflies on the buddleia. With which deft changes of subjects they went in to tea. Georgie and Bridge, and dinner, and more Bridge followed, and Lucia observed with strong misgivings that Elizabeth left her bag and Benjy his cigar-case in the garden room when they went to bed. This seemed to portend their return there in the morning, so she called attention to their forgetfulness. Elizabeth on getting upstairs had a further lapse of memory, for she marched into Lucia's bedroom, which she particularly wanted to see, before she recollected that it was no longer her own.

Lucia was rung up at breakfast next morning by the Padre. There was more diluvian news from the shore, and his emotion caused him to speak pure English without a trace of Scotch or Irish. A tide, higher than ever, had caused a fresh invasion of the sea, and now his bungalow was islanded, and the gale had torn a quantity of slates from the roof. Georgie, he said, had kindly offered to take him in, as the Vicarage was still let, and he waited in silence until Lucia asked him where Evie was going. He didn't know, and Lucia's suggestion that she should come to Mallards House was very welcome. She promised to send her car to bring them in and rejoined her guests.

'More flooding,' she said, 'just as you prophesied, Major Benjy. So Evie is coming here, and Georgie will take the Padre. I'm sure you won't mind moving on to the attic floor, and letting her have your room.'

Benjy's face fell.

'Oh, dear me, no,' he said heartily. 'I've roughed it before now.'

'We shall be quite a party,' said Elizabeth without any marked enthusiasm, for she supposed that Evie would share their sitting-room.

Lucia went to see to her catering, and her guests to their room, taking the morning papers with them.

'I should have thought that Diva might have taken Evie in, or she might have gone to the King's Arms,' said Elizabeth musingly. 'But dear Lucia revels in being Lady Bountiful. Gives her real pleasure.'

'I don't much relish sleeping in one of those attics,' said Benjy. 'Draughty places with sloping roofs if I remember right.'

Elizabeth's pride in her ancestral home flickered up.

'They're better than any rooms in the house you had before we married, darling,' she said. 'And not quite tactful to have told her you had roughed it before now . . . Was your haddock at breakfast *quite* what it should be?'

'Perfectly delicious,' said Benjy hitting back. 'It's a treat to get decent food again after that garbage we've been having.'

'Thank you dear,' said Elizabeth.

She picked up a paper, read it for a moment and decided to make common cause with him.

'Now I come to think of it,' she said, 'it would have been easy enough for Lucia not to have skied you to the attics. You and I could have had her old bedroom and dressing-room, and there would have been the other two rooms for her and Evie. But we must take what's given us and be thankful. What I do want to know is whether we're allowed in the garden-room unless she asks us. She seemed to give you your cigar-case and me my bag last night rather purposefully. Not that this is a bad room by any means.'

'It'll get stuffy enough this afternoon,' said he, 'for it's going to rain all day and I suppose there'll be three of us here.'

Elizabeth sighed.

'I suppose it didn't occur to her to take this

room herself, and give her guests the garden-room,' she said. 'Not selfish at all: I don't mean that, but perhaps a little wanting in imagination. I'll go down to the garden-room presently and see how the land lies . . . There's the telephone ringing again. That's the third time since breakfast. She's arranging football matches, I expect. Oh, the *Daily Mirror* has got hold of her gift to the hospital. 'Most munificent': how tired I am of the word. Of course it's the silly season still.'

Had Elizabeth known what that third telephone call was, she would have called the season by a more serious name than silly. The speaker was the Mayor, who now asked Lucia if she could see him privately for a few moments. She told him that it would be quite convenient, and might have added that it was also very exciting. Was there perhaps another Board which desired to have the honour of her membership? The Literary Institute? The Workhouse? The — . Back she went to the garden-room and hurriedly sat down at her piano and began communing with Beethoven. She was so absorbed in her music that she gave a startled little cry when Grosvenor, raising her voice to an unusual pitch called out for the second time: 'The Mayor of Tilling!' Up she sprang.

'Ah, good morning, Mr. Mayor,' she cried.

'So glad. Grosvenor, I'm not to be interrupted. I was just snatching a few minutes, as I always do after breakfast, at my music. It tunes me in — don't they call it — for the work of the day. Now, how can I serve you?'

His errand quite outshone the full splendour of Lucia's imagination. A member of the Town Council had just resigned, owing to ill-health, and the Mayor was on his way to an emergency meeting. The custom was, he explained, if such a vacancy occurred during the course of the year, that no fresh election should be held, but that the other members of the Council should co-opt a temporary member to serve till the next elections came round. Would she therefore permit him to suggest her name?

Lucia sat with her chin in her hand in the music attitude. Certainly that was an enormous step upwards from having been equal with Elizabeth at the bottom of the poll . . . Then she began to speak in a great hurry, for she thought she heard a footfall on the stairs into the garden-room. Probably Elizabeth had eluded Grosvenor.

'How I appreciate the honour,' she said. 'But — but how I should hate to feel that the dear townsfolk would not approve. The last elections, you know . . . Ah, I see what is in your mind. You think that since then they

346

realize a little more the sincerity of my desire to forward Tilling's welfare to the best of my humble capacity.' (There came a tap at the door.) 'I see I shall have to yield and, if your colleagues wish it, I gladly accept the great honour.'

The door had opened a chink; Elizabeth's ears had heard the words 'great honour,' and now her mouth (she *had* eluded Grosvenor) said:

'May I come in, dear?'

'*Entrate*,' said Lucia. 'Mr. Mayor, do you know Mrs. Mapp-Flint? You must! Such an old inhabitant of dear Tilling. Dreadful floods out by the links, and several friends, Major and Mrs. Mapp-Flint and the Padre and Mrs. Bartlett are all washed out. But such a treat for me, for I am taking them in, and have quite a party. Mallards House and I are always at the service of our citizens. But I mustn't detain you. You will let me know whether the meeting accepts your suggestion? I shall be eagerly waiting.'

Lucia insisted on seeing the Mayor to the front door, but returned at once to the garden-room, which had been thus violated by Elizabeth.

'I hope your sitting-room is comfortable, Elizabeth,' she said. 'You've got all you want there? Sure?'

The desire to know what those ominous words 'great honour' could possibly signify, consumed Elizabeth like a burning fire, and she was absolutely impervious to the hint so strongly conveyed to her.

'Delicious, dear,' she enthusiastically replied. 'So cosy, and Benjy so happy with his cigar and his paper. But didn't I hear the piano going just now? Sounded so lovely. May I sit mum as a mouse and listen?'

Lucia could not quite bring herself to say 'No, go away,' but she felt she must put her foot down. She had given her visitors a sitting-room of their own, and did not intend to have them here in the morning. Perhaps if she put her foot down on what she always called the *sostenuto* pedal, and played loud scales and exercises she could render the room intolerable to any listener.

'By all means,' she said. 'I have to practise very hard every morning to keep my poor fingers from getting rusty, or Georgie scolds me over our duets.'

Elizabeth slid into her familiar place in the window where she could observe the movements of Tilling, conducted chiefly this morning under umbrellas, and Lucia began. C Major up and down till her fingers ached with their unaccustomed drilling: then a few firm chords in that jovial key.

'Lovely chords! Such harmonies,' said Elizabeth, seeing Lucia's motor draw up at Mallards Cottage and deposit the Padre and his suit-case.

C Minor. This was more difficult. Lucia found that the upward scale was not the same as the downward, and she went over it half-a-dozen times, rumbling at first at the bottom end of the piano and then shrieking at the top and back again, before she got it right. A few simple minor chords followed.

'That wonderful funeral march,' said Elizabeth absently. Evie had thrust her head out of the window of the motor, and, to anybody who had any perception, was quite clearly telling Georgie, who had come to the door, about the flood, for she lowered and then raised her podgy little paw, evidently showing how much the flood had risen during the night.

As she watched, Lucia had begun to practise shakes, including that very difficult one for the third and fourth fingers.

'Like the sweet birdies in my garden,' said Elizabeth, still absently (though nothing could possibly have been less like), 'thrushes and blackbirds and . . . ' Her voice trailed into silence as the motor moved on, down the street towards Mallards, minus the Padre and his suit-case.

'And here's Evie just arriving,' she said, thinking that Lucia would stop that hideous noise, and go out to welcome her guest. Not a bit of it: the scale of D Major followed: it was markedly slower because her fingers were terribly fatigued. Then Grosvenor came in. She left the door open, and a strong draught blew round Elizabeth's ankles.

'Yes, Grosvenor?' said Lucia, with her hands poised over the keys.

'The Mayor has rung up, ma'am,' said Grosvenor, 'and would like to speak to you, if you are disengaged.'

The Mayoral call was irresistible, and Lucia went to the telephone in her Office. Elizabeth, crazy with curiosity, followed, and instantly became violently interested in the book-case in the hall, where she hoped she could hear Lucia's half, at any rate, of the conversation. After two or three gabbling, quacking noises, her voice broke jubilantly in.

'Indeed, I am most highly honoured, Mr. Mayor — ' she began. Then, unfortunately for the cause of the dissemination of useful knowledge, she caught sight of Elizabeth in the hall just outside with an open book in her hand, and smartly shut the Office door. Having taken this sensible precaution she continued:

'Please assure my colleagues, as I understand that the Town Council is sitting now, that I will resolutely shoulder the responsibility of my position.'

'Should you be unoccupied at the moment, Mrs. Lucas,' said the Mayor, 'perhaps you would come and take part in the business that lies before us, as you are now a member of the Council.'

'By all means,' cried Lucia. 'I will be with you in a couple of minutes.'

Elizabeth had replaced the fourth volume of Pepys' Diary upside down, and had stolen up closer to the Office door, where her footfall was noiseless on the india-rubber. Simultaneously Grosvenor came into the hall to open the front door to Evie, and Lucia came out of the Office, nearly running into Elizabeth.

'Admiring your lovely india-rubber matting, dear,' said Elizabeth adroitly. 'So pussy-cat quiet.'

Lucia hardly seemed to see her.

'Grosvenor: my hat, my raincoat, my umbrella at once,' she cried. 'I've got to go out. Delighted to see you, dear Evie. So sorry to be called away. A little soup or a sandwich after your drive? Elizabeth will show you the sitting-room upstairs. Lunch at half-past one: begin whether I'm in or not. No, Grosvenor, my new hat — '

'It's raining, ma'am,' said Grosvenor.

'I know it is, or I shouldn't want my umbrella.'

Her feet twinkled nearly as nimbly as Diva's as she sped through the rain to the mayor's parlour at the Town Hall. The assembled Council rose to their feet as she entered, and the Mayor formally presented them to the new colleague whom they had just co-opted: Per of the gas works, and Georgie of the drains and Twistevant the greengrocer. Just now Twistevant was looking morose, for the report of the Town-Surveyor about his slum-dwellings had been received, and this dire document advised that eight of his houses should be condemned as insanitary, and pulled down. The next item on the agenda was Lucia's offer of fifty almond trees (or more if desirable) to beautify in spring-time the bare grass slope to the south of the town. She said a few diffident words about the privilege of being allowed to make a little garden there, and intimated that she would pay for the enrichment of the soil and the planting of the trees and any subsequent upkeep, so that not a penny should fall on the rates. The offer was gratefully accepted with the applause of knuckles on the table, and as she was popular enough for the moment, she deferred announcing her project for the relaying of the steps by the Norman Tower.

Half-an-hour more sufficed for the rest of the business before the Town Councillors.

Treading on air, Lucia dropped in at Mallards Cottage to tell Georgie the news. The Padre had just gone across to Mallards, for Evie and he had got into a remarkable muddle that morning packing their bags in such a hurry: he had to recover his shaving equipment from hers, and take her a few small articles of female attire.

'I think I had better tell them all about my appointment at once, Georgie,' she said, 'for they are sure to hear about it very soon, and if Elizabeth has a bilious attack from chagrin, the sooner it's over the better. My dear, how tiresome she has been already! She came and sat in the garden-room, which I don't intend that anybody shall do in the morning, and so I began playing scales and shakes to smoke her out. Then she tried to overhear my conversation on the Office telephone with the Mayor — '

'And did she?' asked Georgie greedily.

'I don't think so. I banged the door when I saw her in the hall. You and the Padre will have all your meals with me, won't you, till they go, but if this rain continues, it looks as if they might be here till they get back into their own houses again. Let me sit quietly with you till lunch-time, for we shall have them all on our hands for the rest of the day.'

'I think we've been too hospitable,' said Georgie. 'One can overdo it. If the Padre sits and talks to me all morning, I shall have to live in my bedroom. Foljambe doesn't like it, either. He's called her 'my lassie' already.'

'No!' said Lucia. 'She'd hate that. Oh, and Benjy looked as black as ink when I told him I must give up his room to Evie. But we must rejoice, Georgie, that we're able to do something for the poor things.'

'Rejoice isn't quite the word,' said Georgie firmly.

★ ★ ★

Lucia returned to Mallards a little after half-past one, and went up to the sitting-room she had assigned to her guests and tapped on the door before entering. That might convey to Elizabeth's obtuse mind that this was their private room, and she might infer, by implication, that the garden-room was Lucia's private room. But this little moral lesson was wasted, for the room was empty except for stale cigar-smoke. She went to the dining-room, for they might, as desired, have begun lunch. Empty also. She went to the garden-room, and even as she opened the door, Elizabeth's voice rang out.

'No, Padre, my card was *not* covered,' she said. 'Uncovered.'

'An exposed card whatever then, Mistress Mapp,' said the Padre.

'Come, come, Mapp-Flint, Padre,' said Benjy.

'Oh, there's dearest Lucia!' cried Elizabeth. 'I thought it was Grosvenor come to tell us that lunch was ready. Such a dismal morning; we thought we would have a little game of cards to pass the time. No card-table in our cosy parlour upstairs.'

'Of course you shall have one,' said Lucia.

'And you've done your little businesses?' asked Elizabeth.

Lucia was really sorry for her, but the blow must be dealt.

'Yes: I attended a meeting of the Town Council. But there was very little business.'

'The Town Council, did you say?' asked the stricken woman.

'Yes: they did me the honour to co-opt me, for a member has resigned owing to ill-health. I felt it my duty to fill the vacancy. Let us go in to lunch.'

12

It was not till a fortnight later that Georgie and Lucia were once more dining alone at Mallards House, both feeling as if they were recovering from some debilitating nervous complaint, accompanied by high blood-pressure and great depression. The attack, so to speak, was over, and now they had to pick up their strength again. Only yesterday had the Padre and Evie gone back to their bungalow, and only this morning had the Mapp-Flints returned to Grebe. They might have gone the day before, since the insane widow of the Baronet had left that morning, removing herself and forty-seven canaries in two gipsy-vans. But there was so much rape seed scattered on the tiger-skins, and so many tokens of bird-life on curtains and tables and chairs that it had required a full day to clean up. Benjy on his departure had pressed a half-crown and a penny into Grosvenor's hand, one from himself and one from Elizabeth. This looked as if he had calculated the value of her services with meticulous accuracy, but the error had arisen because he had mixed up coppers and silver in his pocket, and he had genuinely meant to give her five shillings. Elizabeth gave her a sweet smile and shook hands.

Anyhow the fortnight was now over. Lucia had preserved the seignorial air to the end. Her car was always at the disposal of her guests, fires blazed in their bedrooms, she told them what passed at the meetings of the Town Council, she consulted their tastes at table. One day there was haggis for the Padre who was being particularly Scotch, and one day there were stewed prunes for Elizabeth, and fiery curry for Major Benjy in his more Indian moods, and parsnips for Evie who had a passion for that deplorable vegetable. About one thing only was Lucia adamant. They might take all the morning papers up to the guests' sitting-room, but until lunch-time they should not read them in the garden-room. *Verboten; défendu; non permesso.* If Elizabeth showed her nose there, or Benjy his cigar, or Evie her parish magazine, Lucia telephoned for Georgie, and they played duets till the intruder could stand it no more . . .

★ ★ ★

She pressed the pomander which rang the electric bell. Grosvenor brought in coffee, and

357

now they could talk freely.

'That wonderful fourth round of the Inferno, Georgie,' said Lucia dreamily. 'The guests who eat the salt of their host, and *sputare* it on the floor. Some very unpleasant fate awaited them: I think they were pickled in brine.'

'I'm sure they deserved whatever it was,' said Georgie.

'She,' said Lucia, mentioning no name, 'She went to see Diva one morning and said that Grosvenor had no idea of valeting, because she had put out a sock for Benjy with a large hole in it. Diva said: 'Why did you let it get like that?'

'So that was that,' said Georgie.

'And Benjy told the Padre that Grosvenor was very sparing with the wine. Certainly I did tell her not to fill up his glass the moment it was empty, for I was not going to have another Wyse-evening every day of the week.'

'Quite right, and there was always plenty for anyone who didn't want to get tipsy,' said Georgie. 'And Benjy wasn't very sparing with my whisky. Every evening practically he came across to chat with me about seven, and had three stiff goes.'

'I thought so,' cried Lucia triumphantly, bringing her hand sharply down on the table. Unfortunately she hit the pomander, and

Grosvenor re-entered. Lucia apologized for her mistake.

'Georgie, I inferred there certainly must be something of the sort,' she resumed when the door was shut again. 'Every evening round about seven Benjy used to say that he wouldn't play another rubber because he wanted a brisk walk and a breath of fresh air before dinner. Clever of him, Georgie. Though I'm sorry for your whisky I always applaud neat execution, however alcoholic the motive. After he had left the room, he banged the front door loud enough for her to hear it, so that she knew he had gone out and wasn't getting at the sherry in the dining-room. I think she suspected something, but she didn't quite know what.'

'I never knew an occasion on which she didn't suspect something,' said he.

Lucia crunched a piece of coffee sugar in a meditative manner.

'An interesting study,' she said. 'You know how devoted I am to psychological research, and I learned a great deal this last fortnight. Major Benjy was not very clever when he wooed and won her, but I think marriage has sharpened his wits. Little bits of foxiness, little evasions, nothing, of course, of a very high order, but some inkling of ingenuity and contrivance. I can understand a man developing a certain acuteness if he knew Elizabeth was always just round the corner. The instinct of self-protection. There is a character in Theophrastus very like him: I must look it up. Dear me; for the last fortnight I've hardly opened a book.'

'I can imagine that,' said he. 'Even I, who had only the Padre in the house couldn't settle down to anything. He was always coming in and out, wanting some ink in his bedroom, or a piece of string, or change for a shilling.'

'Multiply it by three. And she treated me all the time as if I was a hotel-keeper and she wasn't pleased with her room or her food, but made no formal complaint. Oh, Georgie, I must tell you, Elizabeth went up four pounds in weight the first week she was here. She shared my bathroom and always had her bath just before me in the evening, and there's a weighing-machine there, you know. Of course, I was terribly interested, but one day I felt I simply must thwart her, and so I hid the weights behind the bath. It was the only inhospitable thing I did the whole time she was here, but I couldn't bear it. So I don't know how much more she went up the second week.'

'I should have thought your co-option on to the Town Council would have made her thinner,' observed Georgie. 'But thrilling! She must have weighed herself without clothes, if she was having her bath. How much did she weigh?'

'Eleven stone twelve was the last,' said Lucia. 'But she has got big bones, Georgie. We must be fair.'

'Yes, but her bones must have finished growing,' said Georgie. 'They wouldn't have gone up four pounds in a week. Just fat.'

'I suppose it must have been. As for my co-option, it was frightful for her. Frightful. Let's go into the garden-room. My dear, how delicious to know that Benjy won't be there, smoking one of his rank cigars, or little Evie, running about like a mouse, so it always seemed to me, among the legs of chairs and tables.'

'Hurrah, for one of our quiet evenings again,' said he.

It was with a sense of restored well-being that they sank into their chairs, too content in this relief from strain to play duets. Georgie was sewing a border of lace on to some new doilies for finger-bowls, and Lucia found the 'Characters of Theophrastus,' and read to him in the English version the sketch of Benjy's prototype. As their content worked inside them both, like tranquil yeast, they both became aware that a moment of vital import to them, and hardly less so to Tilling, was ticking its way nearer. A couple of years ago only, each had shuddered at the notion that the other might be thinking of matrimony, but now the prospect of it had lost its horror. For Georgie had stayed with her when he was growing his shingles-beard, and she had stayed with him when she was settling into Mallards, and those days of domestic propinquity had somehow convinced them both that nothing was further from the inclination of either than any species of dalliance. With that nightmare apprehension removed they could recognise that for a considerable portion of the day they enjoyed each other's society more than their own solitude: they were happier together than apart. Again, Lucia was beginning to feel that, in the career which was opening for her in Tilling, a husband would give her a certain stability: a Prince Consort, though emphatically not for dynastic purposes, would lend her weight and ballast. Georgie with kindred thoughts in his mind could see himself filling that eminent position with grace and effectiveness.

Georgie, not attending much to his sewing, pricked his finger: Lucia read a little more Theophrastus with a wandering mind and moved to her writing-table, where a pile of letters was kept in place by a pretty paper-weight consisting of a small electro-plate cricket bat propped against a football, which had been given her jointly by the two clubs of which she was President. The clock struck eleven: it surprised them both that the hours had passed so quickly: eleven was usually the close of their evening. But they sat on, for all was ready for the vital moment, and if it did not come now, when on earth could there be a more apt occasion? Yet who was to begin, and how?

Georgie put down his work, for all his fingers were damp, and one was bloody. He remembered that he was a man. Twice he opened his mouth to speak, and twice he closed it again. He looked up at her, and caught her eye, and that gimlet-like quality in it seemed not only to pierce but to encourage. It bored into him for his good and for his eventual comfort. For the third time, and now successfully, he opened his mouth.

'Lucia, I've got something I must say, and I hope you won't mind. Has it ever occurred to you that — well — that we might marry?'

She fiddled for a moment with the cricket bat and the football, but when she raised her eyes again, there was no doubt about the encouragement.

'Yes, Georgie: unwomanly as it may sound,'

she said, 'it has. I really believe it might be an excellent thing. But there's a great deal for us to think over first, and then talk over together. So let us say no more for the present. Now we must have our talk as soon as possible: some time to-morrow.'

She opened her engagement book. She had bought a new one, since she had become a Town Councillor, about as large as an ordinary blotting-pad.

'*Dio*, what a day!' she exclaimed. 'Town Council at half-past ten, and at twelve I am due at the slope by the Norman tower to decide about the planting of my almond trees. Not in lines, I think, but scattered about: a little clump here, a single one there . . . Then Diva comes to lunch. Did you hear? A cinder from a passing engine blew into her cook's eye as she was leaning out of the kitchen window, poor thing. Then after lunch my football team are playing their opening match and I promised to kick off for them.'

'My dear, how wonderfully adventurous of you!' exclaimed Georgie. 'Can you?'

'Quite easily and quite hard. They sent me up a football and I've been practising in the *giardino segreto*. Where were we? Come to tea, Georgie — no, that won't do: my Mayor is bringing me the plans for the new artisan dwellings. It must be dinner then, and we shall have time to think it all over. Are you off? *Buona notte, caro: tranquilli* — dear me, what is the Italian for 'sleep'? How rusty I am getting!'

Lucia did not go back with him into the house, for there were some agenda for the meeting at half-past ten to be looked through. But just as she heard the front door shut on his exit, she remembered the Italian for sleep, and hurriedly threw up the window that looked on the street.

'*Sonni*,' she called out, '*Sonni tranquilli.*'

Georgie understood: and he answered in Italian.

'*I stessi a voi*, I mean, *te*,' he brilliantly shouted.

★ ★ ★

The half-espoused couple had all next day to let simmer in their heads the hundred arrangements and adjustments which the fulfilment of their romance would demand. Again and again George cast his doily from him in despair at the magnitude and intricacy of them. About the question of connubialities, he meant to be quite definite: it must be a *sine qua non* of matrimony, the first clause in the marriage treaty, that they should be considered absolutely illicit, and he need not waste thought over that. But what was to happen to his house, for presumably he would live at Mallards? And if so, what was to be done with his furniture, his piano, his bibelots? He could not bear to part with them, and Mallards was already full of Lucia's things. And what about Foljambe? She was even more inalienable than his Worcester china, and Georgie felt that though life might be pretty much the same with Lucia, it could not be the same without Foljambe. Then he must insist on a good deal of independence with regard to the companionship his bride would expect from him. His mornings must be inviolably his own and also the time between tea and dinner as he would be with her from then till bed-time severed them. Again two cars seemed more than two people should require, but he could not see himself without his Armaud. And what if Lucia, intoxicated by her late success on the Stock Exchange, took to gambling and lost all her money? The waters on which they thought of voyaging together seemed sown with jagged reefs, and he went across to dinner the next night with a drawn and anxious face. He was rather pleased to see that Lucia looked positively haggard, for that showed that she realised the appalling conundrums that must be solved before any irretraceable step was taken. Probably she had got some more of her own.

They settled themselves in the chairs where they had been so easy with each other twenty-four hours ago and Lucia with an air of determination, picked up a paper of scribbled memoranda from her desk.

'I've put down several points we must agree over, Georgie,' she said.

'I've got some, too, in my head,' said he.

Lucia fixed her eyes on a corner of the ceiling, as if in a music-face, but her knotted brow showed it was not that.

'I thought of writing to you about the first point, which is the most important of all,' she said, 'but I found I couldn't. How can I put it best? It's this, Georgie. I trust that you'll be very comfortable in the oak bedroom.'

'I'm sure I shall,' interrupted Georgie eagerly.

' — and all that implies,' Lucia went on firmly.

'No caresses of any sort: none of those dreadful little dabs and pecks Elizabeth and Benjy used to make at each other.'

'You needn't say anything more about that,' said he. 'Just as we were before.'

The acuteness of her anxiety faded from Lucia's face.

'That's a great relief,' she said. 'Now what

is my next point? I've been in such a whirl all day and scribbled them down so hastily that I can't read it. It looks like 'Frabjious.''

'It sounds as if it might be Foljambe,' said Georgie. 'I've been thinking a lot about her. I can't part with her.'

'Nor can I part with Grosvenor, as no doubt you will have realised. But what will their respective positions be? They've both bossed our houses for years. Which is to boss now? And will the other one consent to be bossed?'

'I can't see Foljambe consenting to be bossed,' said Georgie.

'If I saw Grosvenor consenting to be bossed,' said Lucia, 'I merely shouldn't believe my eyes.'

'Could there be a sort of equality?' suggested Georgie. 'Something like King William III and Queen Mary?'

'Oh, Georgie, I think there might be a solution there,' said Lucia. 'Let us explore that. Foljambe will only be here during the day, just as she is now with you, and she'll be your valet, and look after your rooms, for you must have a sitting-room of your own. I insist on that. You will be her province, Georgie, where she's supreme. I shall be Grosvenor's. I don't suppose either of them wants to leave us, and they are friends. We'll put it to them tomorrow, if we agree about the rest.'

'Won't it be awful if they don't come to terms?' said Georgie. 'What are we to do then?'

'Don't let's anticipate trouble,' said Lucia. 'Then let me see. 'Mallards Cottage' is my next entry. Naturally we shall live here.'

'I've been worrying terribly about that,' said Georgie. 'I quite agree we must live here, but I can't let the Cottage with all my things. I don't wish other people to sleep in my bed and that sort of thing. But if I let it unfurnished, what am I to do with them? My piano, my pictures and embroideries, my sofa, my particular armchair, my bed, my bibelots? I've got six occasional tables in my sitting-room, because I counted them. There's no room for them here, and things go to pot if one stores them. Besides there are a lot of them which I simply can't get on without. Heart's blood.'

A depressed silence followed, for Lucia knew what his household goods meant to Georgie. Then suddenly she sprang up, clapping her hands, and talking so weird a mixture of baby-language and Italian that none but the most intimate could have understood her at all.

'Georgino!' she cried. 'Ickle me vewy clever. Lucia's got a *molto bella* idea. Lucia knows how Georgino loves his *bibelotine*. Tink a minute: shut oo eyes and tink! Well, Lucia no tease you any more . . . Georgino will have booful night-nursery here, bigger nor what he had in Cottagino. And booful *salone* bigger nor *salone* there. Now do you see?'

'No, I don't,' said Georgie firmly.

Lucia abandoned baby and foreign tongues.

'I'll send all the furniture in your bedroom and sitting-room here across to Mallards Cottage, and you shall fill them with your own things. More than enough room for the curtains and pictures and occasional tables which you really love. You wouldn't mind letting the Cottage if you had all your special things here?'

'Well, you are clever!' said Georgie.

An appreciative pause followed instead of that depressed silence, and Lucia referred to her notes.

'"Solitude' is my next entry,' she said. 'What can — Oh, I know. It sounds rather as if I was planning that we should see as little as possible of each other if and when we marry, but I don't mean that. Only, with all the welter of business which my position in Tilling already entails (and it will get worse rather than better) I must have much time to myself. Naturally we shall entertain a good deal: those quaint Bridge parties and so on, for Tilling society will depend on us more than ever. But ordinarily, when we are alone,

370

Georgie, I must have my mornings to myself, and a couple of hours at least before dinner. Close times. Of course nothing hard or fast about it; very likely we shall often make music together then. But you mustn't think me unsociable if, as a rule, I have those hours to myself. My municipal duties, my boards and committees already take a great deal of time, and then there are all my private studies. A period of solitude every day is necessary for me. Is it not Goethe who says that we ripen in solitude?'

'I quite agree with him if he does,' said Georgie. 'I was going to speak about it myself if you hadn't.'

Most of the main dangers which threatened to render matrimony impossible had now been provided for and of these the Foljambe-Grosvenor complication alone remained. That, to be sure, was full of menace, for the problem that would arise if those two pillars of the house would not consent to support it in equal honour and stability, seemed to admit of no solution. But all that could be done at present was to make the most careful plans for the tactful putting of the proposition before William and Mary. It ought to be done simultaneously in both houses, and Lucia decided it would be quite legitimate if she implied (though not exactly stated) to

Grosvenor that Foljambe thought the plan would work very well, while at the same moment Georgie was making the same implication to Foljambe. The earlier that was done, the shorter would be the suspense, and zero hour was fixed for ten next morning. It was late now, and Georgie went to bed. A random idea of kissing Lucia once, on the brow, entered his mind, but after what had been said about caresses, he felt she might consider it a minor species of rape.

Next morning at a quarter past ten Georgie was just going to the telephone with brisk tread and beaming face, when Lucia rang him up. The sparkle in her voice convinced him that all was well even before she said '*La domestica e molto contenta.*'

'So's mine,' said Georgie.

★   ★   ★

All obstacles to the marriage being now removed, unless Elizabeth thought of something and forbade the banns, there was no reason why it should not be announced. If Diva was told, no further dissemination was needful. Accordingly Lucia wrote a note to her about it, and by half-past eleven practically all Tilling knew. Elizabeth, on being told, said to Diva, 'Dear, how can you

372

repeat such silly stories?' So Diva produced the note itself, and Elizabeth without a particle of shame said, 'Now my lips are unsealed. I knew a week ago. High time they were married, I should say.'

Diva pressed her to explain precisely what she meant with such ferocity that Paddy showed his teeth, being convinced by a dog's unfailing instinct that Elizabeth must be an enemy. So she explained that she had only meant that they had been devoted to each other for so long, and that neither of them would remain quite young much longer. Irene burst into tears when she heard it, but in all other quarters the news was received with great cordiality, the more so perhaps because Lucia had told Diva that they neither of them desired any wedding presents.

The date and manner of the wedding much exercised the minds of the lovers. Georgie, personally, would have wished the occasion to be celebrated with the utmost magnificence. He strongly fancied the prospective picture of himself in frock-coat and white spats waiting by the north door of the church for the arrival of the bride. Conscious that for the rest of his years he would be overshadowed by the first citizeness of Tilling, his nature demanded one hour of glorious life, when the dominating role would be his, and she would promise to love, honour and obey, and the utmost pomp and circumstance ought to attend this brief apotheosis. To Lucia he put the matter rather differently.

'Darling,' he said (they had settled to allow themselves this verbal endearment), 'I think, no, I'm sure, that Tilling would be terribly disappointed if you didn't allow this to be a great occasion. You must remember who you are, and what you are to Tilling.'

Lucia was in no serious danger of forgetting that, but she had got another idea in her head. She sighed, as if she had herself just played the last chord of the first movement of the 'Moonlight.'

'Georgie,' she said, 'I was turning up only yesterday the account of Charlotte Brontë's wedding. Eight o'clock in the morning, and only two of her most intimate friends present. No one of the folk at Haworth even knew she was being married that day. So terribly *chic* somehow, when one remembers her world-wide fame. I am not comparing myself to Charlotte — don't think that — but I have got a touch of her exquisite delicacy in shunning publicity. My public life, darling, must and does belong to Tilling, but not my private life.'

'I can't quite agree,' said Georgie. 'It's not the same thing, for all Tilling knows you're going to be married, and it wouldn't be fair to them. I should like you to ask the Bishop to come again in cope and mitre — '

Lucia remembered that day of superb triumph.

'Oh, Georgie, I wonder if he would come,' she said. 'How Tilling enjoyed it before!'

'Try anyhow. And think of your organ. Really it ought to make a joyful noise at your wedding. Mendelssohn's Wedding March: tubas.'

'No, darling, not that,' said Lucia. 'So lascivious don't you think?'

'Well, Chopin's then,' said Georgie.

'No, that's a funeral march,' said Lucia. 'Most unsuitable.'

'Well, some other march,' said Georgie. 'And the Mayor and Corporation would surely attend. You're a Town Councillor.'

The example of Charlotte Brontë was fading out in Lucia's mind, vanishing in a greater brightness.

'And the *Hastings Chronicle*,' said Georgie pushing home his advantage. 'That would be a big cutting for your book. A column at least.'

'But there'll be no wedding presents,' she said. 'Usually most of it is taken up with wedding presents.'

'Another score for you,' said Georgie

ingeniously. 'Tell your Mr. Meriton that because of the widespread poverty and unemployment you begged your friends not to spend their money on presents. They'd have been very meagre little things in any case: two packs of patience cards from Elizabeth and a pen-wiper from Benjy. Much better to have none.'

Lucia considered these powerful arguments.

'I allow you have shaken my resolve, darling,' she said. 'If you really think it's my duty as — '

'As a Town Councillor and a fairy-godmother to Tilling, I do,' said he. 'The football club, the cricket club. Everybody. I think you ought to sacrifice your personal feelings, which I quite understand.'

That finished it.

'I had better write to the Bishop at once then,' she said, 'and give him a choice of dates. Bishops I am sure are as busy as I.'

'Scarcely that,' said Georgie. 'But it would be as well.'

Lucia took a couple of turns up and down the garden-room. She waved her arms like Brunnhilde awakening on the mountain-top.

'Georgie, I begin to visualize it all,' she said. 'A procession from here would be out of place. But afterwards, certainly a reception in the garden-room, and a buffet in the

376

diningroom. Don't you think? But one thing I must be firm about. We must steal away afterwards. No confetti or shoes. We must have your motor at the front door, so that everyone will think we are driving away from there, and mine at the little passage into Porpoise Street, with the luggage on.'

She sat down and took a sheet of writing paper.

'And we must settle about my dress,' she said. 'If we are to have this great show, so as not to disappoint Tilling, it ought to be up to the mark. Purple brocade, or something of the sort. I shall have it made here, of course: that good little milliner in the High Street. Useful for her . . . 'Dear Lord Bishop' is correct, is it not?'

The Bishop chose the earliest of the proffered dates, and the Mayor and Corporation thereupon signified their intention of being present at the ceremony, and accepted Lucia's invitation to the reception afterwards at Mallards. A further excitement for Tilling two days before the wedding was the sight of eight of the men whom now Lucia had come to call 'her unemployed' moving in opposite directions between Mallards and the Cottage like laden ants, observing the rules of the road. They carried the most varied burdens: a bed in sections came out of Mallards passing on its way sections of another bed from the Cottage: bookcases were interchanged and wardrobes: an ant festooned with gay water-colour sketches made his brilliant progress towards Mallards, meeting another who carried prints of Mozart at the age of four improvising on the spinet and of Beethoven playing his own compositions to an apparently remorseful audience. A piano lurched along from the Cottage, first sticking in the doorway, and thus obstructing the progress of other ants laden with crockery vessels, water-jugs and basins and other meaner objects, who had to stand with their intimate burdens in the street, looking a shade self-conscious, till their way was clear. Curtains and rugs and fire-irons and tables and chairs were interchanged, and Tilling puzzled itself into knots to know what these things meant.

As if this conundrum was not sufficiently agonizing, nobody could ascertain where the happy pair were going for their honeymoon. They would be back in a week, for Lucia could not forsake her municipal duties for longer than that, but she had made concession enough to publicity, and this was kept a profound secret, for the mystery added to the *cachet* of the event. Elizabeth made desperate efforts to find out: she sprang all

378

sorts of Jack-in-the-box questions on Lucia in the hope that she would startle her into revealing the unknown destination. Were there not very amusing plays going on in Paris? Was not the climate of Cornwall very agreeable in November? Had she ever seen a bull-fight? All no use: and completely foiled she expressed her settled conviction that they were not going away at all, but would immure themselves at Mallards, as if they had measles.

All was finished on the day before the wedding, and Georgie slept for the last time in the Cottage surrounded by the furniture from his future bedroom at Mallards, and clad in his frock-coat and fawn-coloured trousers had an early lunch, with a very poor appetite, in his unfamiliar sitting-room. He brushed his top-hat nervously from time to time, and broke into a slight perspiration when the church bells began to ring, yearning for the comfortable obscurity of a registry office, and wishing that he had never been born, or, at any rate, was not going to be married quite so soon. He tottered to the church.

The ceremony was magnificent, with cope and corporation and plenty of that astonishing tuba on the organ. Then followed the reception in the garden-room and the buffet in the dining-room, during which bride and bridegroom vanished, and appeared again in their go-away clothes, a brown Lucia with winter-dessert in her hat, and a bright mustard-coloured Georgie. The subterfuge, however, of starting from Porpoise Street *via* the back door was not necessary, since the street in front of Mallards was quite devoid of sightseers and confetti. So Georgie's decoy motorcar retreated, and Grosvenor ordered up Lucia's car from Porpoise Street. There was some difficulty in getting round that awkward corner, for there was a van in the way, and it had to saw backwards and forwards. The company crowded into the hall and on to the doorstep to see them off, and Elizabeth was quite certain that Lucia did not say a word to Cadman as she stepped in. Clearly then Cadman knew where they were going, and if she had only thought of that she might have wormed it out of him. Now it was too late: also her conviction that they were not going anywhere at all had broken down. She tried to persuade Diva that they were only going for a drive and would be back for tea, but Diva was pitilessly scornful.

'Rubbish!' she said. Or was all that luggage merely a blind? 'You're wrong as usual, Elizabeth.'

* * *

Lucia put the window half down: it was a warm afternoon.

'Darling, it all went off beautifully,' she said. 'And what fun it will be to see dear Riseholme again. It was nice of Olga Bracely to lend us her house. We must have some little dinners for them all.'

'They'll be thrilled,' said Georgie. 'Do you like my new suit?'

13

Lucia decided to take a rare half-holiday and spend this brilliant afternoon in mid May, in strolling about Tilling with Georgie, for there was a good deal she wanted to inspect. They went across the churchyard pausing to listen to the great blare of melodious uproar that poured out through the open south door, for the organist was practising on Lucia's organ, and, after enjoying that, proceeded to the Norman Tower. The flight of steps down to the road below had been relaid from top to bottom, and a most elegant hand-rail put up. A very modest stone tablet at the side of the top step recorded in quite small letters the name of the person to whom Tilling owed this important restoration.

'They were only finished yesterday, Georgie,' said Lucia hardly glancing at the tablet, since she had herself chosen the lettering very carefully and composed the inscription, 'and I promised the foreman to look at them. Nice, I think, and in keeping. And very evenly laid. One can walk down them without looking to one's feet.'

Half-way down she stopped and pointed.

'Georgie,' she cried. 'Look at the lovely blossom on my almond trees! They are in flower at last, after this cold spring. I was wise to get well-grown trees: smaller ones would never have flowered their first year. Oh, there's Elizabeth coming up my steps. That old green skirt again. It seems quite imperishable.'

They met.

'Lovely new steps,' said Elizabeth very agreeably. 'Quite a pleasure to walk up them. Thank you, dear, for them. But those poor almond trees. So sad and pinched, and hardly a blossom on them. Perhaps they weren't the flowering sort. Or do you think they'll get acclimatised after some years?'

'They're coming out beautifully,' said Lucia in a very firm voice. 'I've never seen such healthy trees in all my life. By next week they will be a blaze of blossom. Blaze.'

'I'm sure I hope you'll be right, dear,' said Elizabeth, 'but I don't see any buds coming myself.' Lucia took no further notice of her, and continued to admire her almond trees in a loud voice to Georgie.

'And how gay the pink blossom looks against the blue sky, darling,' she said. 'You must bring your paint-box here some morning and make a sketch of them. Such a feast for the eye.'

She tripped down the rest of the steps, and Elizabeth paused at the top to read the tablet.

'You know Mapp is really the best name for her,' said Lucia, still slightly bubbling with resentment. 'Irene is quite right never to call her anything else. Poor Mapp is beginning to imitate herself: she says exactly the things which somebody taking her on would say.'

'And I'm sure she wanted to be pleasant just now,' said Georgie, 'but the moment she began to praise your steps she couldn't bear it, and found herself obliged to crab something else of yours.'

'Very likely. I never knew a woman so terribly in the grip of her temperament. Look, Georgie: they're playing cricket on my field. Let us go and sit in the pavilion for a little. It would be appreciated.'

'Darling, it's so dull watching cricket,' said Georgie. 'One man hits the ball away and another throws it back and all the rest eat daisies.'

'We'll just go and show ourselves,' said Lucia. 'We needn't stop long. As President I feel I must take an interest in their games. I wish I had time to study cricket. Doesn't the field look beautifully level now? You could play billiards on it.'

'Oh, by the way,' said Georgie, 'I saw Mr. Woolgar in the town this morning. He told me he had a client, very desirable he thought, but he wasn't at liberty to mention the name yet, enquiring if I would let the Cottage for three months from the end of June. Only six guineas a week offered, and I asked eight. But even at that a three months' let would be pleasant.'

'The client's name is Mapp,' said Lucia with decision. 'Diva told me yesterday that the woman with the canaries had taken Grebe for three months from the end of June at twenty guineas a week.'

'That may be only a coincidence,' said Georgie.

'But it isn't,' retorted Lucia. 'I can trace the windings of her mind like the course of a river across the plain. She thinks she wouldn't get it for six guineas if you knew she was the client, for she had let out that she was getting twenty for Grebe. Stick to eight, Georgie, or raise it to ten.'

'I'm going to have tea with Diva,' said Georgie, 'and the Mapps will be there. I might ask her suddenly if she was going to take a bungalow again for the summer, and see how she looks.'

'Anyhow they can't get flooded out of Mallards Cottage,' observed Lucia.

They had skirted the cricket ground and come to the pavilion, but since Tilling was fielding Lucia's appearance did not evoke the gratification she had anticipated, since none of the visiting side had the slightest idea who she was. The Tilling bowling was being slogged all over the field, and the fieldsmen had really no time to eat daisies with this hurricane hitting going on. One ball crashed on to the wall of the pavilion just above Georgie's head, and Lucia willingly consented to leave her cricket field, for she had not known the game was so perilous. They went up into the High Street and through the churchyard again, and were just in sight of Mallards Cottage on which was a board: 'To be let Furnished or Sold,' when the door opened, and Elizabeth came out, locking the door after her: clearly she had been to inspect it, or how could she have got the keys? Lucia knew that Georgie had seen her, and so did not even say 'I told you so.'

'You must promise to do a sketch of my almond trees against the sky, Georgie,' she said. 'They will be in their full beauty by next week. And we must really give one of our omnibus dinner-parties soon. Saturday would do: I have nothing on Saturday evening, I think. I will telephone all round now.'

$$\star \quad \star \quad \star$$

Georgie went upstairs to his own sitting-room to get a reposeful half-hour, before going to his tea-party. More and more he marvelled at Lucia's superb vitality: she was busier now than she had ever pretended to be, and her labours were but as fuel to feed her fires. This walk to-day, for instance, had for him necessitated a short period of quiescence before he set off again for fresh expenditure of force, but he could hear her voice crisp and vigorous as she rang up number after number, and the reason why she was not coming to Diva's party was that she had a class of girl-guides in the garden-room at half-past four, and a meeting of the Governors of the Hospital at six. At 7.15 (for 7.30) she was to preside at the annual dinner of the cricket club. Not a very full day.

Lucia had been returned at the top of the poll in the last elections for the Town Council. Never did she miss a meeting, never did she fail to bring forward some fresh scheme for the employment of the unemployed, for the lighting of streets or the paving of roads or for the precedence of perambulators over pedestrians on the narrow pavements of the High Street. Bitter had been the conflict which called for a decision on that knotty question. Mapp, for instance, meeting two perambulators side by side had refused to step into the road and so had the nursery-maids. Instead they had advanced, chatting gaily together, solid as a phalanx and Mapp had been forced to retreat before them and turn up a side street. 'What with Susan's great bus,' she passionately exclaimed, 'filling up the whole of the roadway, and perambulators sweeping all before them on the pavements, we shall have to do our shopping in aeroplanes.'

Diva, to whom she made this protest, had been sadly forgetful of recent events, which, so to speak, had not happened and replied:

'Rubbish, dear Elizabeth! If you had ever had occasion to push a perambulator, you wouldn't have wheeled it on to the road to make way for the Queen.' . . . Then, seeing her error, Diva had made things worse by saying she hadn't meant *that*, and the Bridge party to which Georgie was going this afternoon was to mark the reconciliation after the resultant coolness. The legislation suggested by Lucia to meet this traffic problem was a model of wisdom: perambulators had precedence on pavements, but they must proceed in single file. Heaps of room for everybody.

Georgie, resting and running over her activities in his mind, felt quite hot at the thought of them, and applied a little eau-de-cologne to his forehead. To-morrow she was taking all her girl-guides for a day by the sea at Margate: they were starting in a chartered bus at eight in the morning, but she expected to be back for dinner. The occupations of her day fitted into each other like a well-cut jigsaw puzzle, and not a piece was missing from the picture. Was all this activity merely the outpouring of her inexhaustible energy that spouted like the water from the rock when Moses smote it? Sometimes he wondered whether there was not an ulterior purpose behind it. If so, she never spoke of it, but drove relentlessly on in silence.

He grew a little drowsy; he dozed, but he was awakened by a step on the stairs and a tap at his door. Lucia always tapped, for it was his private room, and she entered with a note in her hand. Her face seemed to glow with some secret radiance which she repressed with difficulty: to mask it she wore a frown, and her mouth was working with thought.

'I must consult you, Georgie,' she said, sinking into a chair. 'There is a terribly momentous decision thrust upon me.'

Georgie dismissed the notion that Mapp had made some violent assault upon the infant occupiers of the perambulators as inadequate.

'Darling, what has happened?' he asked.

She gazed out of the window without speaking.

'I have just received a note from the Mayor,' she said at length in a shaken voice.

'While we were so light-heartedly looking at almond trees, a private meeting of the Town Council was being held.'

'I see,' said Georgie, 'and they didn't send you notice. Outrageous. Anyhow, I think I should threaten to resign. After all you've done for them, too!'

She shook her head.

'No: you mustn't blame them,' she said. 'They were right, for a piece of business was before them at which it was impossible I should be present.'

'Oh, something not quite nice?' suggested Georgie. 'But I think they should have told you.'

Again she shook her head.

'Georgie, they decided to sound me as to whether I would accept the office of Mayor next year. If I refuse, they would have to try somebody else. It's all private at present, but I had to speak to you about it, for naturally it will affect you very greatly.'

'Do you mean that I shall be something?' asked Georgie eagerly.

'Not officially, of course, but how many duties must devolve on the Mayor's husband!'

'A sort of Mayoress,' said Georgie with the eagerness clean skimmed off his voice.

'A thousand times more than that,' cried

Lucia. 'You will have to be my right hand, Georgie. Without you I couldn't dream of undertaking it. I should entirely depend on you, on your judgment and your wisdom. There will be hundreds of questions on which a man's instinct will be needed by me. We shall be terribly hard-worked. We shall have to entertain, we shall have to take the lead, you and I, in everything, in municipal life as well as social life, which we do already. If you cannot promise to be always by me for my guidance and support, I can only give one answer. An unqualified negative.'

Lucia's eloquence, with all the practice she had had at Town Councils, was most effective. Georgie no longer saw himself as a Mayoress, but as the Power behind the Throne; he thought of Queen Victoria and the Prince Consort, and bright images bubbled in his brain. Lucia, with a few sideways gimlet-glances saw the effect, and, wise enough to say no more, continued gazing out of the window. Georgie gazed too: they both gazed.

When Lucia thought that her silence had done as much as it could, she sighed, and spoke again.

'I understand. I will refuse then,' she said.

That, in common parlance, did the trick.

'No, don't fuss me,' he said. 'Me must fink.'

'*Si, caro: pensa seriosamente,*' said she. 'But I must make up my mind now: it wouldn't be fair on my colleagues not to. There are plenty of others, Georgie, if I refuse. I should think Mr. Twistevant would make an admirable Mayor. Very business-like. Naturally, I do not approve of his views about slums and, of course I should have to resign my place on the Town Council and some other bodies. But what does that matter?'

'Darling, if you put it like that,' said Georgie, 'I must say that I think it your duty to accept. You would be condoning slums almost, if you didn't.'

The subdued radiance in Lucia's face burst forth like the sun coming out from behind a cloud.

'If you think it's my duty, I must accept,' she said. 'You would despise me otherwise. I'll write at once.'

She paused at the door.

'I wonder what Elizabeth — ' she began, then thought better of it, and tripped lightly downstairs.

★ ★ ★

Tilling had unanimously accepted Lucia's invitation for dinner and Bridge on Saturday, and Georgie, going upstairs to dress heard himself called from Lucia's bedroom.

He entered.

Her bed was paved with hats: it was a *parterre* of hats, of which the boxes stood on the floor, a rampart of boxes. The hats were of the most varied styles. There was one like an old-fashioned beaver hat with a feather in it. There was a Victorian bonnet with strings. There was a three-cornered hat, like that which Napoleon wore in the retreat from Moscow. There was a head-dress like that worn by nuns, and a beret made of cloth of gold. There was a hat like a full-bottomed wig with ribands in it, and a Stuart-looking head-dress like those worn by the ladies of the Court in the time of Charles I. Lucia sitting in front of her glass, with her head on one side was trying the effect of a green turban.

'I want your opinion, dear,' she said. 'For official occasions as when the Mayor and Corporation go in state to church, or give a civic welcome to distinguished visitors, the Mayor, if a woman, has an official hat, part of her robes. But there are many semi-official occasions, Georgie, when one would not be wearing robes, but would still like to wear something distinctive. When I preside at Town Councils, for instance, or at all those committees of which I shall be chairman. On all those occasions I should wear the same hat: an undress uniform, you might call it. I don't think the green turban would do, but I am rather inclined to that beret in cloth of gold.'

Georgie tried on one or two himself.

'I like the beret,' he said. 'You could trim it with your beautiful seed pearls.'

'That's a good idea,' said Lucia cordially. 'Or what about the thing like a wig. Rather majestic: the Mayor of Tilling, you know, used to have the power of life and death. Let me try it on again.'

'No, I like the beret better than that,' said Georgie critically. 'Besides the Mayor doesn't have the power of life and death now. Oh, but what about this Stuart-looking one? Rather van Dyckish, don't you think?'

He brought it to her, and came opposite the mirror himself, so that his face was framed there beside hers. His beard had been trimmed that day to a beautiful point.

'Georgino! Your beard: my hat,' cried Lucia. 'What a harmony! Not a question about it!'

'Yes, I think it does suit us,' said Georgie, blushing a little.